OUR WEDDINGS

BY THE SAME AUTHOR

Persian Brides

OUR WEDDINGS

DORIT RABINYAN

Translated by Yael Lotan

BLOOMSBURY

First published in Great Britain 2001

This paperback edition published 2002

Bloomsbury Publishing Plc, 38 Soho Square, London W1D 3HB

A CIP catalogue record is available
from the British Library

ISBN 0 7475 5767 5

Typeset by Hewer Text Ltd, Edinburgh
Printed in Great Britain by Clays Ltd, St Ives plc

Part One

Matti Azizyan's Birthday, Five-thirty in the Morning

At last, the luminous match was struck and the day was lit. But Matti had awakened earlier – before her father rose from his dreamless bed and went, sorrowful, to the sea; before her sister Sofia's blue baby awoke and shook the house with his cough; before her brother Maurice woke up in a rage at the naked women hanging on the walls of his room; before her sister Lizzie returned from night-shift at the hospital, her high heels clacking on the living-room floor, revealing under her white nurse's smock a shimmering low-necked dress and blue bruises.

Matti woke up knowing she'd had a bad dream, but could not remember what it was.

Her mother had not yet completed her cycle of prayers at the synagogue. Her tearful bed was empty, and on the kitchen worktop flickered the six candles she had lit. Matti's divorced sister Marcelle had abandoned the heroes of the romance she had borrowed at the public library, turned off the light in the living-room and was sitting on the window ledge. The autumn wind and the scent of guavas wafted into the house. Marcelle lifted her sad eyes yearningly beyond the road and over the roof of Grandma Touran's house, where Sofia was wandering about the empty rooms, searching in vain for sleep.

Her past years of sound sleep were of no avail. Sofia Kadosh, beauty queen of the technical-college system, lay alone in a purple silk nightgown on her dead grandmother's bed, sleepless, alert.

Solly Azizyan, short, barefoot, got off the iron bed with the springs that moaned like a weary lover, remembered that his mother was dead, and walked very quietly down the corridor with the Indian gods. Without the creaking of her parents' bed-springs Matti would not have known that her father's small shadow was moving across the statues' stone faces. Every morning at daybreak, as he passed from the iron bed to the bathroom, her father was able to move his body without churning the air with his limbs, without stirring the dust that had settled on the statues, or swirling the warm breath rising from his wife's and children's lungs. He passed among the particles of light that filtered in from the living-room, his footsteps almost ethereally delicate, and only the burbling of water in the basin indicated that he had completed his route and would shortly be going down to the sea.

Matti held her breath and her thoughts when her father's shadow stopped abruptly and a circle of light fell on his face as he stood in the doorway of the children's room. A smile flickered on his scorched fisherman's face, sprinkled with beads of water he didn't care to press into a towel.

Matti's eyelids slammed shut and she pretended to be asleep, but she'd seen how much her father had aged in the six months she'd been away at boarding-school. She noticed his new teeth that replaced the bad old ones, the white stubble sprouting amid the furrows of his face, and that the coppery glint of his hair was fading to a dull grey. His face seemed more naked than his feet, as though it too should be protected with sock and shoe from injury in the street. Her eyeballs darted under the lids and her lashes quivered, but she did not stir. She let her father caress her face and hair with the forlorn gaze of parents who are unable to save their children. And waited for him to walk away.

But he didn't want to move. Her father was full of longings, and not only for her. He missed his mother, Grandma Touran, who had died before Matti was sent to boarding-school. He missed his wife Iran, who had withdrawn from him into an orthodox head-kerchief, psalms and memorial candles. He missed his son Maurice, who was sleeping, shut away and ill-humoured, in the adjoining room. And he missed Matti's older sisters, Sofia, Marcelle and Lizzie, who had been cuddly, laughing girls and were now embittered, disappointed women. He missed the children he used to have years ago, when he was still able to comfort them with boiled milk that he poured from cup to cup till it cooled, and sweetened with lots of honey.

Breathing lightly and furtively, Matti smelled the odour of salt on his clothes and kelp on his skin, and was almost tempted to open her eyes, jump up and sit on the edge of the bed calling out, 'Come, Daddy, come to me, I'm awake now!' But she stopped herself. The previous evening, when she'd come home from boarding-school in honour of her birthday, her father had still been at sea, and she'd fallen asleep before he returned. She knew that this evening, when her birthday was over and she'd gone back to school, he would still be selling his catch at the stall in the wholesale market in Netanya. Solly was torn between his various longings and was about to wake her, and Matti sensed the approach of his smile through her closed eyelids, when Sofia's baby began to cough.

The joy that filled her in anticipation of his kiss and hug marred her pretended sleep, but Solly did not notice. He turned round quickly. His sharp movement struck her face.

Matti peered through her lashes and the dawn seeped into her eyes. Her father, drawn by anguish to the suffering infant, withdrew his gaze and showed her his square bald patch. He left her alone and went to the living-room.

The baby coughed, a hoarse, irritable, persistent cough. It echoed from the living-room to the staircase, leaped from floor to floor, broke out into the street, crossed it and knocked on the door of the house that had been Grandma Touran's where Sofia was unable to fall asleep, fearful that her baby would die.

Looking through the branches of the guava tree, Marcelle saw Sofia coming out of the little house and crossing the lane in her furry pink slippers, her legs as slender as a flamingo's. Matti heard the chorus of Marcelle's bangles tinkling as she went to the kitchen to put the kettle on.

'Did you manage to get some sleep?' Solly asked Sofia when she came in, speaking in a whisper, as though trying not to wake her. She didn't answer. She picked up the sick baby and rocked him on her shoulder. She was so weakened that her entire body shook like a cradle in the wind. Solly looked at her grey face, the face of a twenty-three-year-old beauty queen, and knew that the purple silk nightgown peeping out of her satin robe had not brought sleep to his daughter.

The baby continued to cough, and with every cough Sofia's face grew older. In the azure dawn light that drifted in upon them the diamonds flashed in the many rings her husband had slipped on her fingers. The gold glowed, as though leaking from her bent knuckles, as did the blonde streaks in her hazelnut hair. Between one cough and the next she uttered moans that had no time to turn to sobs, and she and her baby shrank a little more.

Marcelle left the kitchen, her fingers twined around the handles of two cups of scalding coffee, and the numerous thin silver bangles she could no longer take off her wrists groped ahead of her like feelers. Her movements betrayed the extra caution adopted by disabled people not born in that condition. To avoid bumping into the furniture she advanced as though she were walking on a riverbank and was liable at any moment to stumble and fall in. She set the cups on the living-room table, one in front of her father and the other for her sister, putting them down on a three of clubs and a diamond ace that had been left on the finespun tablecloth since the night before.

There was no end to the games of solitaire that Maurice played against his imaginary opponent. The cards were always laid in rows on the living-room table. In the past he had lain them out only in low moments on Saturday night, in the shallows of the weekend, when his sisters followed their admirers to the dance clubs, and his parents took leisurely walks to inspect the window displays of the closed shops. But since the house had become awash with tears, Maurice's loneliness played against itself night after night.

Marcelle returned to the window which let the autumn into the house. The severe-looking glasses she had taken to wearing since her marriage and divorce greatly enlarged her eyes, like the lenses of a microscope through which she examined her pain. To spare herself additional suffering, she had given up her job in the bridal salon and instead took care of a paralysed woman who lived not far away. After her return to her parents' house her eyes had suddenly dimmed. The Turkish films she watched in the daytime and the romances she devoured by night seemed to have coated them with a grimy film of grease. She would go through two and even three such books every night – all of them cheap and simple, as alike as cousins. The failure of her dream appeared doubled before her eyes, and she could smell the greasy dust of the lending-library.

In her loneliness in the middle of the night Marcelle wept fitfully. Across the lane Sofia, alert to the sick baby's lungs, was startled by a cry like breaking glass that would now and then burst from her parents' house. But the sob always died down before she had time to respond to it. A single cry – dry as dust, high as remorse, violent as rape – broke from Marcelle's chest every time her eyes fell on the framed wedding picture, or when she suddenly recollected herself. But she would immediately fall silent and plunge into the next page of her book, as though nothing had happened.

Marcelle Azizyan had been in love with Yoel Hajjabi for so long that, without this love, there was almost nothing left of her. Now she was twenty-two, a patchwork of nights and days, inlaid with characters and plots, stained with the blue bruises of a person going blind, yet desolate amid it all. Only a dusty, bland white vapour lingered between the doorposts of her body, the kind left by a glorious dream that can't be recalled in the morning.

Solly stood between his two daughters, the former hairdressers, clutching the coffee cup with both hands, but he did not drink. The dark liquid was bitter, because the sugar bowl had been empty for a week and nobody had bothered to refill it. Solly liked to sweeten his coffee with two and a half teaspons of sugar and dunk a biscuit in it, but the oven, like his wife's body, had gone cold and neither glowed nor purred. Iran's unhappiness had embittered her pastries and she'd stopped baking them. The colibri birds had also stopped hovering outside their bedroom window in the hope of sweet crumbs.

Time was when the beauty of his elder daughters, those three fruit-trees which had sprung up in the small grove of his life, drew him to them and filled him with astonishment. Sofia, Marcelle and Lizzie – three ringing, giggling bells. Iran had given him one son and three daughters. Then Matti was born, without her twin. But as well as all these – they should live long – there was beauty. The three girls grew and became three women. They were his daughters, but their beauty was wild. Solly scarcely had time to grow accustomed to it before it vanished. Time was when he would fall silent and stammer, embarrassed by the beauty which had sprung from his seed, and now it had all burnt away. Their bodies rounded out like the vases in the living-room, his three lilies bloomed and – snap! – before their fragrance had quite left his nostrils, it soured. Daddy's three dolls. What has become of you? He asked in his mind again and again, as if reciting the question by rote. His three dolls.

The baby in Sofia's arms leaked spit, tears and snot. Suddenly, alarmingly, he drew air into his lungs, as he always did after a coughing fit, every wheeze accompanied by a loud moan. Sofia raised her eyes to heaven, to God who could soothe her son's lungs, or bring her husband Itzik back from his business trips in Africa. Without her luxuriant sleep she was no longer as beautiful as she used to be. The memory of her reign had been usurped from her face. Since her recovery from pneumonia her eyes had been sinking deeper into their darkening sockets. Her father looked at her and thought that she had lost a lot of weight. Too much, he said to himself, it doesn't look good. Solly Azizyan trembled with compassion. He saw his eldest daughter, the most timid of them, her fingers crooked, her fingernails bitten, her lips chewed, nursing her sick infant, and saw the new anxiety which had emerged with the baby from the shrinking, frightened womb that nestled inside her.

Nobody moved, even after the baby stopped sputtering. Sofia's eyelids were too weary to rise or fall. She wept with her eyes half shut, as she always did when she saw death coolly whistling to its faithful hound, turning to go on its way, only to return and try to claim her child. Marcelle's glasses turned to the distance, her eyes glazed, as though she was solving a difficult mathematical equation, while the breeze tugged at her peroxided, frizzled hair.

In the gaping silence Solly wondered if he should wake little Matti and kiss her, or wait for his wife to return from the synagogue and kiss her. Then his thoughts reached his dead mother and stopped there.

The more Iran withdrew from him, wrapped herself in her sorrow and clung to the tombs of holy men, the more Solly missed his mother. While his wife betrayed him with God, his mother advanced towards him. He mourned her quietly, to avoid burdening the others. So secretly did he long for her that it troubled his conscience. He knew, too, that in the world of the dead his mother was awake, smoking, listening for the echo of his longings, the way she used to wait for him when he came home late. His wife was making him jealous. Seeing her muddled with despair, appropriated by rabbinical mountebanks who stole her away from him and bent her to their fancy, he tried with desperate courtship to remind her of his love. But her apple-round shoulders jerked in alarm when he touched her, and her beautiful eyes became agitated, as if she did not recognise in the balding old man with the porcelain teeth the lover who'd planted five children and all that beauty in her womb.

'It's getting longer every day,' he muttered. 'Every day your mother's getting more crazy.'

Solly knew that the sea was swelling and waiting for him, but his wife was dawdling over her prayers in the synagogue, and he decided to wait for her. He sighed and absent-mindedly kissed the lip of the coffee cup, tried to console himself with a sip and was shocked by the bitterness.

Cars rolled down the street; a hoarse engine started up. Marcelle lowered her gaze from the horizon, Sofia from the clouds, and they both saw Lizzie emerging from a taxi, picking out a handful of coins and thrusting them into the driver's palm. Their eyes turned to the living-room, met, then fell on their small father, standing there with his false teeth, holding a cooling cup of coffee in his hand.

Lizzie's heels were high and thin and as wicked as daggers. They clicked on the pavement outside the building, stabbed at the steps and assaulted the front door, as if she were accompanied by ten persistent men.

'Is Maurice awake?' she whispered in the doorway.

Her sisters shook their heads. 'Good!' she breathed and came inside, shedding shoe after shoe. Only when she was barefoot did the thin tinkle of her brass anklet become audible, and she was startled to see her father. His forehead creased as if impressed with a huge fingerprint. The pink snakes of his new gums swam in his mouth, as they did in the glass of water in which they spent the night. His third daughter, just over twenty, was dressed in a too-short party dress, made of a fabric encrusted with an excess of sequins that shimmered pathetically in the early-morning light. Her eyes were daubed with bright green paint, smeared around with tiredness. Piratical earrings dangled from her ears, and a velvet band hung loosely around her neck. Her nurse's uniform, with which she tried to keep her thighs warm and disguise where she was coming from, could not hide the shameful blue marks her cuckolded husband had left on her body.

Lizzie was back from the Mars Club in Ramlah. Her breath smelled of the brandy she had learned to drink from her father on Friday nights long ago, but she was not drunk. Her ears were still ringing with the wailing song the club trio had sung. Dimly she remembered some rhymes about suffering love, but her throat was still choking with the smell of the sweat of the lead singer, who wore his shirt open down to his navel. He had pulled her up on the table to dance with him and pressed her body to his. The musicians surrounded her and tied a scarf around her hips, to emphasise the shaking and grinding movement of her arse. The singer didn't touch her until the show was over, only sang into her cleavage and waved his white handkerchief, soaked with sweat, in front of her nose, making her dizzy.

She had not been to her parents' house for the past four days, nor to her husband's parents' house. Skimpy short skirts wallowed in the sweaty depths of her imitation leopard-skin bag, and her handbag lining was stained with makeup. Unlike her elder sisters, she still had her beauty, though it was bruised, and though in the last few days it had been reflected only in the flaking mirrors of strange bathrooms.

Lizzie was unaffected by the alternation of nights and days, because her work at the district hospital had long ago undermined her natural cycle of sleep and waking. She hardly ever went to her in-laws' house, where she and her husband lived in order to save money for flat of their own. But by now everybody knew why each time she went there she came out covered with blue bruises, and why she preferred to sleep at her parents' house in between hospital shifts and casual fucks, whose odour was not quite overwhelmed by the cheap perfumes with which she doused herself.

Since her marriage all the strength had drained from the Azizyan household. Nobody bothered to defend the family's honour from her bare cleavage, nobody bothered to count the packets of cigarettes she chain-smoked. A couple of months after the wedding Iran suddenly smelled the withered-banana odour that wafted from Lizzie. She lifted her eyes from her tear-stained Book of Psalms and stared at her daughter in naive astonishment. She saw that beneath her opaque honey-coloured eyes, below the splendid breasts in their loosened bra, her belly was perfectly flat, just as it had been before she'd announced she was getting married.

'Where is your baby, Lizzie?' Iran asked, carefully stringing the words into a gentle query.

Lizzie's lower lip thrust out in a pout. 'It was imagined.'

'Then what was everything all for? What did you get married for?' Iran let slip the awful question.

But Lizzie didn't hear her mother. 'It was a phantom pregnancy,' she explained. 'That's a kind of gynaecological phenomenon. It was all in my mind.'

When Iran Azizyan finally shuffled her wooden mules home from the synagogue, Lizzie was still in her disgraceful dress and Maurice had not yet woken up. She advanced like a beetle under the woollen shawl and lavender-scented kerchief that she had adopted together with the other old-age mannerisms, her short stature as close to the ground as an insect, her mind cracking with superstitions.

Her lips were still mumbling the dawn prayer she'd

heard at the synagogue, but her private pleas to God were already trickling in the crannies of her mind. With every prayer and hymn she thought about her son Maurice, her big daughters, Sofia Kadosh, Marcelle Hajjabi and Lizzie Moussafi, about her little daughter Matti and her sick grandson. It was only on their behalf that she spoke to God, and the prayers ravaged her soul – upright vertical prayers, circular and convoluted prayers, winding and singular prayers, recited according to tradition and stammered from the heart, morning, noon and night and in her dreams. Iran Azizyan exhausted herself hollow with prayers. Her soul was running down, like the six candles she lit every Monday and Thursday morning, the days when the Torah scroll is taken out of its ark in the synagogue. Her heart dripped and congealed, and the next day, with a layer of crusted wax underneath, it relit itself and wept.

By now the wise women were mocking Iran's despair.

'I'll make you some tea, missis. You just drink, calm down, then go home,' was how the coffee-grounds reader dealt with her.

'The truth, honey?' the zodiac-reading woman cackled. 'Astrology is rubbish don't you know, just make-believe.'

'You here again?' grumbled the reader of cards. 'Come to shame me in front of all my customers?'

They didn't even charge her any more, because in spite of all the good advice they'd given her with the usual rituals, none of her loved ones were relieved of their miseries. They regarded her as a nuisance and their greed changed to pity and their pity to cold-shouldered disdain. Whenever they saw her shuffling towards their houses, her arms dangling helplessly, they barred their doors, turned off the lights and ignored her urgent knocking. But Iran kept coming back. Terror-stricken, she carried her multiplying troubles out of her house, took one bus after another, and grovelled tearfully before their ample, haughty bosoms. She sought a bride for Maurice in a pack of cards, looked in coffee-grounds for a miracle for Sofia who had lost her strength to live, searched in weird rituals for a solution for Marcelle, whose love had died and no one would want her now, a healing for Lizzie who wandered by night like a hungry whore and whose husband beat her senseless, a genuine rabbinical blessing for the sick baby, and a crack in the Wailing Wall in which to post a letter to God pleading for help for little Matti's confused mind.

More than once she fell victim to crude impostures. She was sent to collect the tears of she-donkeys in a glass vial. She was made to yell mysterious Arab imprecations in all the rooms of the house in order to drive out the demons who had established a kingdom there. But the troubles in her children's lives did not retreat before her yells, irrespective of whether she shouted in Isfahani Persian, in Bengali or broken Hebrew. For every she-ass' tear she collected Iran shed ten of her own. Her house began to stink of disappointment, neglect and the little bagged amulets whose dubious contents soon rotted. Only the praise of love came into her house; love itself had long ago departed from it. It was twenty-seven years since Iran and Solly had launched their bedroom and the colibri birds gathered in front of their window. But since her children had grown up the house attracted only rumours and guesses about love. Lovers and bridegrooms came, even a grandson was born, but these were merely tail-ends, hints and echoes. Love's footsteps could be heard climbing the stairs, coming right up, but it never knocked on the front door.

That was why Iran undertook to abstain from all pleasures. She no longer sipped her tea with a sugar-cube held between her lips, letting it dissolve slowly down her gullet. She took vow after vow, but no one was greatly impressed by her self-mortification and her wagers against fate. Fate itself ignored the small woman whose tea was bitter, who sprinkled salt on peaches and black pepper on pears, who swore that she would never again taste anything sweet until her children knew peace once more.

In the meantime she tied red embroidery threads around their wrists, threads which had previously been looped seven times around the tombs of rabbis famous for their sanctity. The caretakers of the holy places could ease her burden for a little while, massaging her grief with the fragrant oil of promises. When she was faced with living rabbis, Iran trembled. Shrouded in the early-morning mists, she traipsed to their dens and took her place among the despairing. She met the same people time and again in the gloomy entrance halls, where they took their turn in an orderly fashion.

She spent the entire summer with them and became contaminated by their despair. Morning after morning she inhaled their breath as they recounted their troubles to her and the vapour of their grief soaked into her clothes. It blended with the rue tea that was handed round and made her urine give off a sour smell of self-pity. When she was finally called into the inner sanctum, she would make her way in only to tremble before the sweet-cheeked rabbis, who could see the terrified little girl quavering inside her elderly form. She put her anguish to them as if she were in her parents' bed on a winter's night, complaining sulkily about a bad dream. Sometimes she showed them photos of Sofia at her engagement party, or the picture of Marcelle and Joel Hajjabi at the henna ceremony, or the smell of Maurice's disenchantment in a sweaty vest of his, or a lock of Lizzie's hair snipped off while she was asleep. By the time she emerged from the dark rabbinical dens, evening had fallen and she shivered with cold and hope all the way home. Her husband had quite slipped her mind.

Iran approached the house. The guava tree spread its shadow over her and threw thin bands of light across her face. She tilted her head back to look at the third floor and the sweet whiff of neglected guavas blew into her nose. The sky was cloudy, but her eyes were clear. She remembered her youngest daughter Matti, whose eleventh birthday it was today, and who was sleeping in her own bed after so many nights in the boarding-school for crazy children. Seized with a crazy longing for her, to kiss and hug her, she hurried up the stairs.

Sixty steps separated the Azizyan home from the street. As she climbed up, step after step, Iran had one thought in mind, the kind of thought that fills the whole body, not just the head, a simple thought that flashes all at once, but any attempt to describe it becomes convoluted and tiresome.

Her body recalled the simple contact that had once existed between her and her children, the ease with which she used to touch their skin when they were smooth and rosy, the freedom with which she kissed and pressed them against her stomach. Iran's longings rushed backwards, reversing the direction of time, which had complicated and ruined everything. She longed for the time when there was no need to justify caresses, when the self-explained embraces did not produce anguish, when the countless, endless, insatiable kisses were still only kisses. She missed the mighty force of her motherhood, which could heal any insult, remove all misery, resolve all pain. She missed her children's childhood, the body that she and they formed together, one big warm flesh. She thought about the honesty that families lose as they mature, and the gaps which appear when the individualities take shape. She recalled the tickling on Saturday mornings in the iron bed which was filled with children and laughter. Thinking of their separation, she entered her home.

'There! You see!' Maurice shrieked at the sight of his mother's wet, tearful face. 'She starts crying in the morning and doesn't stop till she goes to sleep at night, crying and crying all day just because of you!'

He didn't know that by then Iran wept only for herself.

It was six-thirty on that Monday morning, Matti's birthday and the anniversary of her twin brother's death, but for a moment the Azizyan house became once again a diamond-cutting workshop, as it had been many years before, when Iran and Solly paid 5,754 pearls for it. The tears in Iran's eyes turned into faceted clear gems that diffracted the light into myriad colours. Through her diamond tears she could see Lizzie standing in debauched apathy in the middle of the room, shielding her breasts from Maurice, who was yelling, cursing and raising his hand to beat her. She saw Marcelle abjectly pleading with him to calm down, and Sofia begging him to take pity on her sick baby and stop. And she saw her husband – lonely without her, weary and helpless.

'Look at you! See what you've done to your mother, you deaf piece of shit!' Maurice was screaming. His eyes glared at Lizzie's breasts, as if it was them he was yelling at.

'See what's become of her, how she's eating her heart out? Can you see anything at all, you bitch?' His forehead creased and his eyebrows rose into his hairpiece.

'Stop, stop right now! It's a shame what you're doing to Mama and Papa!' Marcelle sobbed at him.

'Leave me alone, I tell you, both of you – leave me alone!' Maurice furiously shook off Marcelle and Sofia's hands, which were twining around his arms, adorned with their diamond rings, their silver bangles and red embroidery threads. 'You hear what I'm saying to you, you slag? Go to your husband, go! We got enough troubles in this house without you coming here like a tramp, showing your . . .'

'Maurice! My baby . . . enough!' All Sofia cared about was her son.

'You think if you put on these hospital rags I won't notice that you stink of brandy and perfume, ah? And all those cigarettes, ah? The beatings he gives you aren't enough for you? Ah?' Maurice's rage was burning hot, scalding his shoulders, his arms and hands, and he landed a slap on his sister's face.

As Lizzie collapsed under his blows, he bent down over her sequined dress and continued to thump her around the head. She made no attempt to protect herself. Her eyes were vacant like the eyes of a sphinx, which cries from its belly without moving its lips. Her arms quivered across her breasts and her head drooped to the floor.

'You don't understand, do you?' He spat out the words through his rounded mouth. 'Can't you see that you're destroying this whole house? That my mother is crying tears of blood because you are both such dumb cows, one more retarded than the other!'

'Maurice! Maurice, enough! It's a shame, stop it!'

Sofia and Marcelle's screams scratched Lizzie's hearing, but Iran's wails pierced her ears, wounding them.

'God! Oh God!' she wailed in her Persian accent. 'What did I do to deserve this punishment? Look at them, God, look at my children.' A woman of forty-four who looked sixty, she lifted her hands to the ceiling to tug at God's mantle, and wept loudly like a five year old.

'What can I do, God in heaven? What I must do with them? How did all this happen?' Her hands came down on her breasts, which had amply nourished all her children, and slapped, scratched and tore what hurt her most. Her face winced as if she had touched a hot frying pan. She touched it again and again, and was repeatedly singed. The mark left on her forehead in childhood by a monkey which sank its claws into her face throbbed and flickered like a burn.

'God, tell me who to blame that they're like this and I'm like this? I'll kill myself – will that make everything all right?' The cries that broke from her mouth seemed to come from far away. 'That what you all want? That I should kill myself and then you'll stop?'

Matti got up slowly. So slowly that when she stood up she glanced back at the empty bed behind her, to make sure she had gathered up all of her body. She couldn't tell if she was shivering from cold or terror. Very quietly she came out of the children's room, all of eleven years old this morning, slipped past the Indian gods which were exuding dust in the corridor, and crept, limb by limb, into the kitchen. Iran's candlesticks were weeping wax tears on the worktop. Beside them the proud flame of the memorial candle for Grandma Touran burned steadily, while the memorial candle for Matti's dead twin fluttered, shaken by the yelling in the living-room. Approaching the door, she smelled the sweet musty odour of the guavas. She saw her mother's anguish cleaving the ceiling in two and the glass drops of the chandelier vibrating, but she scarcely heard the yells, the crying and the blows.

'Hold your breath, Moni,' she whispered to her dead twin, who was crouching behind her. 'When you hold your breath your ears also close. Shhh . . . come!'

Matti went out through the front door. Her body tensed. Quietly, unobserved, she pressed against the neighbours' door and thought about knocking. In her mind she knocked. Softly. Not a sound came in response. She stroked the door handle. It moved by itself and the door opened. Matti put her head into the silent, empty flat. In it lived two people, a husband and wife without children, who took care of each other as if he was her son and she his daughter. Their bedroom was in darkness, and two glowing strips of an electric radiator heated the unmoving air. Matti wriggled in between the bodies of the woman and the man, who were lying closely and barrenly together. Between them she felt small, even smaller than herself.

They awoke together. 'Little Matti,' they whispered softly in one voice. 'You're back, our little Matti?'

Part Two

Us

On the day that Iran Eliaspour agreed to marry Solly Azizyan, he gave her a big, capacious jewellery box, made of wood and painted green as an artichoke. Inside lay a thin, unadorned silver ring, and he promised Iran that the time would come when he would fill it with jewels to the brim.

On their wedding night his face was so close to hers that Iran could see every pore in his nose, every delicate greenish blood vessel in his eyelids, and the tiny laughter creases around them. Her virginal lips kissed his face again and again. His moustache swept the minute droplets of saliva on her skin and he dried them with his breath. He removed the shoes from her feet then lay down beside her, and the wedding gown her mother had made for her and encrusted with 5,854 pearls on a single white thread gleamed before his eyes with an ivory sheen.

Earlier that evening, when they danced on the checked floor of the wedding-hall in Jaffa, the pearls had rubbed together, their precious glittering tinkle accompanying the music of the band and the joyous exclamations of Iran's brothers and sisters. Even now, on their bed in the asbestos hut, the heavy gown crackled in time with the rise and fall of her breasts and her chattering teeth. Solly undid the buttons with trembling fingers, and was dazzled by the radiant oyster sheen of her breasts. The rosy nipples at their tips were as small as the pearls of her gown, and he bent and kissed them, like a pearl-fisher lifting the gems from the seabed.

Now all that separated them were her white tights and her knickers. Even so, she felt more naked than she had ever been. The nylon tights, fine and wonderfully sheer, were stretched like a second skin on her thighs. Solly's hands glided down the slopes of her breasts and slid over her stomach, but when he tried to pull down the elastic hem that bound her waist and cut across the valley of her navel, Iran captured his hand and soothed the storming fingers with a caress.

'Please, let me keep them on, just for tonight,' she begged, and her pleading refusal sounded as sweet to his ears as a seductive whisper. He responded with caresses and did not unwrap her.

'Tomorrow I take off, I swear,' she promised in her Persian accent with Indian intonations. Like a butterfly reluctant to part from its cocoon, she clung to her nylon virginity. Solly kissed her all night until his wife was wet, trembling and moaning with desire, and her fingers began to dig into the pearly gown lying beside them.

They didn't hear the first pearl becoming detached and rolling off, but once the white thread was broken it released all the other pearls, which cascaded in a great stream on to the floor. A carpet of dancing pearls whirled between the walls, watched by the two of them in amazement until the last pearl found its corner and fell silent. In the morning Iran gathered them all up. She gave her husband 5,754 of them, and the remaining one hundred she poured, smiling her virginal smile, into her empty jewellery box. When we were born and were growing up – first the four of us, then Matti without her twin – in the house which was purchased with the 5,754 pearls, we loved to plunge our little hands into the deep jewellery box and stir the pearls that were left from Mama's wedding gown. We'd pick up handfuls in our fists, trying to produce from the box the cool, delicate sound of that famous gown, and then the same virginal smile would appear on Mama's lips.

In the first months after the wedding, their winter of honeymoons, Solly and Iran lived in an exposed asbestos hut in Givat Olga. There wasn't a single tree anywhere in its vicinity. Their front door faced the empty sea and the sea breezes kept slamming it. The asbestos walls gave off a choking smell of burnt oil, and grains of sand seeped into every gap, into fibres, into the holes of the vegetable-grater and the ear canals. By night, Iran and Solly wound their bodies around each other, like a pair of snakes in a burrow, and shared their warmth equally.

During the day Iran had nothing to do till her husband came back from the sea. She would sit on the sealed dowry chests, looking at the waves through the window and twisting the cheap silver ring on her finger, till she fell asleep. Towards evening she would open her young doe's eyes, leaf through the notebook of measureless recipes her mother had dictated to her, and take the stoppers out of the treasury of spices she had inherited. When Solly came back to the hut his nose was assailed by the powerful aromas of her cooking and the strong odour of her anticipation.

They would eat very quickly, then go back to practising their love lessons. Like a diligent student, Solly learned by heart the map of Iran's delicate bones, fine as a fish's bones, and the story of every little scar on her skin. Iran's lips learned to recognise every hair on his body, and the star-map of his birthmarks became etched in her memory.

They were both virgins and shy, but she was a skilled cook and he was a skilled fisherman.

So Solly's tongue imitated the soft muscles of sea-cats, licked her body with the slithery movements of eels, and his fingers evoked the silky fins of goldfish. She tried out recipes on him. She stripped him delicately like a roasted pepper, licked his bristly neck like fresh okra, made the hairs on his sweaty breast stiffen, as if it were rinsed spinach leaves, a little scratchy, a little nippy, till the skin was shivery. And like a cook she would now and then blow softly on the heated dish.

They had no memories of other beds, nor secrets or terrors left from other beds. So they made discoveries – she his salty sea flavour, he her dark river depths. And when they came out of the water, breathless and panting, they would shout their findings to each other. Then they could not bring themselves to fall asleep.

'Don't go to sleep yet, love, not yet . . .' Not yet, when her skin was smooth, taut and sleek like a female dolphin's, and he could flood her black eyes with translucent caramel light. Not now, when she knew how to gather his honey with her tongue while oboe moans broke from his throat.

By the time they had learned the art of making love, winter was over and they bought the flat in the house on Independence Street in Givat Olga for the price of 5,754 pearls. Solly placed the matrimonial iron bed under the bedroom window, with a chair for a nightstand beside it, and on it Iran put her green jewellery box.

The building on Independence Street had three floors, with three flats on every floor and three rooms in every flat. It stood broad and proud on thick elephantine columns, and resembled a fat woman spreading her concrete legs, her skirt raised above her calves, squatting to piss in the shade of the guava trees. Over the years a housing estate grew around and peeped at her.

The building's foundations were not new. Seventeen years passed from the time they were planted in the ground till the nine families dragged their belongings up the staircase, which twisted in the back of the house like a misshapen spine. For seventeen years it had been a diamond-cutting workshop. Its doors were as massive as a vault's and its barred windows as small as the narrowed eyes of a diamond dealer peering at a precious gemstone through his loupe. The new residents attacked their new homes with hammers and pickaxes. They tore the bars out of the windows and widened them, letting brightness and fresh smells into the cool, shadowy rooms.

The guava trees that surrounded the house were taller than the medlar trees that had sprung up among them. When the third-floor residents widened their windows to let the sunlight into their rooms, it came in accompanied by the branches of the guava trees, outstretched like open arms, feathered with white blossoms. In the early autumn the night air also carried the fruit's potent, crude smell. Every year this smell burst in through our windows and returned Mama and Papa to the days when they were waiting for their first baby to assure them that they had been making love correctly.

Solly carried the dowry chests on his back up to the third floor and Iran unpacked them. She found among the quilts, towels and tablecloths the blanket with pictures of female leopards that had covered her childhood in Isfahan and Calcutta, and spread it on the bed. She filled the kitchen cupboards with the rose-painted china, and decanted her treasury of spices into pharmacy jars with the Latin labels still pasted on their bellies. He lined the shelves in the wardrobe with sheets of paper, hung on the stark white walls of the living-room the needlepoint pictures Iran had embroidered in her maiden days, and she smoothed her cobwebby crocheted mats over the arms of the sofas. Together they polished the brass vessels with lemon halves and placed their wedding photograph in the tall dresser behind glass.

Along the corridor which led to the empty-echoing nursery Solly put up a long shelf, and on it Iran arranged the family of Indian gods that had travelled with her from Calcutta.

When the last chest had been emptied and the moon hung over the balcony they created Maurice with slow love-making under the blanket of the leopardesses.

Maurice was born in the dark stairwell. Iran managed to walk down eight steps, breathing heavily, her feet groping carefully behind the great dome of her belly. On the ninth step she was seized with a contraction and sat down on the cold stone, her legs ajar. Between contractions she slid on her bottom from step to step, and finally gave birth on the second-floor landing.

It was not cries of pain that brought the strange neighbour out of his flat. He heard a juddering metallic noise and opened his front door to see Iran sprawled there, embarrassed and agonised. One of her heavy wooden mules had dropped off her slippery sweating foot, struck the railing as it tumbled down, and fetched him out of his flat. He turned on the automatic light and saw Iran's hands gripping the bars of the railing as though they were her husband's hands, almost ripping them out. Her eyes were black wells of pain.

He was a dentist, his mouth a treasury of gold caps replacing the teeth he had pulled out himself. Without saying a word, he drew Maurice out into the world, the rictus of his effort exposing his golden glory. His hands, Mama recalled, were warm, smooth and soft as the hands of a pampered woman. Their confusing touch eased her embarrassment, because till that day she had been too shy to shake the neighbours' hands. She had certainly never imagined that one day a strange neighbour's hands would gently stroke her damp hair, turn up her skirt and deliver her son.

'It's a boy?'

'Yes. It's a boy.'

The pain stopped at once. Mama lay back on the floor, the man laughed and the baby cried.

She climbed up the twelve steps she had slid down, cradling Maurice in her arms, swaddled in the hem of her lifted skirt. The neighbour carried her wooden mules, his shining bald skull almost striking the stairs as he wiped up the trail of blood and afterbirth with the white coat he had taken off.

'Thank you,' Mama gasped and grabbed her mules, the umbilical cord and his stained coat. 'I wash it. It will be like new.'

Once behind her own front door she undressed and slid, exhausted and trembling, into the bath to wash herself and her baby. The dentist had said he would return in a moment to take them both to the hospital. After drying Maurice she felt all his limbs and made sure that his tiny body was perfect and complete. Everything was as it should be. His testicles were in the right place, his fingers and toes were in sets of five, his ears were neatly made. But there was no heartbeat under his ribs.

Terrified, she locked the front door and crouched naked over her baby. She placed one hand on the left side of his chest and the other on her left breast. Then she switched hands, but still did not feel the tiny heart beating. Only her own heart throbbed against her fingers, pounding anxiously like two hearts, while the neighbour's knocks on the door grew desperate. Mama did not open up. She remained on the carpet, staring at the ceiling, and waited in terror for God to notice that He had made a mistake. Now and then she sensed a dim, distant beat in Maurice's body, but she suspected that it was an echo of her own heart, or a noise from the neighbours' flat. Maurice's cry was a wonder and his hunger for her milk nothing less than a miracle.

When Papa came home he found his wife crouched on the carpet in the living-room, crying. His new son was lying in her lap with his eyes shut. He bore an amazing resemblance to her.

Grief-stricken, Papa also undressed and fell naked on her shoulders, and sobbed for his first son who was born dead and for his beloved wife, whose strange Indian mourning customs broke his heart. Naked, they clasped each other on the Persian carpet, their baby between them, and wept, till Maurice opened his eyes and bawled with them.

Papa blushed with surprise. 'Why then did you cry?'

'From excitement,' she excused herself and covered her face, to hide the tears that would not stop flowing.

Maurice cried for seven days but, like all newborns, he cried without tears. Mama searched for the tears in his eyes the way she had looked for his heart behind his ribs, but couldn't find them either. With her own eyes swollen from weeping and sleepless nights, she kept examining his eyelids. Her fingers pressed the tiny tearducts as through they were pimples, and she licked them with her tongue to stimulate the tears. The fingering of his eyes made him cry harder, but still the tears did not flow. Only Mama's breasts dripped tears of milk.

Mama was afraid of him. With neither heart nor tears, crying his wicked dry cry, his tiny hands gripping her finger felt like a lustful man's clutch, and their nails were as sharp as those of a voluptuous woman. His gums chomped her nipples with violent avidity, and the wound of his navel stared at her like an alien green eye. Seventeen years old and naive, Mama was full of guilt, but kept his absent heart a secret. She said nothing about it either to her sisters or to her husband. She tried to understand what they had done wrong in their love-making, and only begged her husband not to take the child to the hospital or to a doctor.

'But why, my lovely wife, why are you crying so? They'll examine him, see that everything is all right, God willing, and then we'll come back . . . What's so sad about it?'

At the circumcision ceremony her face was still sodden with tears, swollen and crimson like corals, and she still waited for the baby's tears to run. She swallowed his foreskin with a glass of water in the kitchen – a sure remedy for post-natal depression. Once, when Mama fell asleep, Papa managed to sneak Maurice out of the house to show him to Grandma Touran. Finally, when Maurice was ten days old, Papa's patience snapped.

'Crying, crying, crying, but you don't say why. Now I must take you both to the hospital. *Bolansho*, get up, Iran. We'll go to casualty, and maybe they'll get a doctor of souls who will say why instead of being glad you are crying all the time.'

He snatched Maurice from her arms and took him to the hospital. Mama followed him, crying all the way, but didn't say a word.

The doctors found Maurice's heart hiding on the right side of his chest. Their stethoscopes located it and it hummed at them happily. In their delight at the discovery they almost forgot to tell his mother about the faint rustling they heard in its beat. They called each other over, summoned students from all the wards, and bent over the remarkable chest. Mama had to push and shove through the wall of white coats that surrounded Maurice, her eyes blinking with joy about the newly found heart and her lips trembling with fear about the strange place in which it had chosen to sprout. Looking down at the small woman, whose head was at the level of their coat-pockets, the doctors adjusted their glasses, cleared their throats delicately, and explained that the child's heart was weak, that it was whistling like a flute with blocked holes.

'But he has one, he has a heart, he does!' Mama sobbed, and the nurses comforted her, assuring her that her little brother would be all right.

On their way back Iran and Solly stopped in the market and slaughtered five chickens, a sacrifice for Maurice's soul. When they got home, Iran ripped them open with her fingers and tore out their hearts. Plucked and gutted, the fowls lay on the kitchen worktop and stared at her with a final glassy accusation. She rubbed the bluish-crimson hearts with coarse salt till they were pink, then fried them with onions and ginger till they turned yellow. When the five hearts were swimming in a golden puddle of oil she ate them, standing alone, glassy-eyed, at the kitchen worktop. She ate chicken hearts every day until she weaned Maurice, and as soon as he cut his first teeth she minced them for him and softened them with her spit. But his strange heart did not change its place and it did not grow any stronger.

The earliest memories of first children are as shadowy as a closed cupboard. Sometimes, when the rosemary bushes put out their blue flowers, faint embers flicker in Maurice's mind, though he doesn't know why. For a brief moment the ashes of his infantile nights smoulder in the dark nursery which was once his room, then wink out. There is no one to blow on them, no one to tell him about the baby he was, to remind him of our Mama as a frightened seventeen-year-old girl tiptoeing into his room at night to gaze at her sleeping baby, the light from her face falling on his and sweeping across his dreams like the beam from the lighthouse.

She was so short, she did not need to bend over as she furtively undid the buttons of his tiny shirt and moved her ear all over his chest, like the stethoscopes of the excitable doctors at the hospital. Maurice's chin nestled in the thicket of Mama's nape, his breath ruffled the strand that writhed down to her back, and the lamps of her eyes illuminated his world.

Every night she heard the roaring of the blood in his veins, the singing of his lungs and the whisper of his domed diaphragm. In the midnight silence his dormant prostate gland hummed, her milk wound its way through his intestines, the stomach juices burbled, and pure baby urine flowed from his kidneys. Mama listened proudly to the courage welling in his bile-duct, the giggles echoing in his spleen, the vacillations simmering in his pancreas. But gradually the liquid concert in the baby's body fell silent, and the pulsing of his mutinous heart filled her ears. The one thing she did not hear was the rustle.

Sometimes she thought she heard a sound like fingers scratching a dry leather satchel, or the hiss of a banana being peeled, or the purring of a contented cat, but not a rustle.

'Come, Iran, my soul, let him sleep . . .' Her husband would come in and lead her back to bed.

But when Papa did not sense the absence of her small, hard-breathing body, and did not rise like a sleepwalker to bring her back to bed, Mama refused to part from her son, and cunningly invaded his thoughts. She knew that while he slept he could not hear her whispering beautiful words to ornament his dreams, that his mouth was closed to her food, and his eyes were shut and could not be amused with funny faces. So she entered him through his nose. She shook stems of rosemary under his tiny nostrils, soaps smelling of mint and lemon, and sesame seeds which glinted in the dark like flakes of gold. She also tickled his neck with the feathery rosemary, to give him pleasure. She launched sweet fragrances on the waves of his breath, to drive bad dreams away from his misplaced little heart.

'I'm a sacrifice for your little willie,' she laughed when he woke, and kissed and kissed the little member, shorn of the foreskin she had swallowed. She pampered Maurice as if he were a guest who would leave if ignored.

So Maurice knew Mama before the rest of us, when her motherhood was newborn. He drank immature milk from firm, thrusting breasts that had recently sprouted, was cradled in arms as thin as lemon-tree branches, and slept on her lap when it was still clothed with creamy skirts. The baby and the girl sat together in front of the new washing machine, staring at its dark porthole. Bedsheets and socks swirled before their eyes, water slapped at the flying dresses, soap foamed and rolled. The swish of the wash-cycle made them sleepy and the whirring of the spin-cycle woke them up. They played with his toys as if she were his elder sister. Mother and son wandered through the brightly lit daytime world like babes in the woods, lost among the big words and the tall people. Maurice sensed the alarm flickering in her eyes, smelled the anise smell of her diffidence, and tensed when her frightened sweat gave off an aggressive odour of musk. The hand that held his was quite small and tremulous with fear, and at night when she hung over him her tears fell on his closed eyes and leaked through his lashes. Mama's pupils gleamed very near his face, and never withdrew into the black sky of her eyes.

Her heart was always close to us, a child's heart at a level a child can reach.

Mama picked Maurice up in her arms and went to drink black coffee in the kitchen of a woman who read destinies in overturned cups.

'You got nothing to worry about, love,' the coffee-reader said and at once rinsed the cup in the sink. 'What I see in the boy's heart is that one woman will come into it, and she'll never leave again.'

She showed his little palms to another old woman, who peered at them through one eye, keeping the other one shut, and examined his life line, the line of destiny around the base of the thumb, his lines of head and heart – and saw nothing out of the ordinary. When Mama insisted that she look at the other hand, the palm-reader praised the loops in Maurice's fingertips and admired the unusual whirls and arches.

'Just like mine,' Mama said proudly, displaying her own fingers.

'Not like yours and not like your husband's,' the old woman scolded her. 'The fingerprint of one person is like the taste of guava – it's special and not like anything else.'

She asked the astrologer to appeal to the heavenly bodies to put Maurice's heart in its proper place.

'Come on, woman! I have some powers, but don't go

overboard, what do you think!' the stargazer reprimanded her.

Nor did the reader of cards know how to justify God's error, or explain how He had happened to slacken off and mix up left and right.

Maurice's heart remained where it was, rustling like an unsolved riddle in Mama's lap. She saved up and bought a stethoscope, so she could listen to it at night. He drank her milk till he was three, and she carried him everywhere in her arms. She took him with her in the mornings when she went to clean other women's flats, where he would sit in a corner of the strange house and wait for her to finish working. His attachment to her breasts adapted the shape of his mouth to her nipples, made his lips round and pouting as if to suck, and her milk made them rosy. His legs had stretched and his bones ripened, ready to run and jump, but her arms wouldn't let him go. Mama needed that embrace and Maurice grew within it.

'You got a son and made him into a girl!' Papa protested, and begged her to wean the boy. But Papa's scolding and pleas had no effect. Neither did the advice of her neighbours, who urged her to hurry and get pregnant again as soon as possible. Maurice was weaned only when Mama rubbed hot pepper on her nipples. Maurice bit them with his new milk-teeth, drew away quickly from her breast and slid off her lap. He looked at his new sister and said, 'Out the window, Mama. Let's throw her out the window, come on, Mama?'

On her first morning in kindergarten Sofia had a head cold, the collar of her new blouse was chafing her neck, and she saw the faces of unknown children peering at her around the teacher's skirt. But she didn't cry when, from behind the stack of play blocks, she saw her mother slipping out quietly. From the moment she was brought home from the maternity ward Sofia was always a newcomer. Mama and Maurice were involved with each other like a man and wife, and Sofia surrounded herself with towers of blocks.

It seemed as if they had always been together, even before Maurice was born. It seemed as if he was always cradled in her arms, drinking from her breasts, and she was tucking her head between his legs, kissing and laughing and promising to be a sacrifice for his pretty willie. It was Maurice's mother who gave birth to Sofia, as she soon realised. Sofia could never remember when it was that the dry wind which made her heart arid first blew.

In her early years she was a thin and sleepy child. She had no appetite for anything, neither food nor toys. When Mama tried to tickle her she did not wriggle away, but did not laugh either. Her appetite for words was likewise poor. She almost never babbled in that strange, excitable language of babies, and scarcely uttered a word before she was eighteen months old.

On her first birthday Mama made her a dress in scarlet velvet and seated her on the high 'godfather' chair, left in the house since Maurice's circumcision. Our uncles and aunts cavorted in Indian dances around her and sang her Persian good-fortune songs, but Sofia only blinked. Mama sometimes wondered if the child was quite normal, but would dismiss the fear with a mother's practical haste, with the same quickness with which she picked spinach leaves, examined bundles of leeks or chose aubergines from the market stalls.

As for Papa, Sofia did not know him well, and chiefly by touch. In the morning when she woke up he was already at sea, and when he returned from the wholesale market in Netanya she was asleep. Sometimes she woke up in her fancy cot sensing him kissing the top of her head and the image of his face fell on her retina like a hologram, indistinct and radiant as a dream.

On Saturdays, when he had waded wearily home, then sank in his vest into a prolonged working-man's weekend snooze, she would kiss his forehead and feel his sweat blending with the moisture of her lips.

Sofia was lonely until Marcelle appeared in the nursery with her sad eyes. Later they were joined by Lizzie, and Sofia pushed her thumb into the baby's mouth and the baby's thumb into her own, and fell asleep.

'They stick to each other's behinds. They are like flour, water and salt,' Mama said to Papa. 'Like instant glue, these daughters of yours, God keep them healthy.'

Two years separated Sofia and Marcelle, and Lizzie came a year after Marcelle. Mama explored their bodies and they explored hers. She told them that even if you're only going downstairs to throw out the rubbish, you should put on makeup.

'You never know what can happen,' she said. 'What if you meet your future husband on the stairs?'

She organised their sashaying parade on her high heels, and told them that a young woman's waist must be no more than twice her age – at sixteen, not more than thirty-two centimetres.

'All right, maybe an extra year or two, but that's all!'

* * *

Long before Sofia became a hairdresser at the Beauty Palace salon and double-chinned women stuffed her pockets with tips, her footsteps were accompanied by a clinking of metal. She loved the ringing of coins in her pocket and of the house keys which hung from her neck. She insisting on wearing them round her neck even after Mama stopped cleaning other women's houses and was waiting for us at home when we returned from school.

Sofia kept her pocket-money, the coins she won at backgammon and the change from the shops that she didn't bother to give back to Mama, in an empty biscuit tin. She kept this treasure-chest hidden under her bed, behind the pull-out bedding drawer. At night in the darkened children's room she would take it out and finger her fortune with her eyes shut.

Mama pretended to know nothing about it. She would smile with satisfaction when, while cleaning the house, she pulled out the bedding drawer and her broom struck the hidden biscuit tin. She weighed it in her hands and her lips protruded with respect for Sofia's greed, but she never said anything.

Mama didn't intervene even when she found Sofia on the pavement one evening, holding an auction of old belongings and toys she was tired of. She only said to her sisters, our aunts, 'Poor girl, she loves money so much.'

'Sofia has no courage. It's a pity, because a woman needs to have courage. Sofia is too scared,' Papa said.

'She's not scared. Why all of a sudden scared?' Mama protested. 'What she got to be scared about? Just a little nervous, she is. It'll pass by her wedding time.'

Nevertheless, to be on the safe side, she fed her raw and pickled strips of fennel against anxiety, and told her that there were two things she shouldn't pick at – teenage pimples and bad moods. 'That's how things are at your age, and you have to wait till they go away.'

Sofia got into bed and waited for things to pass. In bed she didn't chew her lower lip till it bled, and did not crack her knuckles. Under her bed lay her penny treasury and in the bed she discovered her talent for dreaming. Sofia slept and meanwhile she grew.

Then in the summer when she was eleven years old she began to cry in her sleep. The sound of her crying woke her up, and she couldn't explain it. Mama thought that the girl might be dreaming about her future and that it was awfully sad, but Sofia said that her leg bones were hurting, her spine was hurting, even her skull was hurting!

'I'm torn from inside, Mama, really, I swear I am . . .'

Mama remembered hearing just such a cry when Sofia was a baby and cutting her first teeth. She rubbed her body with oil, just as in those days she had rubbed her gums with honey.

Sofia went on sleeping and crying in her sleep, while her bones went on pushing against her flesh and stretching it. She grew taller and the bed kept growing smaller. Mama was convinced that it was excessive sleep that was making her grow so precipitately, and tried to pluck her torpid daughter out of bed. She dropped pot lids on the floor, sang aloud, slammed doors, and repeatedly shook Sofia, saying that she needed to change the bedding.

'So what if I changed it yesterday? Get up now!'

Mama persisted, as if she was envious of the faraway regions the sleeping Sofia wandered in.

'What are you seeing there – foreign places? Get up I tell you!'

But Sofia woke up only to cry, then fell asleep again.

'Is this what you were born for, Sofie? It's killing me, get up! You'll get worms in your backside from sleeping so much. Get up now!'

She made her drink coffee, forbade her to eat the iodine-rich fish dishes, which are famous as brain-food, and she herself lay awake at night, worrying where she would find a giant bridegroom for the girl. She tied a rooster to the orange tree in Grandma Touran's yard, but to no avail. At the end of the summer holidays, when the dozy Sofia returned to school, her classmates stared up at her in amazement – she had grown thirty centimetres in the interval. Her beauty towered over her teachers, rose higher than the green chalkboard and higher than the mirror in the girls' toilet.

'What does this dream mean, Mama? What is it saying?' was Sofia's perpetual morning chant after she woke up, battered by the night's dramas, her cheek bearing the imprint of the patchwork quilt.

Mama was spreading the remains of breakfast on eight slices of bread, and Sofia's face became strained as if she was walking into a strong wind. By the time the four sandwiches were wrapped up and tucked into four schoolbags, Sofia had caught her dream by the tail and recounted it.

'So what does it mean?'

'That you're an idiot, that's what.' Marcelle and Lizzie made fun of her, and Maurice said dreams were girls' stuff, because his own dreams were embarrassing.

Only our father, on Saturday mornings when we

were all tickling him on the iron bed that groaned with our laughter, was intrigued by Sofia's hectic dreams and wanted to hear the details. He, who muttered in his sleep more than he talked when awake, was never able to recollect his own dreams. Every morning he woke up empty of stories, as blank as a new school exercise book.

'It means that now you must get married,' Mama declared.

'Now? I must get married now?'

The riddle was solved.

'Or else . . .' Mama reflected, 'sometimes they say when a woman dreams about her wedding it means she's got worries.'

'Worries?'

'Yes. But in a few days you'll dream you're having a baby. It will be a difficult birth, but after that you will feel much better. Enough now, Sofia, finish-finish, you're late.'

Alone in the mornings, at home or in one of the houses she cleaned, Mama wondered about her tired daughter. She tried to decode her by her dreams, these being the only opening her daughter gave her, but on the whole she suspected that after passing a dark and empty night she made up the dreams to get attention. Mama was generous and forgave her her fibs, and Sofia, her schoolbag swinging on her back and her eyes still dazed with sleep, waited for it to pass, because Mama's interpretation was true. She did have worries.

Mama told us that since Sofia loved money so, fate would decide if she would be a very rich or a very unhappy woman. Until she met the man who made her both rich and unhappy, Sofia went on dreaming dreams. When she bore his son, she lost those too.

Having got her first silver bangle from Mama when she was a little girl, Marcelle began to collect them, until dozens of these thin silvery hoops rattled on her forearms, from wrists to elbows. They left red marks on her growing arms, and eventually couldn't be taken off because her hands had also grown.

As the number of bangles grew her forearms disappeared. There wasn't even room for a wristwatch. When she talked or played backgammon her movements shook metallic music from the bangles. When she was calm, their sound softened into gentle tinkling. But in the early morning, between about five and precisely seven – after Papa left for the sea and before Mama rose to change the water in the vases – Marcelle's bangles were silent.

When she was four, Marcelle left her bed in the children's room and moved to the living-room sofa. Her liveliness, which excited the admiration of the women neighbours, was draining Mama's strength. Her sad eyes were always wide open, and smiling dimples gaped in her cheeks. When she grew a little older Mama's pride in her became tinged with anxiety, and the anxiety turned to foreboding. All her efforts to rein in the girl's wild vivacity and to close those sad eyes in sleep failed. After three nerve-racking years of struggle, Mama and Papa gave up trying to lull her and themselves went to sleep.

They had carried her in their arms till their muscles screamed with pain, made room for her in their bed, then left it all to her. They sang her lullabies in all the languages they knew, repeated ancient tales and made up new scary ones. They smacked her, tried to exhaust her with tears and entreaties, fed her every kind of soporific drink and every fruit and vegetable that people recommended. They took her for evening walks all over Givat Olga, pushed into her mouth dummies, baby bottles and every one of her ten fingers. They bathed her in scented baths, tucked parchment psalms into her clothes, hid amulets in her bedding, hung pictures of sainted rabbis over her bed, turned her cot to face every point of the compass, even changed her mattress.

But all their efforts failed and Marcelle was at last left alone and did not have to suffer any more. She realised that her sleep was poor and capricious, and there was nothing for it but to let it arrive in its own good time. At five o'clock in the morning, after Papa kissed her and left to go to the sea, Marcelle lay on the living-room sofa, closed her eyes and slowly her bangles too subsided. With the muslin curtains drawn, a warm inner breeze ruffled her diaphanous thoughts and Marcelle learned to drift on shallow, reddish waters to her luminous, brief, two-hour sleep.

Insomnia clung to her. Her hearing was as keen as a wild cat's and she recognised every passing nocturnal noise, while her eyes glowed in the dark, searching for company among the bats in the medlar trees. Before she had taught herself to read and found comfort in her poems and diary, she chased geckos and crushed insects with the flat of her hand. She knew every phase of the moon and could follow the motion of the stars across the sky. She was familiar with every alarm clock that rang in the neighbourhood, and knew which one had a late cuckoo and which an early pendulum. She eavesdropped on the neighbours' quarrels, heard the smashed plates and broken sobs. She told us about the mad fits that gripped people by night, about hungry men who sleep-walked to the fridge and women who cleaned their houses by moonlight.

Sometimes she tried to wake us, thought up tricks to rouse us from sleep and delve into our dreams. But it was no use. Sadly, she would listen to our breathing as it grew slower, lower and softer, heard the last unfinished giggle, and sat in the dark room observing how, limb after limb, our bodies became slack.

'You bothering their sleep again, what?' Mama roared at her when the light was switched on and crying broke out in the children's room. She smacked Marcelle's bottom and dragged her away from us as if she had a contagious disease.

'Get out of here or I tear off your two arms. Scat!'

She was sick of the taste of the hot milk Mama made her drink every night, and she always loathed the lettuce and celery they fed her and which failed to induce so much as a yawn. As for the feasts of sweet red *kiddush* wine, which had cheered her lonely nights in front of the open window on the balcony, these were banned before long.

'Because I don't send my daughter to nursery school drunk, that's why!' Mama announced in the same tone in which she tried to read us stories at bedtime. But she soon decided that the fairy-tale books she'd bought for us at the recommendation of the nursery school teachers were putting her, rather than us, to sleep. So she threw aside the colourful books and instead of reading aloud tales about strangers who lived happy and wealthy lives, she perched on one of the beds in the children's room and told us about our weddings.

'Tell us again about my wedding today!' we all begged every evening.

'How come your turn is again today?' Mama scolded Sofia. 'Just last night I told you about your wedding!'

'That's right!' we shouted. 'Today it's me, Mama, my turn, please . . .'

'But I forgot,' Sofia pouted. 'And I fell asleep in the middle.'

'Ah well, so quick-quick I tell you about Sofia's wedding, then we go on Lizzie's wedding, all right?'

So night after night Mama's tongue sewed white gowns for her daughters and tailored a black suit for Maurice. Long lacy trains fell from her lips, champagne sparkled and *ketubbah* scrolls curled. When we grew sleepy, the hypnotic whispering infected our nightly dreams and Marcelle's daydreams. Years later that magic showed its powers, tightened its grip on our personal wills like fingers closing around the throat, and we all feverishly longed to get married. Then one summer the spell was broken and we all returned home.

As children we always waited for our shy father to come home at night, Marcelle in the living-room and the rest of us in the darkened children's room. In our drowsiness we sensed Mama's anticipation and her impatience hummed in our ears and kept us awake, like a badly tuned radio quavering a sweet lullaby.

'They can feel my flesh waiting for you, when I'm with Marcelle in the living-room,' she whispered to Solly one night after they'd made love. 'Even when they're rolled up in bed in the other room, they're part of my flesh. They feel it, so how can they go to sleep?'

At the sound of Papa's soles scraping on the stairs, three pairs of eyes opened in the children's room and lit the darkness like a bonfire.

'Papa's home! Papa's home!' Marcelle would shout to us. We'd jump up as one and rush to the door after her and Mama, whose mouth was holding back a similar cry behind an awkward grin.

'Wait, wait, let him breathe!' Marcelle would tell us off. She regarded him as her property.

Papa would flop on to the rickety velvet sofa with a dull thud, each time bursting another seam in its upholstery and startling the woodworms that were boring through its frame. He stretched out on the sofa, filling the house with hairy male limbs and iron muscles. His yawns blew fresh air through the living-room as if another window had been opened, and his eyelids fluttered in the effort to keep his weary eyes open.

Papa stroked Lizzie's head, which was snuggling close to his chest, and produced helpless giggles from Sofia's tummy as she wriggled up to his fingers. Maurice lay on the carpet and watched Papa yawning immense, roaring yawns which threatened to swallow into their dark cavern us and Mama, the furniture, even the framed needlepoint pictures, the new wallpaper and the plaster on the walls. Marcelle crouched at his feet like a dog at heel, and took his shoes off.

'Careful, careful, move away or it will spill on you!' Mama would warn us, coming up with a big glass of tea in her hands. She stirred it with the spoon all the way from the kitchen to the living-room, making the glass ring like a bell. As the glass hovered over her head and was transferred from Mama's fingers to Papa's palm, Marcelle could see the soundless storm in its depths, the tea-leaves swirling and the veil of sugar dissolving in the sweet vortex.

The cups of coffee Marcelle made him in the morning were black and opaque.

'Thank you, my soul,' Papa would say to Mama, clearing space for her to wriggle under his arm, taking care not to move his feet as Marcelle was still crouching over them. Marcelle untied the laces one by one, drew out the leather flaps and with an effort wrenched the shoes off. Papa cheered her on with grunts of relief, and thanked Mama in the same way as he licked the sweet rim of the glass. Marcelle's tickling fingers stripped the steaming socks off his feet and Papa's laughter made Mama's breasts jiggle as she snuggled in his arms. On winter nights Marcelle would put the checked slippers on his feet as they rested limply on the table, and on hot nights she turned the electric fan in his direction, and the breeze would make him open his red lips and stir life into his moustache.

'Solly? Solly? Go to bed now, your neck will crick if you stay like this!' Mama would shout when he fell asleep in our midst. 'Hop now, everybody, scat, to bed now!'

Then she locked the front door and Papa darkened the rooms. He left only the living-room light on.

'Goodnight, Papa's good girl, I'm going to sleep.' Papa bent down over the sofa and kissed Marcelle.

As on every night, the house was filled with Mama's noisy breathing and Papa's soft exhalations. She snored like a boiler and he talked in his sleep but couldn't remember a single dream. Marcelle was left on her own.

'Papa? Papa, are you sleeping already?' she would say, like a lame child testing its disability and trying to hop. Sometimes she wept softly, longing for the loud cry that, as an infant, she could let rip, which used to wake our parents and astound them with her permanently open eyes, while their hands stretched out to stroke her head sorrowfully.

'Papa? Are you sleeping?' she tried again, hoping he would read her a story.

'Sleep now, child, go to sleep,' Papa would mumble. 'In the morning, my heart, in the morning . . .' He would turn his back to her and plunge his head into Mama's breasts. He knew there was no point in trying, that the stories would only provoke a million questions and his head would drop on the sofa's arm-rest.

Marcelle whirled under the Cyclops' eye that burned in the living-room, and a silvery halo of moths circled over her head. That is why she grew up so fast, and her sad eyes kept growing sadder. Her years did not creep up on her, as did ours. She grew while we slept. In addition, she received the gift of the evening hours with Mama, who waited for Papa in a carnival of lights, and of Papa, who was the last to part from her every night and in the morning found her sitting under the kitchen sink, listlessly gnawing an unripe persimmon or avocado.

'Papa's good girl,' he said every morning as he drank his breakfast coffee, which she sweetened for him with two and a half teaspoons of sugar and a biscuit.

Marcelle spoke Persian better than the rest of us, because she listened to Mama and Papa till they retired to their bed, unravelling the grown-up syntax and the grammar of disputes. She went on listening after they went to their room, and so learned by heart Mama's subdued love moans and Papa's dreamy murmuring. All of it was in Persian, in order that Marcelle would not understand.

Apart from understanding Persian, Marcelle also learned to read Hebrew. It came about when, in her loneliness, she tried to lull herself by going over our story-books and repeating them from memory, patting her own head, her fingers imitating the fingers of our weary, yawning mother. One Friday evening, when Papa read the *kiddush*, Marcelle corrected him.

'How do you know?' His girlish mouth under the moustache gaped with surprise.

'It's written here,' Marcelle replied, pointing to the black print.

A couple of days later Mama told him that Marcelle's soul had just escaped the fate of a 'fantasist', God help us.

'Fantasist?' Papa's nose twitched with suspicion. 'What's a fantasist?'

'Yes, Solly, fantasist. I talked with the nurse at the clinic, so don't make faces like I don't know what I'm talking about.'

'I didn't say you don't know what you're talking about,' Papa apologised. 'But I did say this child is clever, that's all. Can't I say that? She's a clever girl.'

On Thursday Mama discovered that Marcelle's appetite for words was driving her to read the notebook with measureless recipes and the labels on the box of soup mix, the jar of honey and the tin of olives. She took Marcelle back to the nurse at the clinic, who sent them both to the public library.

From that time on the living-room lamp was not turned on and off in frustration, but shone through the night. A soft rustling of turning pages replaced the shuffling of bare feet wandering aimlessly all over the tiled floor. Marcelle's bangles tinkled gently and her hungry tongue licked her fingertips. Then the pencils squeaked as they strung words on the pages of her diary. Marcelle began to shed verses in place of tears.

Of all of us, Marcelle was the one whom Papa knew really well. They met at dawn, the coldest hour of the twenty-four, when souls rub against each other to keep warm, and seek comfort by becoming acquainted.

Every morning Papa kissed her and blushed. His mouth, plumply visible under his fisherman's moustache, embarrassed men and attracted the babies. He kissed Mama on her eager lips, and kissed Grandma Touran, whose flesh was as soft as cheese, on her furrowed cheeks, but he kissed us on the backs of our hands.

'The lady is married already?' he would enquire, forming his hand into a deep bowl and pouring our small paw into it. It always made us laugh.

'Your husband will not get angry?' he would ask and, like a man bending over to drink from a river, he would lower his face into the bowl of his palm and deeply inhale the odour of our skin. His closed eyes and his eyebrows rising to the blushing bay of his receding hairline told us how sweet was the scent of childhood that he was sniffing.

'Mmm . . .' he would mumble pleasurably.

Unlike Mama's short moist kisses, which found every fold in our body, Papa would push out his handsome lips like a pair of cushions, bristle his moustache up into his nostrils and revel in a long kiss, shaking his head with relish.

On Friday nights, after drinking half a glassful of brandy, when the alcohol glistened like oil on his siren's lips, his red sunburnt cheeks became quite fiery.

In addition to the cheap brandy, the drinks shelf in the dresser held a bottle of banana liqueur left from Maurice's circumcision, a bottle of white wine that had long turned into vinegar, though Mama insisted that it was growing better as it grew older, and a forgotten bottle of champagne, which had served as a prop in Papa and Mama's black-and-white wedding photograph.

But it was the tall bottle of brandy with the vulgar shoulders that was squeakily uncorked on Friday nights. Papa would pour the golden liquid into a plain glass, then ceremoniously slice two cucumbers lengthwise and sprinkle them with glistening grains of salt. By the time the brandy was down to the bottom of the glass, his flushed bald brow was covered with beads of sweat.

In the early days of their marriage, when they were still living in the asbestos hut, Solly had placed before Iran an imitation cut-glass goblet with a thin stem and shelled pistachio nuts for her.

'Cheers, my beautiful wife!' he saluted her, and put into her mouth one green nut and two small sips of brandy.

He saw her lovely eyes glaze over and her head slip slowly down to his lap. Friday after Friday, she left him behind and withdrew to a high, unreachable plateau of sleep.

'Come, my soul, come to bed, your neck will crick like this. Come on.' He would stroke her hair, carry her to bed, and wait for a son who would drink with him.

Maurice was ten years old when Mama allowed Papa to give him some brandy. Papa celebrated the occasion by pouring the brandy into the silver *kiddush* goblet for the boy.

'Drink! You're Papa's man. Cheers!' Papa kept ruffling Maurice's fine hair and lavished caresses and salty pretzels on him.

'What's the matter, Maurice? It's strong? That's good, it warms your insides. Now what's wrong with you?' Maurice's face twitched, he clenched his eyes and mouth tight, as if harnessing his inner strength, then vomited into Papa's lap.

So Papa went on drinking his brandy on Friday nights, alone and without pleasure, with the girls lolling all over him. Marcelle even sniffed the alcohol, Sofia toyed with the squeaky cork, and Lizzie dipped in a finger and tasted the drink with a grimace.

'Want some more?' he asked one night, and his velvety moustache floated over his red lips as he poured a few drops of brandy into the blue bottle cap and offered it to us.

'Come on, Solly,' Mama laughed, peeling a kohlrabi. 'This is little girls. You want somebody to throw up on you again?'

Maurice filled his mouth with kohlrabi and Mama attacked the radishes.

'It tastes like something insulting,' said Sofia. Marcelle did not care for it either. She preferred the sweet *kiddush* wine. Lizzie alone needed no urging. When she grew up she learned to use liquor as a device to catch men and pierce their hearts. They thought it was the alcohol that was dimming her eyes and blocking her ears, that it was the brandy which made her such an easy fuck.

Papa's face was generally associated with darkness. His eyes reflected the glowing lightbulbs and his daytime presence in the house meant it was the Sabbath. But there were remarkable weekdays, though rare and unexpected, when he came home early because his teeth hurt and he had an appointment with the golden-mouthed dentist who had delivered Maurice on the second floor. At the height of our afternoon games, when the night seemed as far away as tomorrow, we'd hear Papa's voice calling from below:

'Missis Azizyan!'

'What?' Mama would rush to the balcony.

'Is your husband home?'

'No!' she'd shout back, hanging meltingly over the balcony rail.

'Good, I'm coming up.'

'Papa! Papa! Papa!' Bursting with violent joy, we'd stampede down the Indian gods' corridor, crowd around the kitchen table and breathlessly watch every forkful that rose to the delicate girlish mouth. And while Mama heaped on his plate second and third helpings out of the pots of weekday dishes, we giggled, clustered around him and exchanged looks of delight at his apparently unlimited appetite.

'Papa, you want more?' We'd urge Mama to refill his plate.

When at last he'd had enough we'd go wild trying to do everything with him, show him everything, make the utmost use of the occasion. We clung to him, clasped his hands, hung on his neck, held his chin and dragged him downstairs, into the neighbourhood.

Because downstairs was where we were growing up, out in the boundless world open to the sky. In the afternoon Mama would send us down to confront each other, compete for a friend, measure our strength, win, lose, grow bigger. During those hours she allowed us to be ourselves, and Papa's rare appearance gave us immense power. With our chests thrust out and our noses in the air, we paraded him through the neighbourhood, drawing deliberate beelines around our best friends.

Because Papa was not there on the many occasions when we desperately wished he would show up, if only for a moment, when blood burst from a knee, when an insult burnt the tongue and scorched the eyes, or when one of the neighbours' children walked past us with their dad who'd just woken up from his siesta, strolling casually, arm in arm.

Only on Saturdays did Papa drop anchor at home. We'd watch him sleeping, clad in a vest, till evening, and when he woke up the rooms seemed too small for him. During the week he was far away from us, and the salt water of the Mediterranean sloshed in the great distance between us. The sea contained the fish, and the fish earned him money. At home Papa was a tourist, a visitor from the world of sailors and fishermen, where we did not belong. His exhaustion meant that our father was a blurry, almost invisible, presence in the house. We always missed him, even while he was with us.

His homecoming at night, together with the moon, cast a shadow on him which hid him from our eyes. Our love for him was entirely pure, untainted by the struggles of everyday existence. The punishments, the weeping and whipping, the severity of scolding and cold-eyed pardons – all these belonged to the realm in which Mama was empress and Papa was a commuter. From Mama we learned what sort of people we should be, and we loved her as a confidante; but Papa's image was the mould of our dreams. Marcelle was the only one who saw him every day, under the last rays of the moon and the first light of the sun. That was why she missed him more than the rest of us, and could not forgive Mama for forgetting him and preferring the dead saints over him.

* * *

By the light of the startling Persian moon, in the town of Maku near the Turkish border, at the foot of the mountains of Ararat, Michael Azizyan undid the hooks of the shift worn by his cousin Touran. At that time she was fifteen years old.

In the darkness of her father's leather-working shop, in which Michael was learning to be a tanner, he untied the butterfly knots and extracted the buttons from their holes. Amid the shadows cast by the raw pelts of sables, bears and deer, her exposed pale skin looked like a cloudy sky with a scattering of freckles twinkling on it.

Michael stroked her shoulders, his fingers gathered up the throbbing freckles on her smooth neck, and they dropped one by one down the path between her breasts and into the tremulous bowl of her navel. There he licked them with his greedy tongue, sucked them and crunched them between his rotting teeth.

Sulphur, acids and antimony salts made the air caustic.

A powerful odour of raw hide rose from the bed of fox-pelts he had spread under her back. Only when he had drawn out the iron chain, which was threaded through his trousers and served as a belt, and lain down on top of her did Touran realise how big her cousin had grown. When he took off his shirt she breathed the smell of oak bark that had soaked into the roots of the hairs on his chest, saturated his skin and formed black crescents under his fingernails.

'Touran, my beautiful, beautiful, beautiful . . .' he whispered. As he moved above her he seemed bigger still. His face, which had been deformed by the adolescent changes in his skull, became even more distorted by pleasure.

A strange sadness wafted in with the wind that blew from the summits of Ararat, passed through the dirty curtain and ruffled the pelts that were hanging from hooks. She loved him, she wanted to caress and kiss him in return for his desire, but her hands fell asleep and her lips were too lazy. Night after night she saw through the window how the smudged Persian moon changed the quality of its light. Night after night she returned to her bed with the taste of oak bark in her mouth, and dreamed that a great conflagration had broken out in the workshop.

'Mama! Papa! Fire!' She would jump out of the dense smoke in her dream. Choked by the fumes, she ran outside in her flannel nightgown and vomited in the mushroom patch behind her parents' house.

Pregnancy did not agree with her. The women in the bath-house in the centre of Maku, who had seen Touran Azizyan growing up, had always complimented her body, saying it was soft and pleasant like a bed made with a fragrant sheet of skin, and said that her breasts invited a man's head to rest on them. They were shocked to see what happened to the Jewish tanner's daughter when she became pregnant and looked neglected like a rumpled bed after a wild night of love. Touran grew very fat, her white skin became spotty and her freckles vanished.

'They say that there are such flowers,' the naked women whispered in the bath-house, 'that you can't pick and put in a vase. Women like this, marriage makes them wilt and pregnancy poisons the smell of their body, God preserve us!'

When Michael was late coming to the wedding canopy which had been set up over the mushroom patch, Touran realised he would not show up. She had known he wouldn't come the moment she told him she was pregnant. She heard him promise in the darkness that they would be married. She put on her bridal dress, twined lilies into her veil and knew that he was moving away, no one knew where, his teeth aching and an iron chain tied around his waist.

The murmur of the guests waiting for the bride and groom rose and fell, like the panting of a man in flight. The drums grew fervid with impatience, followed by the violin's whining quavers. Nobody was dancing; only the flames of the torches flickered in the mountain breeze.

'Your bridegroom will be here in a minute, keep your tears inside your eyes, you're a bride, you mustn't cry!' Her mother circulated self-consciously among the guests, and her father slipped away to avoid them. Michael's mother wept and his father perspired. A row broke out among the brothers and the sisters-in-law, who loved each other like sisters, until Manucher, Michael's younger brother, entered Touran's room.

He was short of stature and he kept his eyes down. His long eyelashes seemed to sweep the floor when he knelt down before her and took hold of the train of her gown.

'Touran . . .' he said, trembling, and touched her hand. 'They sent me to you to . . .'

Through her tears and the veil Touran saw his eyebrows climbing up into his hair. His mouth was open with amazement at what he was about to say to her. His words were dry, but his voice resounded in her ears as though it rose from a deep well.

'Me . . . Would you like me to marry you? Me? In place of Michael? . . .'

He thought he could hear her heartbeat, but in fact he could see her pulse throbbing in her temples, ticking like a clock, counting the moments which passed and still Michael did not appear.

'What?' Her heart dropped into her belly and thudded there, as fast as her lover's receding footsteps.

'Me – will you marry me? Now?'

An eternity passed before she gathered her wits and decided not to say anything about the baby growing inside her. Manucher counted a hundred wild poundings in her temples before she said yes.

The striped suit his father had had made for his brother was several sizes too big for him, and he looked like a passerby who had found himself by accident under somebody else's wedding canopy. All Maku was amazed, and the wedding resembled a funeral. The betrothal prayers were said softly like elegies, the songs wailed and the blessings were shrill with disgrace. The drums stammered and the violin screeched. When a sorrowful wind blew down from the summits of Ararat, shook the flaming torches and put them out, snatched the lily veil from Touran's ferny hair and bore it out of sight, the musicians stopped trying to force the gaiety. Everyone went home and the gates were fastened with iron chains.

One night Touran dreamed that she lifted her flannel nightgown and saw her pregnant belly as transparent as glass. Instead of a baby, there was a fish floating inside. She woke up. Manucher was working with her father in the workshop when she walked quietly past the dirty curtain and on to the midwife's house by herself. There she gave birth to Solly, waited till he grew a little and left Persia.

Solly didn't remember his father's face, nor the dubious look Manucher gave him when the rumours that buzzed in the bath-house reached his ears. He only remembered the oak-bark smell of his father's sweat when he came home from the workshop at night, and the snow his mother used to scrape up from the window-sill, roll into a ball and rub him all over with. Solly cried, his skin turned alternately red and blue, but Touran wanted to toughen him against the cold, so he wouldn't shiver. She also withheld sugar from him, to keep his teeth from rotting. In addition, she beat him hard and often, to make him a man like his father.

When he was seven years old Touran bundled him in bear, sable and fox furs, put on all her jewellery, and crossed the Turkish border on foot. At first the moon was sharp and piercing like the wind. Dry and evil, it lashed at them, until Touran sold a ring and a bracelet in exchange for a horse and cart. When Solly fell asleep she wanted to cry but the tears froze in her eyes like the wayside streams. When they reached the port of Ordo the moon was again sharp.

'What about Papa?' Solly asked when they were on the deck of the dark ship and it had cast off to sea.

'There's no more Papa. From now on it's just me and you.'

'Just me and you and that's all?' Solly turned back to look in the general direction of Persia and held the leather strap of his wristwatch to his nose.

'Yes, and that's all.'

If he were not so sorry for his mother, his heart would have burst with resentment. Resentment about abandoning his father in Persia, about her pretty freckles that turned so soon into age-spots, about the half loaves of bread, chunks of salt cheese and black olives that she sent him to buy on credit when she could no longer pay, and about all the cigarettes he stole for her in Jaffa.

'But they refuse to give credit,' he sobbed in Persian. 'Not one grocer agreed to give me credit.'

'Then who's going to bring me things if not you? Who have I got except you? Stop blubbering like a girl and go back!'

When Solly lit her cigarette for her and saw her bald, plucked eyebrows twitching with every puff, he felt his love for her weighing on his heart, as thick and heavy as the tyres of fat that had grown around her hips.

He slept with her in their one bed under Tel Aviv's humid moon, her head resting in the curve of his shoulder and the inky veins of her wrist draped over his neck. Before she made him a fisherman's apprentice and sent him out to sea, Solly had sold lottery tickets in the streets and evaded the watchful eyes of school-teachers. He would wake up in the middle of the night in his mother's bed, pale and awash with sweat, his eyes full of terror, because in his dreams the numbers on the lottery tickets kept multiplying to infinity. His sobs would wake his mother, who yelled at him to stop because he was a man, and banged on the floor tiles with the cherrywood stick she had taken to using. He would calm down on the heaving mounds of her breasts and fall a sleep on the cinders of her freckles.

Solly knew that it was just her and him 'and that's all', as it had been on the ship in the Black Sea and in their early days in Jaffa, when they didn't know a word of Hebrew. Touran never looked for another man but him, neither husband nor lover. That was why Solly paid no attention when his wife grumbled about his mother's goings on, her absurd lies, her pretences and her hypocritical flattery. He had left his father in Persia and his mother in South Tel Aviv, but when Mama spoke ill of Grandma Touran he reacted as if her mouth smelled bad and turned his back to her. He gave his love to our mother, but his compassion was reserved for his own mother.

When Maurice was born Papa took him to Grandma Touran's house, laid him in her arms and said, 'Well, Mama, now you also have a grandson.'

Grandma Touran blew her nose, wiped her tears and was about to ask that the baby be named Michael Azizyan. She did not propose to explain why, did not mean to tell Solly that Michael was his father, or describe how he would pull the iron chain from his trousers when Muslim boys pestered him in the streets of Maku.

'We called him Maurice,' Papa informed her solemnly,

'God keep him healthy. Named after Iran's daddy, who was really a good man and never did anybody any harm.'

Grandma Touran stuck the ivory mouthpiece of her cigarette-holder into her mouth, waited for Solly to light her cigarette, and her face grew grim. In her mind she resolved to wait for the next grandson. She had no eyebrows left to express her displeasure, so Papa didn't notice anything. She even commanded her great double chin, which hung from ear to ear, to stay still. Maurice began to cry in her arms.

'Take him to his mother,' she said without any emotion. 'Every child should be with his mother. Take him!'

When Mama gave birth to Sofia, then to Marcelle then to Lizzie, Maurice was sent to stay at Grandma Touran's house. When he said he wanted to visit Mama at the hospital, Grandma said: 'What for I should take you to the maternity? Anyhow, it going be a girl again.'

Eventually she left the neighbourhood in South Tel Aviv on Maurice's account. She said she was worried about poor Maurice, because our mother wasn't looking after him properly. So Grandma Touran came to live opposite our building, in a one-storey house with orange trees standing around it like sentinels and ducks waddling in the yard. She spent her days at the window, a cigarette stuck in her slit of a mouth, staring at our balcony. As she watched us her black eyes moved like the beads on the abacus of a grocer tallying up his profit and loss. When she addressed us she usually spoke either Persian or Azeri Turkish, and grew angry when we failed to understand her. In her final years she and Mama were no longer on speaking terms, and Grandma no longer climbed up, huffing and puffing, to complain about Mama's cooking.

'Your wife knows nothing about Persian cookery!' she would say, pushing away the rose-painted plates Papa placed before her in the evenings, heaped with delicious dishes.

'She cooks like she has a chilli pepper in her arse! Tell her one more time, so she'll understand – food is either sweet or sour! The food for a Persian has to be tinted just a little bit sourish, and tinted a little bit sweetish. But hot? Who ever heard of such a thing in our country . . .'

'All right, Mama, no more complaints this time. Eat a little!' He soothed her pains with his massaging hands and hushed her complaints with a vague mumble.

'Don't want to eat this poison!' she would shout. 'It's so spicy, it's poisonous!'

'But Iran says it's good for your bones . . . So eat a little, all right? It's really very tasty . . .'

'Oh yes? Tell her that's why children aren't made in the streets!' She smashed plate after plate. 'Otherwise anybody could come up and tell us what to do and how to do it better!'

Even when she attacked the bad upbringing Mama was giving us, Papa went on silently combing her ferny hair. Before she died all the calcium had run out of her body, God knows where it went, and her brittle bones broke easily. She would wrap herself in her Turkish bearskins and wear all her necklaces at the same time. She asked Papa to draw with a black pencil on the bald patches left by her plucked eyebrows, and Papa drew a black arch over each eyelid, but his mother's mothbally sweat soon made them run. But right up to her dying day Touran's toenails were carefully lacquered with the red varnish her son painted on them.

* * *

Mama's parents died before we were born. Maurice and Sofia were named after them. Mama was nine years old, small and light as a piece of luggage, when they stuffed everything they had into tin chests, rolled up the carpets and migrated from Isfahan to Calcutta. They didn't want to upset her, so they told her that it was just a trip and 'we'll soon be back'. That was why she never said goodbye to her native city. They placed her with her back to the driver on top of the baggage on the lorry, but she twisted around, turned her back to the receding Isfahan, and peered at the horizon through the windscreen.

'You'll hurt your neck like this, *omri*,' her mother said in a quavering voice, trying not to cry. 'Go to sleep now.'

'But I don't want to sleep, Maman, I'm looking out.'

Sofie Eliaspour waited till later, when she covered her lap with the woollen blanket woven with pictures of leopardesses and got Iran to rest her head on it and go to sleep, before she allowed herself the soundless tears of emigrants, in which were blended her regret for the place she had left with fears of the place she was heading for.

As the road began to wind towards the marshes in the heart of the kingdom and the lorry rocked from pothole to pothole, Iran woke up and felt her face wet with tears she had not shed.

She wiped the dust of the road and the tears off her cheeks, and said to her mother, 'Maman, look – did I cry? Did I have a bad dream? I can't remember what I dreamed.'

'Me too, my *omri*.'

'You too, Maman?'

'Yes,' Her mother stroked her face. 'Every child at this

age has a bad dream. That's what your father says. Every child has a bad dream, he says, and after that he's not a child any more.'

From the moment Sofie Eliaspour was married, her husband stood behind her shoulder and, like a theatre prompter, whispered things into her ear. After he was run over by a bus in Calcutta she almost stopped speaking altogether, and she never learned to speak Hebrew after she settled with her children in Israel.

'Your father, God rest his soul, liked to eat aubergines,' the widowed Sofie would say sadly to her daughter. 'He used to say to me, *omri*, I do very much like to eat aubergines.'

It was so difficult for her to part from him, from the mouth which had planted the words in her ears, that she silenced her own voice and left him to speak out of her throat.

'My poor Maurice suffered so much in the summer,' she would sigh. 'He used to say to me, *omri*, I feel too hot in the summer.'

Eventually her overworked heart became weak and she also died, and then the two of them fell silent.

They left Isfahan after Maurice had received a letter from his brother, along with the usual consignment of pearls, urging him to close down the Isfahan branch of the family business and move to Calcutta. Maurice Eliaspour whispered the news in his wife's ear, wiped her tears, arranged the marriages of Iran's sisters to their fiancés, and bought a lorry. On it he loaded his belongings and children, his daughters- and sons-in-law, and his two small grandchildren, and set out.

Maurice sold the lorry in the town of Bushehr on the

Persian Gulf and he and his family boarded a steamship which belched thick black smoke and did not submit to the monsoon winds of the Indian Ocean. Five weeks after passing through the Straits of Hormuz they dropped anchor in the port of Bombay, exchanged the high seas for the railway and travelled to Allahabad. There they took a sailing boat to cross the dark currents of the Ganges, which streamed into Iran's body, flooded her little heart and wended through her flesh like a throbbing, rousing new artery.

'The goddess Ganga, the goddess of this river, lives deep down in these waters,' the sailors told Maurice. They stroked the turbid current with their wooden oars, and Maurice stroked his daughter's head with both hands.

'What did they say, Papa?'

'That she came down through the hair of the king of their gods and poured into this nasty water. Look, dolphins – can you see?'

But Iran ignored the blind river mammals and her eyes strained to see Ganga and the crocodile that they said she rode on.

Where the river raged and foamed on its way to Mirzapur, Iran thought that the goddess was being coy, like the Jewish girls who ran away from the cheeky Muslim lads who pestered them in the streets of Isfahan. Only when they reached Varanasi did Iran realise that Ganga was playing with her, hiding behind the hills, lying in breathless ambush in the valleys, and like her own small niece, who leaped at her from behind doors, shouting 'Tararam!', the goddess too would suddenly leap out from behind the rocks and startle her with a loud cry. She knew that she was somewhere out there, among the waves of the river, curious and smiling, winding from town to village, hiding and appearing, retreating and peeping out, pouring fresh streams into the river and carving new riverbeds, and that eventually they would meet.

Iran's uncle met them in the town of Ghazipur with three black English cars. They arrived in Calcutta in the small hours of the night. There was no moon and the city was dreaming. Only a few lights and fires burned on the banks of the Hooghli, the Ganges' great tributary, but they were enough to reveal figures going down and coming out of the water, cows reclining on the shore, and the outlines of domed temples and steepled palaces.

They met the uncle's family in a spacious hall with cloth hangings billowing on the ceiling like giant fans, the floor heaped with layers of silk carpets which sighed softly under the bare feet of the servants. Here in this house the two families would live together for four years, surrounded by huge ficus trees with numerous trunks that thrust their branches in through the windows, and golden-haired long-tailed monkeys which swung through their foliage.

'Can you take me to your river?' Iran asked the cousin who was sitting beside her, when they had all settled down on the colourful cushions for a noisy, joyous meal.

His name was Jamshid and he was about her age, being the eldest of five boys. His face was flushed, his head inclined forwards, and his eyes looked down shyly at his toes that were twitching under the leather straps of his sandals. His voice sounded bell-like and girlish and tended to crack when it rose. He was embarrassed by its quavering when he replied to her in the broken Persian his homesick father had been drilling into him.

'Now? You want to go now?'

She nodded, and he led her through the alleys, her body tired but her soul crowing with excitement. Iran saw the dawn rising over Calcutta, heating the air and confusing the lingering moths. Jamshid held her hand when they passed among lepers, who were yawning in the face of the new day, sleeping monks curled up like balls beside the road, and painted elephants lying on their sides.

Hand in hand they descended the mossy steps and sat down beside the carcass of a donkey that had died in the night. She looked around her, breathless, and he peered at her surreptitiously, trying in vain to catch her great, astonished eyes as they swept the scene. But Iran did not notice his gaze and did not sense the delicate, silent courting song that his body began to sing her that first morning.

Before long a throng of people surrounded the two children. Washermen slapped wet cloths with weary, rhythmic slaps and sighs. Huge, thoughtful-looking buffaloes sank up to their necks in the river, housewives who came to wash dishes frolicked in the water like little girls, servants scoured silver platters and played at dazzling people with their mirror-like reflections, children washed their hair, barbers with severe expressions shaved barefoot men, women depilators used threads to strip moustaches from their female customers, their eyes welling with sympathy for their suffering, a woman picked headlice out of her daughters' hair, people scrubbed their teeth with moist twigs, an ear cleaner inserted a long spill into waxy tunnels, roosters walked down to sip, old men dried their thin muslin loincloths and babies squealed with delight when slithery trout tickled them with their tails.

'Today is their Sabbath?' Iran asked her cousin.

'No.'

'What then? Do they have a family wedding this evening? Is that why they're all getting ready?'

'No. It's like this every day.'

The red sun, round as the full moon, also played in the water and shook golden flakes all over it. Iran closed her eyes and let it cast shimmering lights on her eyelids. Jamshid thought she was tired from the journey, but Iran only wanted to listen. India bent over her small visitor and whispered to her the great secret she tells her lovers.

Suddenly Jamshid saw her eyes open, her head came up like a snake rising from the basket at the sound of the flute, and her gaze became intense and bewitched. The smell was so good, and the air felt so sweet. Iran stood up, approached the water's edge and saw its murky tongues licking and frothing. Obscure whirlpools swirled in the river when it felt her bare feet entering. The colour of the water turned rosy and violet when Iran slipped into it, warm currents kissed her skin and her skirt spread out like fins.

'Come out! Oh please come out! This is not for us! Come out, it's dirty!' She heard her cousin's voice changing from that of a child to a man's and from a man's to a child's, while Iran rose and sank in the water, rose and sank with her eyes shut.

In the course of the years that her family lived there Iran told Jamshid all the bawdy Persian jokes she could recall, translating them into Bengali. Even in those days she always burst out laughing just before the punchline, when she would throw her head back, open her mouth and show her teeth, and the little clapper in her throat jiggled.

It was Jamshid Eliaspour who bought her the statues of Indian gods in the sculptors' quarter in the city, he who told her that the sad singing that rose from the house of the widows spoke of their longing for Krishna, and it was in his company that she climbed on the many-trunked ficus trees and hung from the branches with the monkeys.

He also went with her every day, hand in hand, to sit on the bank of the river, and together they dispatched to its depths a wish in a banana-leaf saucer, decorated with jasmine flowers and bearing a bit of burning camphor and smoking incense.

'Please God let us never leave Calcutta, let us stay here for ever, amen,' she whispered her wish audibly one evening. With her eyes shut and her braids hanging on her shoulders, she sent off the offering with her face glowing in concentration as if she were setting free a dove. A soft ripple snatched the tiny boat with its flickering flame.

'But it's only a trip, Iran. You'll be back in a month, why are you worrying?' Jamshid said to her on their way home, stroking the soft moustache fledging on his upper lip.

'I don't want to go on a trip, don't want any Israel.' The third eye painted between Iran's eyebrows glittered angrily.

Maurice Eliaspour had really intended to take his

family on a visit to Israel and then return to Calcutta, but that very week he fell under the wheels of a bus and died.

'My Maurice wanted to go to Israel,' his wife Sofie wept. 'He said to me, *omri*, I want to go to Israel. That's what he said to me.'

She crammed everything she could into the tin trunks, bundled up the pearls, gathered his children and grandchildren, his sons- and daughters-in-law, and travelled to Israel to bury him.

Before they all squeezed into one of the uncle's black cars, Iran climbed with Jamshid on the ficus trees. She patted the furry monkeys in farewell and Jamshid stroked her hair. Before he could ask her if she would agree to marry him, and that way she could stay on in Calcutta, a long golden monkey arm reached out and scratched her face. Three of its claws carved three bleeding furrows on her forehead, which would leave a trident-shaped scar.

Looking out of the window of the plane that took her and her family to Israel, Iran saw the Ganges opening many arms in the delta plain, and the goddess riding on her crocodile, struggling against the silt and the tide, and at long last sweeping into the vast Indian Ocean.

Before Matti was born without her twin, when we were still small, childhood ailments swept through the house like epidemics. In the late summer afternoons we would sprawl around Mama in the kitchen after the midday meal, almost swooning under the impact of her massive dishes, while the heat of the emptying pots rivalled the heat of the wind. A column of golden ants marched up to the worktop and into the heap of dirty dishes in the sink, and the orange sun blazed on the remains of tomato sauce clinging to the plates still on the table, and the whole house seemed to shimmer in the heat haze. In those fragrant moments of Mama's tiredness and our boredom, amid the tedious buzzing of flies, when our childish sweat was like honey stains on our clothes and the thirst felt like a puddle of jam in our throats, Mama would suddenly take that deep loud breath that housewives remember to take between one chore and another, and launch a new assault on the headlice.

In the summer especially, when the sweat coated our hair with brine, making it stick to itself in strands and deepening its black hue, the headlice would hatch by the thousand.

Softly-softly Mama would stalk our bare feet as they searched for cool corners on the floor tiles in the shuttered rooms. When she saw that the heat and play had drained our vast childish energies, she would pounce and catch us between her arms and suppress our loud protests against her lap, which she used like a powerful vice. She pushed our rebellious heads, one after the other, into the fat hoops around her belly and subdued the young muscles struggling to escape from the trap of her thighs.

'Don't move, I said, don't move!' She restrained each of us in turn.

Her features grew pointed, as if she was trying to decipher difficult handwriting. Her eyes met near the bridge of her nose and she squinted cross-eyed, her cavernous breaths making her nostrils flare, while her fingers moved crabwise over our scalps, searching here and there, burrowing into the dry crust, her scarlet nails drilling into the roots of the hair.

Time after time we almost managed to escape from between her capturing arms, but we didn't stand a chance against the hunter's keenness that sharpened her instincts. She'd catch us, sulking and whining, and push our foreheads against her navel. Our faces butted against her womb, our tears ran with her sweat, and the smell of her private parts flooded our noses through the onion juice that speckled her dress.

'There! . . . There! . . . There! . . .' she would exclaim triumphantly when she found a whitish headlouse egg clinging to a hair on our head and utter a vindictive snort, and we held our breath as she did. Grimacing with horror, she would pluck the minute egg from the hair, balance it carefully between two fingernails, and crush it with a tiny *crack* in her red lacquered pincers.

'It hurt? It hurt a little, it did? Never mind, it will be all right on your wedding day.'

A light, efficient kiss was planted on our necks, on the vertebrae that poked out at the nape, to make up for the pain and the plucked hair. Her fingers grew ever more avid for the hunt, more skilful, and again and again she grunted with horror as she picked and killed, rubbed off and flung away.

Having forgotten the struggle, we would continue to loll on her lap after the ritual delousing was finished. Lovingly we stroked her floury forearms, revelled in the pleasure of her fingers wandering through our plumage, and surrendered to the smell of sweat in her armpits which grew sharper till it resembled the smell of boiled lentils.

Mama's arms were wide and trunk-like, heavy with flesh, soft and sweet with fat. Their strong muscles were linked to her bulging deltoids and round shoulders by the plumpest, softest flesh – the pampered, lazy rolls of fat that hung down from her underarms. These sagging folds, which remained cool when her whole body was bathed in sweat, were our special delight. Our tiny hands made them swing to our amazement, our cheeks pressed against them with love, and our tickling fingers toying with them produced yelping giggles from Mama, which hinted at her little girl's bashfulness about the big heavy woman's body that had grown around her.

'Enough now, stickies!' She would shake us off like a bitch shaking off her pups and reclaim her body. 'Leave my hands alone, you make me hot.'

Softly and persistently, like midnight lovers, we'd slip the watch off her wrist and expose the full-moon mark it had left on her skin. Once the moon waned, we loved to sink our thumbs into the round snail-shaped scars on her upper arms, left by the vaccinations she'd had as a child in Isfahan. We would casually roll up the sleeves of her blouse, kiss the rough spiral with its curiously shiny whorls, and sniff at her fingers for the odour of bleach she brought from other women's houses.

Sofia, Marcelle and Lizzie tried to imagine Mama as she was in her childhood, as small as they, her arms as thin as lemon-tree branches, dressed in a well-behaved pleated skirt, and her black plaits braided primly around her head.

'Mothers, you see,' Papa tried to explain to us, 'before they become mothers they are all little girls, just like you are now. Honestly, it's the truth, so help me!'

'Oh sure, so you say,' Marcelle grinned.

'Then whose mummy was she when she was little?' Sofia asked. Lizzie too could not quite work it out. Only Maurice knew that despite the thick pads on the backs of her hands, despite her ample, rocketing bursts of laughter, the thunder of her voice that ruled the house, Mama was really a little girl with no breasts, no husband and no children.

'There, Sofia, look at her now and you'll see,' Papa whispered when Mama roared with laughter at the joke she'd been telling, a second before the punchline, closing her eyes like a little girl and showing the fillings in her teeth and the bell-clapper in her throat.

'There now, Marcelle, take a look at your mama now. Lizzie, you're missing everything!' he said, pointing at his wife when she was surrounded by her big brothers and sisters and became once more a small obedient child.

She was fifteen when he first met her on the beach at the southern end of Tel Aviv when the sun was going down over the sea. Her mother, Sofie Eliaspour, widowed and silent, passed the afternoon hours in her house in the Shabazi quarter sewing a wedding gown for her daughter, stringing pearls on a single long white thread. At night the two of them slept in the same bed, and Iran made sure that her mother's heart did not beat too strongly, because she said it hurt her. Iran already knew that not many beats remained in that sore heart before it would stop altogether and cease tormenting her mother, so she refused to leave her and go to school. She sat at her feet and took down recipes without measurements, because recipes were all that remained in Sofie's mouth, since her husband was no longer standing behind her back, stroking her nape lovingly and whispering words into her ears.

'How your father loved to eat *sefenjun*,' Sofie wept in Persian. 'Whenever I made him *sefenjun*, he would say, "Sofie, *khaili khoshmazes*, it's very tasty." He really loved *sefenjun*.'

Iran went to the Carmel Market to buy lamb meat, walnuts, coriander and pomegranates in order to learn how to make *sefenjun* without specified quantities. Her sisters had instructed her when they came to see their mother on Saturday: 'All you have to do is stand in front of the man, point at the thing you want and say, "*Kamah?*"'

'*Chi-chi e* "*kamah*"?' Iran asked. 'What does "*kamah*" mean?'

'*Se chandeh*, it means, "How much?" in Hebrew.'

Iran clutched the coins in her fist, learned by heart the ingredients needed to make *sefenjun*, and all the way to the market kept repeating, 'ka-mah', 'ka-mah' . . .

When she stood in front of the herb-seller's stall she pointed to bunches of coriander, gave him an immigrant's broken-hearted smile and asked with her mouth full of spit and a heavy accent, '*La-mah?*' [Why?]

'Eh?'

'*La-mah? La-mah?*'

'Why what, girl?'

'*La-mah?*' she repeated, her doe's eyes filling with tears, and showed him her sweating palm with the coins she'd been clutching.

At home she fried the lamb in the fat of its tail, threw tomatoes into its juices, drenched it with crushed pomegranates and coriander, and all the while mumbled to herself, '*Kamah? Kamah?*'

'The walnuts are added at the end.' Iran read what she had written that morning at her mother's dictation. 'Walnuts make our food bitter if we add them in the beginning . . . *Kamah* . . .'

Sofie wept as she ate the *sefenjun*.

'But I put them in at the end, like you said!'

'It's not on account of the walnuts, my soul,' Sofie said, pushing the steaming dish aside. She picked up the needle and went back to stringing pearls. 'Now go and find yourself a bridegroom,' she pronounced. 'Your father said to me, let Iran find herself a husband she loves. So go, my soul, go. In the meantime, I'll be sewing the wedding dress for you.'

So Iran went to look for her bridegroom on the shore, the place where bridal couples stopped on their way to the wedding, stood with their backs to the sun setting over the sea and smiled at the clicking cameras. As she walked south towards Jaffa a pale daylight moon hung in the radiant blue sky, and her heart ached wistfully for her faraway river.

Solly was rowing his boat towards the shoreline when he noticed her and immediately blushed. He saw a girl hovering on the shore, her long hair flying like wings, her dress trailing like a tail, and turned the bow in her direction. She walked on the sand in small, thoughtful, almost imperceptible steps, her pelvis swaying easily in a semi-circular motion. As he drew nearer, Solly saw how beautiful she was and how small, and realised that he was afraid to reach the shore. He felt his mouth going dry and salty at the sight of all that beauty, and his tongue stuck to his palate.

So he turned his boat out a little and went on rowing alongside her in the direction of Jaffa. The fishes he'd caught flapped on the bottom of the boat while her hair billowed in the breeze. Her great eyes glanced at him for a second, then shyly flickered back to the water. He also felt shy and stared at the sand at her feet. He saw her feet leave imprints of her heel and big toe, which the sea soon lapped and effaced. He saw the shells she stepped on, and her long skirt trailing behind her, wet and foamy.

When they reached the precinct of the Armenian monastery he dared to look directly at her, at her pink, creamy, shiny eyelids. Then he took another look and saw her thin shoulders where the vaccination snails gleamed. A shy, virginal lad was Solly. He looked again and saw her beautiful breasts. The blue of the sky deepened into the blue of the sea, and her skin took on a plummy tint.

Soon it was evening and the moon came up. The bridal couples had left. The seashore and the summer were at an end. She hovered barefoot over dry land and he bobbed, blushing, on the water, having reached as far south as the Rock of Andromeda.

'Can you take me back?' the girl said to the darkness, the stars twinkling in her eyes.

'Come!' But she didn't move. Her crescent eyes did not understand.

'Please – come on board,' he gestured with his body, and she understood.

'Thank you, thank you.' He saw a little girl climbing into his boat.

Even when she was clothed in the gown that was heavy with thousands of pearls strung on a single long white thread, Solly still saw a small, silent, barefoot girl gliding over the strip of beach. Even when her lovely breasts were filled with milk, it was the small girl from the seashore who was nursing his children. And even when her daughters grew up, towered over her and filled his house with all that beauty, his mouth still went dry and salty whenever he looked at her.

Maurice's birth surprised Papa, perhaps because during that first pregnancy her belly hid itself under the blanket with the leopardesses, or because right up to the ninth month she was taken by strangers for a schoolgirl playing truant from games lessons, and Solly couldn't believe that she was about to produce a baby from under her skirt. One day he returned home from the wholesale market and found her naked and crying on the living-room carpet.

If he hadn't thought that Maurice was dead, he would probably have said, 'Oh a baby – how nice! Where did it come from?'

But Sofia, Marcelle and Lizzie he made quite deliberately. He loved to see the woman's body growing around the little girl from the seashore. He loaded her with bananas, coconuts and peanuts, in order to infect her with their warm nature and make her pearly nipples turn purple. From childbirth to childbirth her hips rounded out, the areolas around her nipples expanded, and a woman grew in the iron bed with the groaning springs. Year after year the veins swelled in her calves, her arms grew flabby, and her belly lost its tone. Sometimes when she slept he would turn back the covers and gently kiss the stretchmarks that glazed her stomach and vibrated with her breathing. When she laughed, he would bite the hoops of flesh that covered her womb. And when she hung over him, he was submerged by the bounty of tender fat, the soft worn-out muscles and the spinning whirlpool of her navel.

'Income Tax will never guess that I'm hiding all my millions here in your belly,' he whispered, clasping the fatty folds of her belly with both hands. His body curled around her back and so he slept.

It happened sometimes on a Saturday afternoon that he got up and found her lying stretched out on the sofa, her dress pulled up to her thighs, a glass of hot black tea with a sliver of ginger, while the four children ran around the house. As the liquid slipped down her throat she spread her legs and rested the glass on her waist. The heat of the tea spread through her inner organs, soothed her intestines and eased the roots of her simmering pains.

'Send them to the neighbours for black chickpeas . . .' Solly would breathe into her ears. The hot glass of tea and his gentle hand stirred her flesh.

'Now?' she giggled.

'Yes, right now,' he urged and clung to her.

'All right.' She smoothed down her skirt, gathered up her children and sent them out of the door.

'Yes, you go too. Tell her to put some black chickpeas in a bag for me . . . Yes, you go with them . . . OK? Again – some black chickpeas, you hear . . . ?'

When the neighbours' wives heard what we'd come for they grinned with pleasure and delayed us at their place. Meanwhile, in the bedroom, shaded by the honeysuckle in the windowbox that attracted many thirsty little beaks, between the worn cotton sheets and the flowered velvet bedspread, Solly rowed through the waves to his new immigrant, who mumbled '*lamah?*' between her moans. At the height of the tide, when the woman shook and a tremor went through her crevices, out swam the little girl who had hovered barefoot on the shore, and muttered a sweet river of Isfahani Persian, Bengali and fractured Hebrew.

She dedicated to the business of the house and family chores her plain cotton dresses with the round collars and the chaste hems that hid her knees. These pieces of cloth, sewn straight up and down and lacking all character, had originally been a rich shade of cream, but over the years they'd faded and become worn almost to transparency. Stains of spices and gravy spread on them, babies held over the shoulder to burp had spewed and left dim maps on the cloth, and our fingerprints, grabbing hold of Mama's skirts, added their own little decorations.

We loved those dresses, which were light and tolerant, as pleasant to the touch as her skin, and felt that their weave held the fragrance of our childhood sweat. Perhaps we dimly remembered how her beautiful breasts were taken out of their pale softness for us. As infants, we looked for their fluttering hems when we raised our heads like tortoises and crawled after her, and in their amplitude we buried our faces in shyness or tears, and snuffled their sweet vanilla scent. Only Papa, returning home at night, didn't like to find her in those orphanage dresses.

'An apron, Iran,' he would plead. 'Why don't you simply put on an apron?'

Mama also wore those worn-out old dresses when she

went to work in strange women's houses. The owners watched her when she swept their floors, and embarrassment made her work faster.

For other people's celebrations she took off those nymph's clothes, stood naked in front of the wardrobe and chose a dazzling dress with a raised collar like dogs' ears, or a colourful skirt with accordion pleats. She made up her face before putting on the dress. The shiny lipstick thickened her delicate lips, clouds of rouge hid her clear complexion, and olive eye-shadow gave her a look of astonishment. Then she would kick off her wooden mules, pull tights over her legs, and hunt for the missing mate of the pointed, high-heeled shoe.

'Where you lost it,' Maurice quoted her usual dictum, 'is where you should look for it.'

She would hurriedly brush her hair loose and screw long earrings into her lobes, hang gold chains round her neck and put on all her rings. Only her square wide fingernails betrayed her when she examined her new image in the mirror. She had imagined that the little nail-varnish brush would disguise the cook's fingers and the smell of bleach.

When she was all dolled and primped up, Maurice would cling to her backside and cry. He wanted her to be always in the house, wearing one of her stained white dresses, her heavy wooden mules clattering on the floor tiles. He believed that she was in all the rooms at once, thumping pillows in the bedroom while at the same time sharpening knives in the kitchen, watering the jasmine beside the door and clicking her knitting needles in the living-room. He believed that she was watching him from every corner of the house out of her big black eyes which showed hardly any white, so that you couldn't tell which way they were looking.

So when she wanted to go to other people's festivities and dressed up for the occasion he was afraid that she would disappear. That's why he hid the missing high-heeled shoe. His anguish infected Sofia, who was always sad anyway, and he accused Marcelle of being indifferent and pinched Lizzie to make her cry too.

'No, Mama, please don't go, Mama! Please!' The three girls would writhe at her feet, wet and tender. Maurice would stand helplessly by, pretending to be a man, keeping apart from his sisters' tears and their quavering cries.

'Don't go, Mama, can't you see they're crying!' he would plead, dry-eyed, but when our parents came back they would find the babysitter – a neighbour's daughter – sleeping on the sofa with her mouth open, Lizzie and Sofia asleep in their clothes on the carpet, and Maurice weeping like an orphan, reading Marcelle stories with sad endings.

Mama was the sun and we her four little planets, orbiting around her. In the shops of Givat Olga, under the white neon lights, we would hold on to her skirt and watch her pointing, uncertain and shy, at a pair of gleaming high-heeled shoes or a curvaceous vase that was on display.

The saleswomen smiled at her sweetly, patronisingly, and lavished compliments on the small customer who seemed suddenly to have grown taller.

'Oh you have such good taste, Madam! You've picked the most expensive item in the shop!'

Mama would repay them with her laugh, which rang like a pocketful of coins, and swelled with subtle pride.

Back in the street she clutched our hands as though they were gifts. Comforted by the flattery, she forgot the smell of the costly merchandise, and would later tell Papa, proudly, that once more she had been told that she had good taste.

'The most expensive in the shop!' she boasted.

'Again, the most expensive?' As always, he was entranced.

'Oh yes, again,' she confirmed with a sigh.

Whether things were tight or easy, Mama ran the household in the manner of Persian merchants' daughters. From her father she'd inherited a gift for negotiation, and from her mother she'd learned the secret pleasure of haggling. When dealing with the market vendors of meat and vegetables she would perform the shimmering dance in which housewives shook the soft fat of their arms as if they were thighs, dazzled the men's eyes with their bangles and rings, and offered a smile in return for a discount and an extra piece for free. Using her piping laugh and the tambourine jingle of her coins, she wove a spell, devised a tactic and rolled her eyes. The pimentos in her cheeks jiggled and her tongue became hot as if she'd been nursed on fiery red peppers.

Sometimes it had no effect, and Mama had to walk up and down the market lane three times in order to save a penny or two, but mostly the stall-keepers took off their hats, if they wore any, curled their moustaches, if they had any, joined the dance that Mama was so good at, and lowered their prices.

We would stare in astonishment at our provocative mother, and pull at her skirt, our faces red with embarrassment: 'Come on, Mama, what are you doing? Come on, let's go.'

No sooner was she back with the bags full from the market, her face flushed like a courted girl, than the four gas-cooker flames blossomed like violet flowers, and the neighbours' children danced around her, holding empty plates.

'The hands of a woman in the kitchen is like swords, that's her weapon! It's like cannons!' she would shout at her daughters, who tried on her aprons in front of the mirror but preferred to plunge into the pages of women's magazines and refused to learn recipes by heart.

'Not me. I'm going to have a rich husband who'll take me to restaurants – every day a different restaurant,' Sofia would announce, fluttering her false eyelashes and yawning indifferently.

Mama was sewing up a turkey that she'd stuffed with rice, dates and cloves. She raised her hands with the needle and thread, tugged at her earlobes and felt her earrings. She had no retort for her daughter, because she'd never known any rich men, nor men who ate in restaurants.

'I see . . .' she said at last, drawing on her limited experience in life, 'a man who'll take you to a different restaurant every day . . . Well, Sofia, then you better make pretty damn sure he don't sleep in a different woman's bed every night also!'

'What's wrong with an omelette?' Marcelle proposed on behalf of her sleepy sister. 'Sofia can always make him an omelette.'

'An omelette?' Mama frothed as if she herself was being whisked. 'No, Madam, omelette is not food to feed a man!'

'How about if he cooks it for me, Mama?' Lizzie said coquettishly, opening and shutting her eyes.

'Ah . . .' The turkey's stitching was almost pulled out as Mama again raised the needle and thread, this time to pinch the bridge of her nose and rub in Lizzie's bizarre idea.

She didn't know any men who cooked for their wives, either. Her own husband only netted the fish for her, brought them up the stairs and slid them into the sink, swaddled in newspapers.

'Don't know what to tell you, Lizzie.' Mama broke the thread between her teeth, patted the fowl's stuffed belly with one hand and her own belly, stuffed with a pair of twins, with the other. 'Your father once made cabbage soup for me. It was really nice.' Her eyes grew thoughtful.

'Cabbage soup?'

'Yes,' Mama laughed like a woman who has everything. 'But he makes children better.'

Mama raised us the way she herself had been brought up, faithful to the educational methods she had learnt from her mother – as a solid package of children, wholesale, the way she shopped in the market, buying whatever possible in large quantities that made for savings. When one of us came down with a childhood ailment, chickenpox, measles or rubella, she made sure that the rest of us caught it, so we'd all be equal. But Maurice was a male child and his foreskin floated inside her. She walked around him on tiptoe as if he were asleep, as if she was afraid to stir up dormant memories in his mind.

Before her daughters turned their proud backs on her kitchen, Mama taught Maurice to cook without measurements, for the simple reason that he was there, he followed her wherever she went, always sticking close to her arse. She would swing him up in her warm bread-loaf arms, his giggles ringing and his little legs kicking like bell-clappers, and seat him on the cool marble worktop with the purple veins. She'd stick a yellow courgette flower in his hair and a pink radish garland in her own, and show him how to mix sugar and cinnamon in the palm of his hand till it took on the aroma of a contented woman, how to deepen the skin's amber tint with turmeric, how to soak fenugreek seeds till they lost their bitter flavour and awakened the tired flesh to love.

'I don't like it. It stinks.'

'It's not for you. It's for Papa.'

By the time Maurice moved to the balcony, which was enclosed with shutters to make it into a room for him, his voice had deepened and his heart had shrivelled in his hand and he had learned to enjoy the exciting feel of a knife peeling an aubergine as though it were himself, to share the thrill of the fine noodles as they plunged into salty boiling water, and rejoice with the seeds of a pomegranate broken open by Mama's fingers. He sensed the alarm of the peas flung into a seething skillet, understood the squeal of the pecans between the arms of the nutcracker and the subtle shivers of a ripe avocado.

When he became a man and his sisters filled the house with their bodies – big women, numerous as a herd of she-elephants – he was embarrassed to sit with his mother in the kitchen, and tried to eject it from his murmuring heart. Only sometimes he felt as if he were coring apples in the bedrooms of his ragged mistresses, whose beds were as cold as their kitchens.

* * *

Apart from the long-beaked colibris which were attracted to the honeysuckle growing on the windowsill of Mama and Papa's bedroom, a different bird would sometimes accidentally fly into the house, bump desperately against the walls of the small rooms, and look for the sky in the bluish damp patches on the ceiling. We became as terrified as the captive bird, pressed against the walls and twittered with fear, till the bird found an open window and flew out.

But when Sofia was nine and an owl flew by mistake into the living-room at the height of her birthday party, flapping its wings frantically, bumping its head against the walls, we thought we'd never get rid of it.

As it hovered sightlessly over the heads of Sofia's school friends, the girls shrieked with terror and hid their faces in their arms, and the boys rose as one and clustered one behind the other in the corner. The owl flew heavily up to the ceiling, struck the glass chandelier that glittered like crystal and set its teardrops tinkling.

Then it dived down, its talons outstretched in front and its wings outspread behind, landed on the birthday cake and knocked it off its stand. The cake overturned and its whipped cream topping fell on the carpet.

'Out, bastard sonofabitch, out!' Mama screamed at it, trying simultaneously to calm the guests with caresses and drive out the invader with flailing kitchen towels. Then she banged spoons on frying pans and struck two pot lids together like cymbals. The owl flew right over her head, its ghostly wings vibrating as though it were hunting its prey, smashed the glass doors of the dresser with a thunderous bang, and knocked over Mama and Papa's wedding photograph and the row of wine glasses that stood on the shelf. Glass shattered, flew all over the place, and sent the last guests scurrying from the house.

Alarmed by the uproar, the owl flew up to the top of the dresser and there stopped still. Its witching eyes opened wide, huge and yellow.

It looked at us, one after another, at our festive clothes, at Mama who was swearing and sweeping up broken glass and blobs of whipped cream, and at Sofia, who had huge accusing tears hanging like crystal drops from her lashes. She thought it looked like a stuffed animal come alive, like a bad dream she was sentenced to dream. Its striped feathers were the colour of sand and a couple of tufts rose from the round platter of its face. Its frigid stare cast a deathly hush on the house, and the moon rose.

For a long time the owl remained still, as if it too was holding its breath, as if it too was alarmed by the invader who had driven away all the little owls from the birthday party.

Suddenly it began to swivel its head with terrifying slowness and blinked its black-rimmed eyes like a tired human. It began to pace back and forth in the space between the top of the dresser and the ceiling, like a trained circus parrot walking on a high wire, A cloud of fine dust rose in the shadowy height which our short mama's duster never reached. The owl walked on its curved claws between an imitation cut-glass vase and a painted ceramic bowl, moving cautiously, having learned from experience that a great hullabaloo might ensue if it knocked over one of those vessels and it broke.

Suddenly the owl noticed a white shape behind a pot holding a plastic fern. Our gaping mouths opened wider, and in the silence only the tears running down Sofia's cheeks and dripping on the floor could be heard. We saw it hopping excitedly around the white china bird which we had always thought of as a barn owl.

The glazed black eyes of the china bird and its proud upright back were grey with dust. Its flattened beak, that seemed to be smiling contentedly, gleamed yellow in the light from the chandelier. The owl fluffed up its feathers with excitement, showed off its outspread wings and slapped them together like hands clapping. The fear in its eyes turned into single-minded determination. It showed the china bird its profile, swayed from foot to foot and swung its tail in a slow, precise dance.

Its rhythmic call was so amazing that the owl itself was stunned to hear it echoing from the walls of our small flat. But it was not discouraged by the impassivity of its lady love. Even when Papa came home in the evening with the smell of the sea in his hair, the strange bird continued its courtship dance, threw out its chest, flapped its wings and blinked its eyes in the bright light of the chandelier.

'Darkness, that's what he needs, this bird. Turn off the light. This bird needs darkness,' said Papa and switched off all the lights. The owl's eyes glowed like two yellow lamps in the gloom that filled the house.

'Now he'll go. Just leave him like this and he'll fly through the window.'

Maurice couldn't sleep that night. The sound of wings flapping in the living-room hummed like the wind in his ears. Mama tried to recall who had given her the female china owl, and on what occasion. But she couldn't remember and at last she fell asleep in Papa's arms, while he muttered in his sleep all that he had left unspoken during the day. Lizzie also slept. Marcelle curled up with her books in the bathroom, because that was the only place Papa had agreed to leave the light on. Sofia wallowed in her grief for the birthday gifts that the children had snatched back in their flight. In her dreams china dolls flew about and strange birds stood still without a breath in their beaks.

Only Maurice heard the blaze that love kindled in the owl's cold blood, and the energy which hope poured into its wings. All night long the bird picked blades of grass with its beak, tore small twigs with its claws, collected dropped feathers and scraps of wool. Maurice lay in bed rigidly and listened to the owl flying briskly through the open window and the flutter of its wings when it returned to its immobile beloved.

At dawn Maurice heard Papa kissing Marcelle, shutting the window against the invader, and leaving for the sea. In broad daylight he ventured out of his bed and discovered on top of the dresser what Papa had not noticed – a thin hollow globular nest, looking like a hastily woven bowl of hair. Maurice rubbed his tired eyes with his fists and saw a wondering glint twinkling in the glass eyes of the china bird – exactly the same as the glint in Mama's eyes when she'd had a long lie-in on a Saturday morning.

He ran to her to wake her up and show her that the owl was gone.

'Good riddance to him!' Mama said when she took in what the boy was saying, and shook off the remains of the night.

'But what is this?' she exclaimed, disappointed, when she saw the woven bowl at the feet of the china owl. 'That crazy bird wants to bring all his family to our house?'

Full of self-confidence, Mama carried one of the kitchen stools up to the dresser, kicked off her wooden mules and with a slight sigh and a corrugated brow climbed up to the living-room ceiling. Her hands reached out to grab the little twig nest and take it off the dresser top, when suddenly she dropped her arms and bit her lips as if tasting an idea.

Maurice thought that his own anxieties had somehow seeped into Mama's stout heart. She opened the windows her husband had shut and left Maurice, small and alone in his underpants, to gaze at the beady black glass eyes and search the summer sky for the roaming owl.

'Are you going to let him stay, Mama?' Maurice ran to the kitchen and clung to her bent back as she rummaged in the open refrigerator. Mama took three eggs out of their cardboard nest, but instead of breaking them to make the breakfast omelettes, she stomped back to the living-room on her wooden hoofs, loosening Maurice's arms from around her waist.

'You wait and see what I'm doing.' She smiled at him confidingly. She felt for the outline of the little round nest and then very carefully deposited the three eggs in it.

When she'd climbed back down in her bare feet, she sent Maurice to wake up his sisters. Maurice was so happy about Mama's generosity, her offering a meal to the visiting bird, that he hurried to do as he was told. At that moment he heard the awaited beating wings, and the owl flew down from the sky and landed on the windowsill. It perched there staring at Maurice with its ringed yellow eyes, and from its curved beak dangled a small grey dead mouse.

Maurice didn't notice Mama's shrieks or her horrified

curses, nor did he pay attention to his sisters, who woke from their dreams of flying china birds and came rushing into the living-room. He was fascinated by the wonderful bird of prey and the gift of love it had brought. Excited and bashful, as if he were the eager lover, Maurice peered at the white china figure and saw that a smile had appeared under its beak and her dusty beady-eyes shone.

He was amazed. So was the owl when it fluttered down to the nest and saw the alien eggs. Its raptor eyes did not perceive that they were hen's eggs, did not notice the moisture that condensed on the shells from the refrigerator's chill, nor even the red markings stamped on them. Offended, it flapped its wings at the faithless bird, knocked her off the perch and flew away over her broken pieces.

Later Mama fried the eggs which had been mistaken for a stranger's, and then remembered that her sisters had given her the china bird as a good-luck barn owl.

Part Three

Matti Azizyan's Birthday, Ten in the Morning

MATTI LEFT THE NEIGHBOURS' flat to go home. She pressed her ear to the door and heard the silence inside. There was a smell of something burnt, but no echoes of Maurice's yells, the jangling of Lizzie's brass anklet, Marcelle's silver bangles, Sofia's baby's coughing and Iran's despairing groans. Only the clock sighed. Matti knocked once, twice, then opened the door. The silence was very intense, like the hush that used to trouble her mind when she was the first to wake up on Saturday mornings.

But today was Monday, and Matti entered her home like a thief sneaking into a strange house.

She wanted to shout, 'Mama? Who's home? Sofia, you there?' But instead she tiptoed in, looked around with sleep-sticky eyes and behaved correctly like a tourist at a museum.

Near the entrance she stopped, because she saw that the two brass dancers holding up the mosaic lampshades high above their heads had shut their eyes. With a fingertip she wiped the dust off the moulded eyes, and they opened. Behind them was a mirror which looked to Matti like a hole in the wall.

She didn't know what to do, so she sat very delicately on the edge of an armchair, as if careful not to hurt it. The ruins of the sofa stood in the living-room like ancient shrines commemorating Matti's wild days before she was sent to the special school. Something inside her was eager to start jumping again from seat to seat. On the table lay Maurice's playing cards, laid out in rows, and on them stood two glasses of coffee, one of which had been drunk and the other not.

Suddenly she spotted Lizzie lying there on the broken three part sofa. Matti saw that under the coat of makeup that still encrusted her face her sister was having a really good sleep. Her body, blotched with old and new bruises, was cradled between her arms, as if it were a baby she'd put to sleep, then fallen asleep with. Matti glanced at Sofia's baby's cot, but before she approached it she knew that it was empty and held only bedding and old nappies. They wouldn't leave him on his own – not with Lizzie, and certainly not with Matti. She strained her eyes and stared hard all around to see if there was anyone else in the room.

On the walls hung plain pieces of cloth in gilt wood frames. In her maiden days Iran used to embroider needlepoint pictures, and in the tradition of Persian weavers made sure always to leave some small defect, so as to avoid perfection. But this summer all the fine embroideries had faded and disappeared behind their thick glass panes, as if they'd been made with the kind of cheap silks which lose their colour after a while.

Gone was the sleeping woman in a loose orange gown, with the rounded breasts and hair that writhed like snakes, and gone were the marble pillars of the rose garden in which she would never wake. Gone too was the king of Persia in his stiff military uniform, and the enormous peacock that hung over the dining-table. Only their dull and hollow frames remained hanging on the walls. Matti examined every picture closely, but saw only her own reflection and the twitching of her facial muscles caused by the Ritalin. A neighbour laughed heartily, and his voice resounded like a French horn from floor to floor and broke into the flat. It startled her. But Lizzie went on sleeping, and Matti went to the kitchen.

The formica doors of the cupboards, swollen from the humidity, hung creakingly open, exposing the shelves which were looking bare and ashamed. Gone were the packets of sugar, bags of rice and boxes of tea with which they used to be crammed. The spices in the pharmacy jars had congealed into lumps, and in the pickle jars floated wrinkled cucumbers in a murky liquid amid webs of dillweed and rotting cloves of garlic. Most of the slats of the kitchen shutter were broken and seemed to wink at the tops of the medlar trees, whose fruits were pecked by birds and bats. Matti felt a mouse scurrying past her feet.

The wall behind the stove was yellow with greasy muck. The electrical sockets, the ceiling light and the windowpanes were coated with damp grey fur. Matti examined the kitchen knives, whose blades had become blunt, the worn-out towels and the remains of the rose-painted china set. The corpses of moths and flies clustered in the corners. The last insects of summer buzzed over the leftovers someone had eaten standing up at the table. The sides of the saucepans heaped in the sink and the bottoms of the frying pans overturned on the work-top reflected Matti's image – blurry, scratched and smeary, wreathed with the sooty imprint of the stove flames which hadn't burned for a long time.

Neglect, both visible and imperceptible, had fallen on their house. Stains had crept in, were wiped here and reappeared there. The bedrooms, having been strenuously stripped of their downy gowns of dust, were overnight re-clothed in the same. Tears that were shed in the house mingled with the dust and raised greenish mould in the cracks between the floor tiles. Tiny pinkish flowers of saltpetre blossomed along the skirtings. Matti hadn't realised how much they had all wept throughout that summer and she hadn't expected the carpets to retain so much of its scorched reek.

She bent down to look at two small corpses that had dried under the kitchen table, and saw two yellow snails which had come up the wastepipe overnight and died while mating. She found other such corpses stuck with their slime to the carpets or tangled in the fringes, having left glistening silvery trails over the intricate patterns.

Nobody had watered the jasmine. The camellias had wilted. The delicate leaves of the Busy Lizzie had withered and turned yellow, the earth in their pot looking parched like Iran's face. Matti imagined that the honeysuckle at her parents' bedroom window was still spreading memories of fragrance, but in fact it was the exhalation of the sweat-soaked sheets. In the aquarium on the dresser shelf, globular like a huge egg, swam the last survivors, two goldfish whose scales had long since faded to silver. Matti stood and gazed at them for a long time, till she saw her eyes reflected in the turbid water, misty black with the fish swimming between them.

No one was looking after anything any more. Matti

leaned against the wall with the flower print and smelled the wallpaper glue that had softened in the all-consuming summer heat. The paper flowers drooped from the wall in tired curls, exposing the strange cave paintings done by Matti's older siblings when they were children and bursting with gaiety and inspiration.

Passing through the Indian gods' corridor, she was accompanied by a small cloud of dust when she went on to the balcony that had been enclosed to give Maurice some privacy. There she encountered new and unfamiliar naked women. They gazed at her with eyes that were tortured with desire, offended and raging with lust. Beside her brother's tumbled, damp and sour bed stood a skull-shaped wooden block on which he hung his false hair by night, with his old stethoscope dangling from its neck. On the floor lay a towel and beside it a pair of old underpants. Matti stepped over these to reach the stethoscope and hung it around her own neck. A faint whiff of fennel and a thick smell of sweaty socks drove her out of there. She went to the room which had once been the room of all the children, then of her elder sisters, and finally her own. It had always been redolent of nail-varnish remover and hairspray, but these were now compounded with the odour of damp clothes and profound sleep. Handsome if faded film stars gazed at her from the walls and the open wardrobe doors. A tortured woman, bound with ropes, shrieked at her from the soft cover of a book Marcelle had almost finished reading.

She sat down on the revolving stool with the purple fur cover and spun round. The seat turned on its spiral shaft and rose higher, and Matti sat straight-backed and looked at herself in the mirror.

Her hair was dishevelled from sleep and she rumpled it some more. Her arching eyebrows were thick and looked like feathery snakes that kissed over her flat nose, forming a prickly hairy hedge. Matti frowned as if in anger, and the eyebrows merged into a black stream that crossed her face horizontally and divided it in two. Thought was concentrated in the creased brow above the black stream, while the senses were arranged below. Matti observed her thin lips, her prominent ears, and the neck tendons twitching above her high T-shirt.

Her sisters' cluttered dressing-table stood between her and the mirror. Among the tweezers and hair-rollers, hairpins and brushes with tipped bristles she spotted some pairs of silvery barbers' scissors. Matti picked up a slim pointy pair, slipped her fingers through the iron loops and snapped at the air.

Snick-snick-snick went the blades, meeting and parting, but the air remained whole. She held the open blades against her neck and they made a thin squeak as they stroked her skin, but did not cut it either. The fine fleshy hollow between her fingers and thumb deepened; the fingers curled and bent their joints. Matti spread the scissors wide open with a thumb thrust deep into each loop, and watched the lump in her throat rising and falling in the angle between the two blades.

Snick . . . snick . . . snick – she snipped the threads of air that curled from her nostrils. Her arms went up and down like flapping wings, and the scissors chirred. Their jaws snipped and snapped and climbed up before her eyes to her forehead, and suddenly took a bite out of her fringe. Small bits of hair fell on her knees. Her fingers shook and the blades went on biting and devouring, more and more. Fine clumps of hair fluttered between her head and the mirror, fell apart on their way to the floor, and Matti heard the neighbour's French-horn laugh again resounding through the building.

Seized with anger she pulled at her hair, chopped it in front and chopped it behind, cutting off more and more of it. By now she couldn't stop the savage rattling of the blades and the avalanche of black chunks that fell on her eyes. The scissors twittered as if suppressing a shriek, and the hair squeaked as if hurt. The metal grew hotter as it rushed through her hair, and did not cool down even when the whole head of hair was ravaged and only bristles remained. Matti looked at herself, at the twitching muscles in her face, and the scissors snickered in her trembling fingers.

She laid them on the table and stopped still. Then she blew carefully at the hairy fallout on her face, which had left black shadows on her cheeks and lashes. When the shadows fell off, she saw very big eyes, immense, weird, like shiny black glands, staring at her in astonishment.

'Moni,' she said hoarsely, 'what have I done? I'm dying, look what I've done!' and a thick, coarse laugh broke from her mouth.

She turned her head this way and that. Tufts of hair stuck out at her temples and the scalp showed in patches all over her head. She picked up the scissors and trimmed some more, this time very slowly, her face close to the mirror. Then she opened her mouth and examined her teeth. Her nose pressed against the glass and the two heads touched. Matti came very close to the scary eyes that seemed to grow even bigger, blacker and brighter, as they focused on her.

'Mmmnn . . .' she grunted, and a strange growl rose from deep in her throat. 'Grrrrah . . .' The fist holding the scissors stabbed at the face in the mirror, while the fingers of the other hand spread open, curled and prepared to scratch.

Matti blinked. She passed a hand over her face and wiped off more chopped hairs, and was again astounded by the sight of the bare stubble. The house was very quiet. She rose, stepped back to the end of the room, glanced at the mirror and went out. Only when she reached the living-room did she notice the pain in her palm and found the scissors clutched tightly in her fist.

Matti cut a lot of things before she came to the family album. She cut fringes off the Persian carpets, snipped off a branch of the spreading avocado plant, even sliced apart the two mating snails, which exuded a disgusting living fluid. Lying on the corpse of the sofa, Lizzie was sinking deeper and deeper into her best sleep. Twice Matti checked to make sure that she was breathing, that she hadn't died from the beatings she'd taken from her husband and Maurice. Suddenly she remembered that before she was sent away to boarding-school, Lizzie had been pregnant, which was the reason she'd got married.

'Lizzie, Lizzie . . .' Matti bent down low over her sister, still clutching the scissors. 'Where's your baby?'

Lizzie trembled.

'Your baby, where is it?'

'It was a phantom,' Lizzie murmured in her sleep. 'There is such a thing, a phantom preg—' She drifted off again with a bitter sigh.

Matti thought that Lizzie didn't want to tell her where her baby was, because she was afraid Matti would throw him downstairs too. Her eyes glazed as she looked at her sister's slumped neck, from which her head dangled as though it had been cut off, and at a vein as thick as a rope that bulged from it. She was mesmerised by the velvet band tied around the vein which pulsated with Lizzie's strong heartbeat, fluttering and throbbing with the pounding of her blood. She felt her own neck in search of a similar vein, but the metal of the scissors felt hard and cold where it touched her hot flesh.

Only when she sank into her parents' iron bed, making the springs groan hoarsely, and looked at all that had been before her time, did the scissors slip from her hand, forgotten, like the jaw of a child that drops when he listens to a story. Between the leather covers, stuck on black pages and protected by thin transparent sheets, were the family photographs, held in the corners by tiny triangles. Some of the snapshots were faded, others shone with a colourful twinkle.

Mama and Papa on their wedding day. The bride in a pearly dress and gloves, the groom in a tie and funny bushy hair. Papa swinging Mama up in his arms. Papa drinking wine from her shoe, and Mama barefoot. Mama's thin arms and almond eyes. Papa and Mama surrounded by champagne bottles, and Mama's brothers and sisters. Grandma Touran standing to one side, blinking at the camera. Grandma Eliaspour before she died. Other people whom she didn't recognise.

Maurice as a baby, Mama washing him in a bowl, while carp swam around him in the bath. Maurice a year old, with two candles on a birthday cake. Mama beside a river in India, holding hands with a boy. Sofia and Marcelle as naked babies, and behind them the embroidered picture of the sleeping woman in the rose garden. Maurice a year old, with a drum, with a ball, with a toy telephone. Mama and Papa kissing in the kitchen, a pair of doves behind them. Sofia with a key dangling from her neck in a school photo with her classmates. Marcelle with all her bangles on a school trip. Lizzie on her fifth birthday in nursery school, a garland on her head and someone playing an accordion for her. Everybody except Matti on a picnic beside the Sea of Galilee.

Maurice beginning to go bald under the guava trees. Grandma Touran and Papa in formal dress at a photographer's studio. Lizzie at Maurice's bar-mitzvah, wearing the poppy dress that Sofia wore in another picture. Mama and Papa kissing by the sea, with strangers in the background. Mama pregnant, Sofia going to nursery school at Purim in a Queen of the Night costume, Marcelle as a clown and Maurice as Peter Pan.

Papa, a skinny red-haired boy, holding a big fat fish and smiling without a moustache. Mama as a girl, singing in the school choir in India. Mama nursing Marcelle on the velvet sofa cover, while Maurice, his front teeth missing, is holding up two fingers behind her head. Sofia, Marcelle and Lizzie in swimsuits by the swimming pool, their bodies beginning to round out. Sofia, Marcelle and Lizzie in the amusement park, eating ice-cream on the swans of the merry-go-round and sticking out their tongues.

Papa biting on a pipe, wearing a beard and army uniform. Lizzie with a fellow. Lizzie with another fellow. Yoel Hajjabi playing football in the distance. Sofia and Itzik Kadosh on their honeymoon in Europe, Lizzie with another fellow.

'You don't have a picture here, Moni, you're dead,' Matti said and remembered the scissors. They were lying open on the bed beside her. Their iron eyes looked expectantly at her page-turning fingers, blinking and begging to be picked up.

The scissors crept up to her side and slipped on to her fingers like a pair of silver rings.

'Now I must really look like you,' she said to Moni. 'I'm sure, now that I don't have a girl's hair. Pity I can't be photographed now, so you'd have at least one picture in the album.'

A colibri flew near the window and didn't notice her. Matti took out a picture of the whole family photographed on the evening that Sofia was crowned beauty queen. The scissors broke into the paper, sliced across it till they reached Matti's face, went around it and came out again. Matti saw her face falling from Papa's shoulder. Only her cut-off legs remained hanging on him, but everybody went on smiling proudly, showing no grief that a hole had opened in the family. Then she mutilated all the pictures from Marcelle's henna party, cutting out all the funny faces she'd made at the camera. She freed Sofia's wedding from her own smirking smiles, meanwhile separating everybody from their bodies. She also eliminated herself from Lizzie's wedding, leaving gaping holes. In one picture she was a bored bridesmaid, in another she was yawning and a third showed her dozing on a chair. The Purim photographs of her dressed as a cowboy, as a gypsy and again a cowboy, were left with hollow costumes and no faces. At the *brith* of Sofia's blue baby a black cavern opened on Grandma Touran's fat knees. In the picture of Lizzie's bat-mitzvah, the scissors lopped the baby Matti from Mama's embracing arms.

She collected all the circles of her faces into one heap.

'Take a look. That's how I used to be,' she said to Moni, picking through false smiles, silly grins and vague expressions. She peered into dozens of her black eyes, looking for the glint of madness. To herself she seemed cute and naive. Maybe half girl, half boy. Perhaps her ears that stuck out a bit, or the imperfect bridge of her nose, indicated something she didn't understand. For a moment she did not recognise herself. Her eyes glazed, then filled with tears. Suddenly she suspected those smiles of hers of being evil. Could it be that the clue lay in them? Perhaps the facial muscles that showed the teeth, lips and gums could reveal to her what everyone else knew. She searched for her evil in her smiles. Slowly, because she knew that evil was a slippery thing. Certainly her mischievous evil was elusive. She went on hunting for it, because it had to be lurking in some feature. She glanced at the beautiful faces of Sofia and Marcelle, Lizzie and Mama, even the faces of Maurice and Papa, but it wasn't there – evil couldn't be hiding in beauty; beauty would expel it immediately from the face, or else it would be spotted on sight.

'Wait, wait, wait . . .' she whispered to Moni.

'Maybe it's not what's there, but what isn't!' she shouted.

How could she have failed to think of that? Maybe something was missing in her, some hidden organ inside the body, something that everybody else had but she didn't, or else it didn't work, or had died.

'Calm down, Moni, calm down. I'll look into it, leave

it to me.' Matti stuck the earpieces of the stethoscope she'd pinched from Maurice's room into her ears, slipped the sliced photographs from which she had excised herself back into their little triangles, and stuffed the paper coins with her pictures into her right pocket along with the scissors. She continued to walk around her parents' room, one hand moving the stethoscope amplifier over her belly while the other rummaged in the drawers. Only when she opened the green jewellery box and found that there were only eight pearls left of the hundred it had once contained, as well as a small, dry piece of skin, did she hear her mother's voice calling her, raw from shouting for some time.

'Matti! Matti! Where are you, Matti?'

Matti shivered, pushed all the pearls into the left pocket which held her six Ritalin tablets, and slammed the box shut. She hid the stethoscope under her shirt.

That was when Iran found her. For a moment she didn't recognise her daughter. It was a brief blink of a moment, which began with astonishment and ended with horror. Not only Iran's mouth, her whole face opened up. Matti had been so absorbed that she quite forgot her haircut. But when she saw her mother's eyebrows, eyes and mouth spreading apart on her face, like a carpet being unrolled, she remembered and smiled, thinking that her mother was admiring her looks.

'Aye!' The horrified cry finally burst from Iran's lips. 'What did you do to yourself?'

Iran chocked as if about to vomit. A bag full of vegetables fell from her hands.

Fragments of dreadful images filled Iran's mind. She could see the scissors scratching Matti's eyes, wounding her delicate scalp, sticking into her neck. Iran shuddered with terror, Matti with disappointment. They stared at each other as though meeting for the first time.

Matti had already seen Iran the previous evening, but it had been late. Now, in the glare of broad daylight, she saw that her mother's eyes were red and tired and looked like two open sores in her face. The running pus of her tears deformed the slant of the former almonds, and numerous new wrinkles that Matti didn't recognise had broken out around them. She saw twin Mattis, shorn and shamefaced, reflected remotely in Mama's eyes. Whether because of the headscarf Iran had taken to wearing, or the grey hair that straggled out of it, her face seemed very far away, making Matti feel she was looking at an embroidered picture of a strange woman on the wall.

Iran looked at Matti and saw what she had missed the night before, that she had grown much bigger. Iran could never make up her mind whom Matti resembled, this girl whose muscles twitched because of the Ritalin, who had become so thin at the boarding-school, who had horribly destroyed her beautiful head of hair, and whose birthday it was. She looked like somebody else's child who had accidentally stumbled into the house, or flown into it through a window, rather than emerged from her own womb after its tubes had come untied.

'Now you really look like a crazy girl.' She shook her head and clucked at her, her eyes veiled, to express her despair of Matti.

'A real crazy girl now,' Iran said again, this time to herself, quietly and sadly, and bent down to gather up the potatoes and courgettes which had rolled out of the bag. Matti heard what she said and thought about the children who walked past the boarding-school fence every morning and saw her hanging on to the high iron posts and making scary faces at them.

'Loony! Dummy!' they yelled and ran away, and Matti would take another Ritalin with a glass of water and feel tired. At this moment they were probably returning from the school behind the cactus hedge, and didn't know where she was or at whom to yell.

Part Four

Our Weddings

GOD CREATED MONI AND Matti Azizyan together. He divided Iran's womb in two, installed two placentas, tied two umbilical cords to two navels, and laboured over the twins day and night. Using the remains of the rolls of skin from which He had previously made Iran's four older children, He cut two new lengths and made two new body wraps. Out of the immense chest of souls He picked two, held each one between His fingers, and tremulously inserted them into the soft fleshy cores – two clear, luminous, pure souls. He formed hands and feet, shaped noses and creased ears, hollowed out eye-sockets and dropped light into them, rolled up strings of intestines, weighed livers, blew up lungs, threaded in vertebrae and planted nails in their fingers and toes. After nine months the spool of black hair and the jars of blood were empty and God listened to the two beating hearts and smiled with satisfaction. He made sure that the two testicles hung at roughly the same level between Moni's legs, and patted him on the back. He counted the eggs in Matti's ovaries and stroked her hair. But just then Iran's contractions began to speed up, something went wrong, and Moni was born dead. Matti was left alone.

For nine whole months Moni and Matti had swum together in the amniotic fluid that swarmed with tiny bubbles inside Mama's womb. From bright, translucent pips they grew larger, rolled over, sprouted new limbs, opened and closed their astonished eyes, pressed against the partition between them and made funny faces at each other. Sometimes they slept back to belly like spoons, and scratched or kicked when Mama ate something tasty. One tight evening, after guzzling pea soup, when Moni's head was already turned downwards and his feet tickled Matti's nose, the muscles around them began to squeeze and swell again and again, like a frightful earthquake. Suddenly the water was gone. They heard cries and wanted to cry too. The force surrounding them squeezed tighter and tighter. Matti pressed against the partition, wanting to hug Moni till it passed, but saw him suffering, twisting, kicking and going wild. She got a dim, painful blow in her face, a brilliant light shone on her, and a hand pulled her out into the world. Matti screamed and screamed and screamed for Moni, but she never saw him again, and she never stopped missing him.

After Lizzie's birth the doctor tied Mama's tubes, and she forgot her womb. She didn't know that the knot had come undone until one Saturday morning she rose, naked and glowing, from under the blankets.

'I'm mad about your arse, my love.' Humming with pleasure, Papa kissed her warm backside. 'As big and beautiful as when Lizzie was born.'

Mama turned happily to the mirror and was abashed

to discover that she was pregnant again. As on the four previous occasions when she'd been stung with her husband's seed, she saw plainly the signs of early pregnancy. Embarrassed by her age and shy before her big children, she decided to have an abortion. And just as years ago, when Maurice was born and she suspected that he had no heart and his eyes were without tears, now again she kept a secret from her husband.

'I swear on my mother's grave, I'm going to do it myself if you don't help me! I'll do it with a knitting needle and Turkish raki!' she cried bitterly at the doctor's.

He gave in and agreed, but when he informed her that she was carrying twins in her forgotten womb, she didn't have the heart to kill them both. She told Solly about it, and he looked forward to a son.

Maurice, his eldest son, resembled Grandma Touran, and Solly wanted a son whose face would remind him of his long-lost father, abandoned at the foot of the Ararat mountains.

'I'm going to have twins,' he informed his mother gaily. 'A son and a daughter.'

Touran hesitated, unsure what to say to him first – that twins in a woman's belly are a sign to the husband that his wife is betraying him; or that at long last his wife was doing him a favour and producing sons; or that she wanted the boy to be called Michael. In the meantime she stuck a cigarette in her slit of a mouth and waited for Solly to light it.

'I made a vow in the synagogue,' he went on solemnly, 'that I'll name the boy Manucher, after my father, God willing.'

'You do what you like,' Touran snapped at him. 'But you should know that twins in the belly is a sure sign to the husband that –'

'But Mama, don't you –?'

'I said, you can do what you like!' She blew the smoke at him and decided to wait for great-grandsons.

Despite her embarrassment, Iran greatly enjoyed her fifth pregnancy. Her children longed for the twins. Her days were filled with ease and pampering, and once again heaps of butter, dates and honey appeared on the kitchen worktop. Solly adored her extra pads of fat, went out late to the sea and returned home early in the evenings.

Matti and Moni were ripe inside Mama when we adopted the white cat with the green eyes. We didn't know it was a she-cat, and that she too was pregnant.

'I said no! Because it makes dirt, that's why!' Mountainous Mama stood in the doorway and we crouched at her thickened ankles, fawned on her huge twins-filled belly, and shed tears on her wooden mules. Between us sprawled the cat, white and sway-backed, its eyes expressing innocence and its fine fur gleaming in the stairwell light that came and went.

'Please, Mama! Oh please, please, Mama!' we whined, caressing the cat as she caressed us, and pulling at her dress like bell-ringers.

But Mama stood firm and looked down at us from the height that mothers achieve in order not to give in to their spoilt children's pestering. Her mules clattered on the floor tiles, loud and determined. She stood like a sentry in the doorway, waiting for the pea soup to come to the boil, and making sure that the soft paws of the alley-cat did not cross her threshold. In her mind she saw it stretching its flea-ridden body on the Persian carpets, shedding its white fur on the sofa, and filling the rooms with the stink of the garbage under its claws. The trident scar left by the monkey's scratch swelled on her forehead.

'Your friends can keep pigs in their houses. I don't care!' she snapped, but when she kicked off her mules and stood barefoot, she added, 'He looks sick, on top of everything. Marcelle, go and get him some milk.'

The cat blinked at her and lapped up the milk that was placed under the flowering jasmine. Then it licked Mama's thick-veined feet, and the timid flattery made her laugh like a spoilt little girl. She bent down over our clustered heads, no taller than us, and discovered that under its white fur it was a pregnant female. She recognised in the green slitted eyes the same weary look she saw in her mirror, the gaze of a pregnant female close to term.

'Aye aye aye, he's a woman cat, that's what he is! He'll soon drive us all crazy.'

She replaced the milk in the saucer with pea soup, carried the cat from the shadow of the jasmine to the fern corner in the living-room, and put down some rags for her to lie on.

Sofia and Lizzie were dazed with happiness. They stuffed themselves with bowl after bowl of soup, and fell asleep exhausted with gratitude and excitement. Maurice went to sleep at Grandma Touran's, as the balcony had not yet been enclosed for him. Only Marcelle's sad eyes remained open. She saw Mama bending over, her legs planted apart, picking up the snowy cat from its ferny shelter and placing her in the hammock of her weekday dress.

'Oh, you are heavy. How many you got in there, tell me?'

Mama sank on the sofa and laid the cat above her belly.

'You're sweet, you know? You're really a little sweetie.'

Mama put her nose to the cat's nose, and the chitchat continued in whispers.

Feeling Moni and Matti's thumping heartbeats, the cat's five embryos suddenly stopped fighting inside her. The twins also pressed their little ears to the wall of Mama's womb and listened to the pattering heartbeats of the cat's embryos. The furry belly rubbed against the belly of skin, and the cat's slanted eyes looked caressingly at Mama's almond eyes. Marcelle wrote about them in her diary, and watched them dozing together, one raking the snowy fur with her fingers, the other licking the olive skin with her tongue. Until the contractions woke them up.

Iran suffered greatly in the delivery room, and finally the doctors decided to cut her belly open with a knife, and pulled out of her a dead male baby and a living female one, with a crushed nose and bleeding nostrils. The male had blocked her way out, and in his struggle had kicked her in the face before he died. Then Iran's belly was zipped up with a whiskery scar.

When she awoke and heard that the male baby had died and only the female survived, she was so demoralised that she didn't bother to check if Matti's fingers were properly arranged in fives, and if her ears were correctly creased. Nor did she listen to the tiny breast from right to left, to discover the site of the heart. After seven days Iran and Solly went from the hospital to the cemetery and then home, with Moni buried in the babies' section and Matti bundled in Iran's arms.

Maurice had been staying with Grandma Touran and the girls had been distributed like cuckoos' eggs among the neighbours. Iran and Solly reached their front door as the automatic stairwell light went off. Solly unlocked the door and reached out to switch on the lamp of the dancers that held up the lampshades. Iran immediately smelled the milk of the she-cat, and felt her soft fur stroking her calves. Alone in the empty house, on the bed of rags that Iran had made for her under the ferns, she had given birth to five steaming kittens.

The cat purred with weary contentment as she welcomed her new mistress. Iran petted her and complimented her on her beautiful kittens. The cat gazed admiringly at the baby bundled in the woman's arms, and her eyes narrowed sadly when she failed to find the other baby. She licked the outstretched hand consolingly.

'Go home, your mama's back,' Grandma Touran informed Maurice the following morning.

'Mama's back! Mama's back!' Maurice rushed from neighbour's door to neighbour's door and they opened to him in turn. Marcelle forgot her shoes on the first floor, Sofia left her dreams on the second, and Lizzie left her breakfast of cocoa and fruit unfinished. The four of them stood in the doorway, stunned.

Inside they saw their mother, her feet very bare, her face streaming, her breasts overflowing. On the carpet at her feet lay the cat with four kittens sucking at her teats. The cat raised her head and licked the tears that dropped from Iran's cheeks and fell on her ankles.

Iran pushed one nipple into Matti's mouth, dandled her and shivered.

'The other one died on me,' she sobbed. 'The one you wanted to call Moni.'

She gave the other nipple to the fifth kitten, the smallest, weakest and most delicate of the litter. She had seen him struggling all night, searching in vain for an unoccupied teat, till she gathered him up to her bosom.

Sofia, Marcelle and Lizzie volunteered to bring up Matti, and they looked after her as if she was one of their dolls. They told her about the dead baby boy, about Mama's sorrow because she'd tried to give Papa another son, about Maurice's disappointment, because he'd wanted a brother, and Papa's unhappiness, as he'd hoped to name the boy Moni, after his own father Manucher.

'But where is he?' Matti asked them.

'We told you – he's dead,' said Sofia.

'Yes, but why isn't he here, at home?'

Sofia threw a pleading look at Marcelle, who took Matti's hand in hers, stroked it and opened the palm. She explained to her, very slowly and clearly, that on Iran's hand there were only five fingers – Maurice was the thumb, the three big girls were the first, the middle and the third fingers.

'And you are the pinkie,' Marcelle concluded and twiddled Matti's little finger.

'So you see,' said Lizzie, 'there just wasn't any room for him.'

Every night Matti made room in her bed for Moni to put his head on the pillow and lie under the covers. She did not resent Moni for having kicked her in the face and crushed her nose, and didn't get mad at him even when he wet the bed. As she grew up, so did her sisters, who found other amusements, and Matti was left alone with her little brother. She taught him to say 'Mama' and 'Papa' and 'light'. She told him all her stories, refused to wear dresses and didn't play with dolls, because Moni said that girls' games were boring. She never sat still for a moment and made a lot of noise, so that her mother wouldn't feel that instead of a pair of twins she had her alone.

When the white cat disappeared one day, because Mama wanted to forget what she reminded her of, Matti whispered softly, 'Don't cry, Moni, Matti's here with you. I'm looking after you.'

Even when she was playing with the neighbours' children she felt his shoulder rubbing against her arm, and his bare feet digging into the sandpit, tickling her toes deep below the surface.

Matti knew that her mother was sad because she was missing Moni. Whenever she heard Iran crying in her room she'd run to her, pick up her heavy arms and place them round her ribs and snuggle between them for a hug.

She would hum and wriggle her shoulders under Iran's stiff arms to nestle against her. When Iran calmed down a little she wanted to tell her about Moni, that he was with her the whole time, that he was hungry when she was, slept when she slept, stayed with her when she was ill, and that he was a good boy.

'Enough, Mama, you mustn't cry, enough.' She breathed warmth on her mother's wet face, blew on the three black beauty-spots and stroked the trident scar.

'You mustn't cry all the time. You know why?' she'd say, her mouth filling with saliva, and her eyes searching for the two little Mattis who would soon appear in Iran's black almonds. In a moment she would tell her that though Moni was dead, he was not sad or angry, and then her mother would be very glad. Then they would appear, a laughing Matti in the left eye, a cheerful Matti in the right, as alike as a pair of twins. 'You know why? Because our Moni . . .'

No sooner did Iran hear the name Moni, than she was again swept away by sorrow.

'He's dead, my little boy is dead,' she sobbed. Her nostrils flared, her arms dropped and the embrace was broken. The two identical Mattis disappeared among the wrinkles that closed Iran's eyes and locked up her face. Matti wanted to say that it wasn't so, that if Moni was dead, it meant that she too was dead. She wanted to show her that she had another pinkie, a little one just like herself, on her other hand. But by then Moni didn't allow her to say anything about him to anybody.

Because the two of them went everywhere together, Matti had a double measure of vitality. Already in her early days in the double cot, playing with the worn toys of her brother and sisters, she made enough noise for two babies, rolled over back and forth, swung on her hands and knees and crawled. At six months she could stand up, and two months later she started to walk. Solly boasted about her nimbleness as if she were a child prodigy. He didn't know that it was Moni, curled up inside her, who urged her on and made her rush around all over the house. Moni wanted to see everything, touch everything, taste everything. Sometimes Matti would have liked to stop and rest a little, but Moni persisted and she was punished.

'Now look what you did, dummy!' Iran would yell, and Moni was hurt.

'That wasn't nice, Moni, look what you did, you made Mama angry again,' Matti would scold, but at once forgave him. 'Never mind, you're my baby and I love you.'

Fits of energy drove her on. She whirled around the way a summer insect zooms around a lighted lamp, teasing a hunting cat. Her black eyes were so alert that they looked as if they never closed. They were always wide open, smouldering and scheming.

'Eyes full of mischief,' Iran would say in moments of affection.

'Eyes full of craziness!' she yelled in moments of rage.

Her father saw her as a small playful animal, an amusing child animated like a rowdy circus band, bursting with love of life, with a permanent carnival in her mind and spotlights shooting out of her eyes.

'Matti!' he always shouted when he addressed her. 'Your father is speaking to you!' He tried to shake her up, but sometimes he came across her sitting deep in thought and her eyes full of sadness, and he was alarmed. Her body seemed so small and her clothes too tight for such a huge pain.

Her parents were too old to bring her up, so she was brought up by everybody and nobody. No one saw the inner pounding that drove her on. They didn't understand that in the morning she wanted to put on a shirt like Moni and trousers like Moni, because that's how it was supposed to be with twins, and persisted stubbornly till she was late for school. They didn't realise that it was he who competed with her in jumping from the roof of Grandma Touran's house, who dared her to smash the window of the children's bathroom in the nursery school and then run away and hide in the oleander bush till nightfall. They didn't see that of every portion of chocolate they gave her she kept a square for Moni, till it melted in her clutching fist. That she divided every sheet of paper in half, so that Moni would have room to draw too. That she woke up in the night because Moni was frightened by her dreams.

Iran was hanging the washing on the lines strung outside the balcony, and peering between the wet bedsheets and socks at Matti running around downstairs. The courtyard was empty, quiet and idle in the midday sun. It looked as if the flats on the estate had been vacated, the residents departed and taken their children with them. Iran could see Matti's desperate desire for play, her hunger for the neighbours' children, who were confined to their homes for the siesta. She thought that Matti was down there on her own.

'Come up and do your homework!' she yelled at her, shaking out a damp shirt.

'Don't have any!' Matti shrugged off the call, kicked with her sandals at invisible pebbles, bent over the standpipe, peeped into the electricity meters' cupboard, investigated the crooked letter-boxes at the entrance to the building, plucked some dry stalks of wild oats and flung them at her shirt, where their prickles caught the fabric and prophesied how many children she would have.

'We'll have seven babies, Moni!'

Iran thought Matti was talking to herself out of boredom.

A couple of hours later Iran came out to see if the washing was dry. She rubbed the sheets and her fingers were cooled by the still-damp socks. Peering between the lines and the coloured clothes-pegs she saw Matti surrounded by the neighbourhood children, her face radiant, blazing like a match that had lain too long in the box. Her laughter resounded to the end of the street, her cheering and boos hooted like engines that pulled the other children's voices after them. Her hair flew in the heat of battle like a victory banner, her sweat ran golden, her skin was flushed and her shirt gleamed.

Iran did not see Moni panting and puffing beside her.

She never felt tired. She cavorted on Grandma Touran's roof, climbed the guava trees, came down and climbed the medlar trees, rode a bike and kicked a ball home, slid on the rusting iron railing and climbed up on the roof again. When all the other children were exhausted, Matti was still going strong.

There were neither sun nor moon, neither Mama nor Papa, only she and he. The third floor was as far away as the clouds. Beyond the treetops was only the sky. If the ball didn't escape from the kicking foot and fly over the fence, if the kids didn't threaten to call their big brothers to deal with her, if no grown-up entered the back yard and crossed its infinite space in three paces, then she and Moni were free on all sides, and when evening came it took them by surprise, like a pair of drunks who'd fallen asleep in the middle of the day on a bustling railway station.

In the end she was said to be hyperactive, sent to a special boarding-school and given a Ritalin tablet every four hours. But before her parents despaired and agreed to turn her into a drugged, apathetic puppet, Matti was a blurred patch of feverish activity. She simply couldn't sit down, and when she did sit, her legs would jump and kick and her eyes darted in all directions. Her heart followed every car that rushed down the street, every plane that crossed the sky, even the blades of an electric fan. She devastated the house and smashed its furniture. The three-part sofa in the living-room became three broken armchairs, the stitches of its upholstery burst open and its foam-rubber stuffing spilled out. Iran and Solly had no strength left, not in their arms when she went on a rampage and they tried to restrain her, nor in their hearts when they tried to love her despite everything. Only Maurice's arms were strong enough, and he beat her. Moni cried with her when she was hurt.

Iran, whose speciality was motherhood, occasionally bent down to listen to the sound of Matti's growing bones, but even she didn't hear the ticking of the clock hands inside her, a big hand and a small one.

'Stand still a moment!' Faithful to her own system, Iran tried to press her ear to Matti's little heart. She even took the old stethoscope from Maurice's room to hear with, but failed to detect the double beat.

'Naughty, that's all,' she sighed. 'Should have a tail on your arse.' She would give Matti a smack on the behind, then leave her to run wild, rush around, search for hiding places. Forgetting how heavy was the burden of child-hood, she hung a schoolbag on her shoulders and sent her to school. And there everything became that much harder for Matti Azizyan.

In her heart of hearts Iran blamed her own father, Matti's grandfather, and his wanderlust. She thought it was he who had passed on to her daughter a passion for movement, which grew into a compulsion. She asked the nurse at the clinic if there could be a connection, but the nurse said no. The family doctor said that perhaps the difficult birth and the problems with the womb that Matti had shared with her dead twin had deprived her of air, and that might be the reason she was like this. Iran couldn't see what it had to do with the fact that Matti was so unruly, and, acting upon her sisters' advice, she made her punishments harsher.

'Now you really got a reason for crying!' Iran would announce when Matti was going berserk in the locked house, crying and screaming that she wanted to go downstairs. But Matti was incapable of sitting still, either at home or in the classroom. Nursery schools rejected her, one after the other, and she finally ended up in a special-needs class. That was where all her rage burst out. There, too, she first heard a teacher saying, 'Don't pay her any attention, children. She's crazy.'

She really caused no end of trouble, but she was not sent to the boarding-school because she stuck the finger of a child who annoyed her into an electric socket, or because she tied up another child on top of a nest of red ants, or peeped into the boys' toilets, or locked the maths teacher in the music room, or turned off the stopcock of the mains water supply for the whole school, or sneaked away from a games lesson and rummaged in all the schoolbags that were left in the classroom and took a bite out of every sandwich.

Her parents despaired of Matti only after Iran locked her in the flat to keep an eye on Sofia's baby, and went out. That was when they began to be afraid of her and realised that she could not remain at home.

It was a spring day, and Matti was sitting in the branches of a guava tree without her shirt, all heated up from the frenetic games she'd been playing. Up on the top branches crouched curly-tailed chameleons in ambush for buzzing insects. Matti's teeth were on edge from eating a hard green unripe guava, because she had bet one of the kids that she'd eat it all up. Her tongue felt rough and her insides were rumbling. She had incited a gang of children from over at the estate to climb after her and throw hard green guavas at a group of children who clustered under the medlar trees. Battle raged from the foliage, shrieks flew to the treetops, and laughter rang from the branches. The kids on the ground, assaulted by the barrage of guavas, shook the lower medlar branches, guzzled the fallen orange-coloured fruits and used their hard pips to fire back.

Matti was overjoyed, because that afternoon no mothers, fathers or older brothers had set foot in the yard and diminished its boundless space. There was a good smell in the air, the smell of a great bonfire, of spicy freedom, of approaching summer.

Suddenly she needed to pee. She decided to hold it in, as she often did, feeling the pleasant evening breeze, which combined warm and cool draughts, passing over and under her skin. The breeze stroked her underarms and passed between her legs. Matti stopped playing and shivered. Her body felt as if she was afraid of something, and all her little hairs stood on end. She felt she herself was a medlar pip, big and black and painful. Suddenly the street lamps hummed, the lights flickered on, stammered briefly, then came back on and burned steadily. The air shimmered. Her mother shouted to her from the balcony, 'Matti! Matti! Come up quick, I need you to come up here quick!' Matti bared her teeth, knitted her eyebrows and was about to yell back, 'Get off my back, can't you see I'm in the middle of a game?' But the need to pee was pressing and she had a funny sensation, like an earthquake in her belly, and she heard herself saying, 'All right.' She climbed down from the guava tree, put on her shirt like a good girl, and went upstairs.

In the kitchen she was met by a stinging smell of chopped hot red peppers.

'I got to go out a moment,' Iran said to her. 'Got to. But Marcelle's at the hair salon and Lizzie's still not back from hospital. So you keep an eye on baby – he's sleeping fast – and I'll come right back.'

Matti didn't hear Iran locking the door after her because at that moment she was flushing the toilet.

The reek of the hot peppers scorched her nostrils, as though she'd bitten them with her nose. She drank three glasses of water one after the other, greedily and noisily. Then she removed the plasters she'd stuck on her arms and knees as if to cover wounds, because it was understood that there was no hitting sore places, wiped the splatters of medlars from her bare skin, and just when she was beginning to feel bored, Sofia's blue baby began to cough.

At first Matti ignored him. She paced back and forth

past his cot her back straight and her head held high, peering at him from the corners of her half-shut eyes. She pretended she couldn't hear anything, hung out of the window, hummed tunelessly, and stared wide-eyed at the gathering dusk that hovered between day and night. The sun spat out streams of red across the vast sky, which blushed. Black flocks of birds hurled themselves violently at the clouds, flew back towards Matti and swung back at the clouds, skimming back and forth.

'Enough, enough,' she muttered at the baby from afar.

She went nearer and whispered, 'Grandma is coming right back.'

Her childish voice squeaked when she tried to keep it low. She circled around the baby the way Sofia did, tried to pray like Iran, even promised to sacrifice half her life for his pretty willie. But it was no use. His coughing pressured her, squeezed her throat and made her head ache. She heard the delighted cries of the medlar gang overcoming the defeated shrieks of the guava kids.

'Stop! Stop! Stop!' she roared at the baby. The coughing turned to barking, and distant dogs, intimidated by the approach of night, began to bark back from around the estate. Matti felt a great wave of anxiety rising inside her, swelling into fury, overflowing, desperate for a shore to break on. The smell of the peppers brought stinging tears to her eyes. She went to the kitchen, walked into all the rooms, as far as the walls, then to the front door. She gripped the handle to open it up, to shout for the neighbours to come and help, to whine with fear. But the door was locked.

'Stop, I said! Stop it right now!'

There was nothing on which to slide, to climb, to

attack, because the front door was locked. Only the inner doors opened and shut. So Matti opened and shut them, opened and slammed hard, till their glass panes shattered and her arms became bloody. But the baby didn't stop.

'Moni!' she cried for help. 'What can I do, Moni?' She screamed at her bleeding hands. 'What can I do?'

Matti picked up her nephew from his cot, trembling like a medlar tree shaken by the children. He coughed in her arms. His deep dark throat opened and closed, gaped and convulsed, turned blue and filled with phlegm.

'Stop it or I . . . Stop now, or I'll . . . Stop stop stop!' she shrieked. The neighbours also shouted, but she didn't hear them. The door didn't break under their blows, the lock didn't give in to their kicks, only Matti and the baby were shaken by each other. They dripped blood, tears, saliva and snot.

'Stop – or I'll throw you out the window, you hear me?'

She shoved off the row of pebbles she kept on the windowsill to throw at the cats. She shook the baby between heaven and earth, but he didn't stop coughing. She stuck out her head but couldn't see the mothers and fathers and big brothers who had gathered under the window. She saw only the tops of the guava trees she'd struck with her pebbles, their trunks spattered with shiny medlars, and the eyes of the children glowing through the foliage in the sudden twilight, twinkling like stars that had just come out in the sky.

'There, I'm going to throw you out!' she screamed and sobbed.

Her screams seemed to rip open an old seam in her throat. Her big eyeballs leaped out of their sockets and jumped downstairs. A picture flew across her darkening mind like a stone flung at a cat's tail. She saw how the baby would drop from her bleeding hands like a blue leaf in the autumn, his tiny fingers struggling to catch the prominent cornice, the medlar children abandoning the tree trunks, their faces aghast, and the guava children striking their heads against the branches in surprise, the whoosh of air in the tiny ears, the second floor, the rooms of the flats she had never seen, the first floor, the nudities hiding in the bedrooms, the lumber on the balconies, the rustle of the fall which would sound as soft as a nut being cracked in the mouth. Then the silence.

'Moni, I'm counting to three! One . . . two . . .' she screamed, and heard a hundred voices shouting her name. The landscape retreated to the horizon, the baby choked and she wept without a sound. The unripe green guava revolved in her stomach and the medlar pip of her own self was caught in her throat, big and black and painful.

'Three!'

That spring evening, which was marked by the harsh sting of chopped red peppers, all over the housing estate, in all the flats around all the supper tables, the residents talked about Matti Azizyan. Her actions dwarfed the fathers and mothers and big brothers, made their voices crack with shock, and reduced their world to the dimensions of the back yard. They had all seen, and those who hadn't seen heard, how Iran saved the baby at the last moment, and beat Matti so hard that Matti hit her back, that blood was spilt, and that at long last those Azizyans had grasped that Matti couldn't be kept at home any longer and had to be sent to a special school for disturbed children.

* * *

Three pots were simmering on the stove and into them Iran dumped withered peaches, elderly quinces and over-ripe plums. It was her custom to prepare thick, morass-like jams at the end of the month of Ellul, when the skies were very starry, and at the same time think about the rose-petal jam her mother used to make but died before she got round to dictating the recipe.

Coated in sweet sweat, Iran shook herself free of the childhood taste that had welled in her mouth, and looked at her fingertips which were tingling. She discovered that while thinking about her mother her fingers had unconsciously stroked the cheeks of the peaches that had escaped stewing in sugar and were judged fit to eat. Their flushed skin and firm flesh had tempted her hands to caress them, and they had shed a mass of fine glassy bristles. Iran was forty-one, and the wrinkles that had formed in her eyelids tightened when she strained her eyes, brought her hands closer and picked the peach fuzz out of her fingers.

'So pretty,' she muttered. 'That's why they sting the fingers.'

It was stifling in the kitchen and she went to the living-room. Sweet vapours spread throughout the house, absorbed in the humidity which came in through the screened windows and the clouds of vapour that came from the bathroom. There her big daughters were taking a joint shower. She could hear their wild laughter gurgling with the rushing water, and opened the door to look at the naked threesome.

'Oh Mama, you made such a good smell,' Marcelle said, licking the stream of water that ran down her shiny shoulders, and soaped Sofia's back. Sofia did not turn round, only suppressed a pleasurable moan and showed her mother her plump buttocks with their dimples. Lizzie was washing her hair, deep in thought, her eyes shut.

'Did someone come in?' She shook herself and straightened her back, her hair twining like leaves and the foam trickling through it like resin and dripping down her breasts.

'Your mother came in.'

Iran shut the door. In the past few nights she had been bothered by dreams that thieves had got into the house and were rummaging in the jewellery box, where the number of pearls had greatly diminished in the course of the years.

'Who knows what's going on in those clubs they go to,' she said in Persian to her husband, just back from the sea. 'Who knows what kind of people are there.'

The three girls painted their toenails with pink polish, curved the arches of their feet into shoes with high, chisel-sharp heels, and the fabrics of their dresses sang the praises of the beautiful legs that showed below their hems. The powder they dusted on their faces hung in the air like mist. Using exquisitely fine brushes they gave themselves giraffes' eyes, sketched eyebrows slender as a whisker, and rushed out.

'God help you if you're not back by twelve! You hear me?' Their mother's shout accompanied the drum-beat of their high heels pattering down the stairs, and her anxious heart pounded faster. She noticed that their shoes contorted their walk, that they pushed their swaying bottoms up and out, and that their necks boldly invited kisses.

Occasionally she was seized by a fit of modesty and

forbade them to 'go out like this with all the family secrets on show'. They never protested but put on a dowdy shawl or a sweater, blew kisses from their flaming, lipstick-swollen mouths, and flew off.

They realised that she was finding it hard to part from the little girls who used to live at home and reconcile herself to the women who had taken their places. After leaving the house they hid the virtuous coverings behind the oleander bushes in Grandma Touran's yard, and allowed the moonlight to caress their humid breasts.

When they returned home in the middle of the night their toes were bleeding, torn by dancing. The narrow shoe straps had grown hot in the darkened clubs and left blisters that would accompany them to work the following morning – Sofia to the hairdresser's, Marcelle to the bridal salon and Lizzie to the hospital.

Though they tried to walk quietly when they entered the house to avoid disrupting the family's dreams, Iran heard them and woke up. Solly at her side had dived into the ocean depths of his sleep. Suppressing her anger, Iran clenched her teeth and held a pillow over her ears, to avoid hearing the noise. Those sharp heels punched holes in her heart.

She heard them wearily kicking off their shoes and whispering, 'I'm dead. My feet are finished!'

'I won't have any feet to stand on tomorrow, nothing . . .'

'Shhh . . . quiet . . .'

She pitied Maurice, who had been asleep in bed for hours, the soles of his feet smooth as a baby's, his dreams empty of adventures. She heard him scratching himself in his sleep and knew that his skin was itching with envy.

The next morning she had to shake her daughters who were clinging to the sweet remnants of sleep. 'Come on, get up now, how many times I have to wake you?' She smelled the traces of their perfumes which she knew would inflame her son's resentment, and urged them to wash them off at the sink. Despite her best efforts, Maurice would wake naked and alone, get dressed in front of the staring nude women he'd hung over his bed, and emerge from his room. His sisters' dull eyes, the traces of lipstick on their mouths, the crumbs of mascara that fell into their breakfast plates with every huge yawn, made him irritable.

He said he could tell what they'd done the night before by the whites of their eyes – fucking causes the whites of the eyes to become clearer, he maintained. So Sofia, Marcelle and Lizzie learned to lower their heads when he looked at them, and gaze at the floor tiles instead.

When he returned, listless and bored by another day in his poky little spice shop, he would find them sprawled on the sofa, their limbs entwined like the branches of a rampant bougainvillaea. Sometimes he found their mother among them, surrendering her body to their caresses, laughing and cracking white pumpkin seeds.

'It's true, it's true,' Iran would sigh. 'Every woman has a poison snake in her heart, a crow in her brain and bugs between her legs. That's how it is with all of them . . . But God kill me if I'm lying – it all goes away, pouf! when a woman gets married. I swear!'

Sofia's face was plastered with a yeast mask, Marcelle had on a mask made from avocado, and Lizzie a cucumber one. Three pairs of eyes twinkled with laughter through their disguises.

'All right, you can laugh at your mother.' Iran's head

sank into her body and her body into the sofa. 'You can laugh till tomorrow, but you better hear good what your mother is telling you . . .'

'Just tell us, Mama darling, and we'll do everything you say.' Sofia's voice was sugary as she played with the rings on Iran's fingers.

'I promise you I'll do just what you say – at least everything I can remember,' Marcelle smilingly assured her, slipped a ring off one of Iran's fingers and tried it on.

'Go on, you make jokes about your mother, I know you,' Iran responded, pinching them affectionately and giving them little loving bites.

Lizzie stretched out her hand and looked sternly at the ring on her middle finger.

'On the next finger, Lizzie, I tell you! A wedding ring goes on the fourth finger of the left hand!' Iran raised her voice to make sure Lizzie took it in. 'That is the finger that can't stand up by itself, it loves the other fingers so much, they all come along with it.'

Lizzie tried to make her fourth finger rise alone out of her closed fist.

'You hear what I'm saying, Lizzie?' Iran shouted. 'And you must never never throw away the shoes from the wedding, you hear? Wedding shoes must always be inside the wardrobe, so you will have love all your life, yes? I'm talking to you!'

'Yes, Mama, I understand. In the wardrobe,' Lizzie echoed, and carefully moved the clasp of Iran's gold chain, which had slid down between her breasts and joined the pendants, to its place on the back of her neck.

'Yes, we know how good you hear,' Iran grumbled as if to herself. 'Just control yourself a little. Not go mad, like a wasp got into the inside of your bra. I don't mind that you all grow legs from underarms to the floor, or you squeeze your liver with belts to give you an arse like an ant. That's all right. But if you could grow not just tits – *mashallah*, spit on the evil eye! – not just tits, but also grow some brains . . .'

The three girls, redolent with the scents of lilac, vanilla or white musk, would nod in mock humility and smile knowingly and with condescension, but it was not long before every one of them accepted the first man who proposed to her, and turned all restless and impatient, like a person who has been travelling for many weary hours when the train finally approaches its destination.

Maurice came in and Iran immediately stood up, startled and confused, covered her daughters' exposed thighs and disowned the warm, scented mass of flesh in which she'd been wallowing.

'Ouf! You stick to me like you need burping!' she complained, emerging from the clouds of face powder. 'Maurice, my soul, what's the matter, you look so tired?'

But Iran was unable to distract her son with fancy dishes and drinks. He would look out from the kitchen and observe his sisters clustering together into an octopus, exchanging earrings and bangles, which they held in common and kept in the old artichoke-green jewellery box. Their fingers fluttered on each other, barely touching, in that distant way of women who keep their nails long and perfectly manicured. Stretched out on the flabby sofa, they whispered together, giggled or kept quiet, smoking one cigarette between them which they passed from hand to hand, tipping the ashes into overflowing blue enamel saucers.

Their clothes and shoes were also held in common and wandered from body to body, from foot to foot, and when taken off were kept in the one wardrobe in their room, a bulging store of fabrics and colours, scents of perfumes and traces of sweat. They had formed a unified taste in clothes, a single size and a single figure, so that sometimes Maurice imagined that they not only loaned each other their finest lingerie for a special occasion to which only one of them was invited, but even their splendid limbs, as though together they added up to a jigsaw puzzle of a perfect woman's body.

When they reached the age of eighteen and one after the other were called up into the armed forces, each of the three put on the same modest expression and the same shapeless flowered skirt down to the ankles, and declared in a whiny pious voice that they were religious, and were therefore exempt from national service. They continued to dance and to work, and their feet continued to hurt. On winter nights they heaped up blankets and quilts and stuffed pillows in the foot of the bed, to prop up their six ankles and restore their circulation. On hot summer evenings they sat with their feet in buckets of cold water up to their calves, to cool the blood that pounded in their veins.

They would lock their door as if it were a secret feminine workshop, but their voices came out of it and deafened the whole house.

'What have I got here? See, touch here, what is it?'

'Here?'

'No, no . . . right, that's it. Can you feel it?'

They never stopped chattering and sucked all the air of the house into their room.

Under the eyes of their favourite film stars, whose pictures they cut out of the centrefolds of the magazines that they read from first page to the horoscopes, they undressed and anointed themselves with oils and creams and perfumes. They comforted each other with slow, painstaking massages of tired feet, kneaded each other's shoulders and backs, petted and caressed. They showed off their nude figures, gleaming with lotions, suntan and pleasure, and turned this way and that in front of the double mirror in their room.

They were forever measuring the circumference of their hips with ruthless precision, and mourned bitterly when the skin of their thighs took on the texture of orange peel. They tucked pencils under their breasts, to see which dropped, the breast or the pencil, tried to grip coins between their legs hoping they would fall because there was not enough fat to hold them, touched nipple to nipple and navel to navel, and hung over each other to squeeze waxy worms out of skin pores.

'Not bad! . . . Not bad! . . .' they would breathe in admiration of each other's fine bones, would cross their outstretched arms and slap open palms on giggly, succulent buttocks.

'It's me, open the door, please, it's me!' Matti begged. When she came into the room with Maurice's stethoscope hanging round her neck, she saw her reflection in the double mirror, looking small and black.

Matti loved this room more than any other part of the flat, loved its fresh, indecipherable liveliness, the overflowing blue enamel ashtrays, the cups of morning coffee with lipstick kisses on their rims, and the music her sisters recorded from the radio hit parade.

'Matti, Matti, what do you think – you think it looks better this way . . . like so . . . or like that?' For her benefit they tried on the clothes they had bought on their last shopping spree, when they'd left behind a cloud of worthless cheques like a flock of yellow butterflies.

Matti would throw herself down on the big bed and couldn't take her eyes off her beautiful sisters. The three would dance in front of the mirror which doubled them into six, sometimes by candlelight, sometimes with the ceiling light on, waggled figures-of-eight with their pelvises, spun around, shook their hips and made their stomachs ripple.

'Just imagine you've got a pencil stuck in there and you draw shapes with it,' they instructed her. Sitting among their jiggling pelvises, Matti observed the tints of the triple body, noted the fine differences between its various versions, and with her heart going pit-a-pat tried to distinguish between the original and the copies. She searched for resemblances to her own self, and found none.

I just look like you, Moni, she thought, and moved the stethoscope amplifier over her chest. You hear me, my Moni? Only you.

When Iran noticed Maurice pricking up his ears at the chorus of female flesh behind the door and flushing with embarrassment and loneliness, she marched in, slammed off the singing tape, chased Lizzie, Marcelle and Sofia away from the mirror and ordered them to get dressed.

'Will I be like them when I get big?' Matti asked her mother.

'You need legs for walking. You got legs, thank God. That's enough.'

'And tits?'

'Tits you'll have when your husband looks at them. You are still small.' Iran brushed her off and got on with the job of mothering. 'Go on, put on some clothes right away!'

Matti approached the double mirror, emptied now of her sisters, stared at the two Mattis who were as alike as twins, and failed to resemble either of them.

'That Matti, she will be a fancy lady just like her big sisters.' She heard her mother's voice through the tubes of the stethoscope that were stuck in her ears.

'That's true. If Matti could climb into the mirror she would,' said Solly, laughing, and added something in Persian that she couldn't understand. Then she was sure she heard Iran saying to Solly that God wanted Matti to come into the world with a twin who would be like her and make things easier for her, but it didn't work out.

'What?' she asked, pulling the earpieces out. She turned her back to the mirror and stared in amazement at her mother, trying to catch what she was saying.

'Your three princesses, what delicate skins they got!' she heard her teasing her husband. 'Any little pinch in their flesh, right away it leaves a blue mark!'

'What does that mean? I bet you have an interpretation for it,' Solly mocked, his mouth opening and closing like an oyster.

'It means they have a talent for loving, your daughters.' Iran's shoulders shook and rose up to her ears with laughter that contained a tinge of fear.

The lurid stains which appeared on their skin, love's bruised stamps, turned blue, green and finally yellow, like the damp patches on the ceiling. The three hid from their mother's all-seeing eyes the bites that their lovers had left on their necks when they pressed avid lips to the fine olive skin and sucked it passionately. They also hid the whites of their eyes from Maurice's gaze, but their bowed heads gave them away.

'I feel sorry for other people's mirrors,' said Solly, tucking his moustache into the hollow of Iran's neck as she combed her hair in front of the mirror. 'They can hang on the wall for years and years and never see all the beauty that I've got in my house, eh, my soul?'

'Never mind all the beauty – good luck is what they need,' Iran grumbled and hunched her shoulders, resisting his kisses. 'Good luck is what really matters.'

'If you could just for a moment come out of yourself and see what I see,' Solly retorted, giving her goosebumps with the tip of his tongue, 'you wouldn't stop looking at yourself. But unfortunately you need a mirror to do it, my poor beauty.'

Sofia was the tallest and most beautiful of Iran's daughters. She was born a beauty, but only when her body began to grow tall did everyone notice how lovely she was, and held their breath. Solly kept looking at her, bashful and smiling, but Iran worried. She saw her daughter ceaselessly cracking her knuckles, watched her fingers becoming bent, and noticed the tremor that clung to them like a persistent shiver.

In primary school Sofia was twice made to repeat a year. Her year-six exercise books were covered with pierced hearts and their corners were torn out for notes. Only the first pages still retained a few unsolved maths problems and unanswered questions. When she was fourteen she got tired of sharpening her pencils and shedding yellow butterflies. Taller by a head than the rest of her classmates, with a bitter and listless beauty, she left secondary school and entered a technical college. She tightened the belt around her wasp waist and her speech acquired a thoughtful tone like a person recalling a dream. Her sister Marcelle followed in her footsteps. Her own schooling deteriorated because of her unrequited love for Yoel Hajjabi. Their mother's face became creased with anxiety, but Sofia broke the hearts of the boys who took electrics and metallurgy at the technical college. After school hours she shampooed heads at the Beauty Palace salon, and as her pockets became stuffed with banknotes her eyes filled with sparks.

Sofia didn't know what she was doing to her admirers, what illusions she was planting in their hearts, when she fell asleep on their shoulders at the cinema, yawned in the cafés and blew clouds of smoke in the dance clubs. Like all truly beautiful women, she appeared serene and distant. She would cross her legs, press the big toe of one foot against the arch of the other, and allow men to drape her on their shoulders like an enviable decoration. They believed that what they saw in her sleepy eyes was the thoughtful gaze of an experienced woman, and interpreted her anxious uncertainty as a challenge, as amused teasing, as unvanquished pride.

Of all the admirers who took care to bring her home by midnight, Sofia chose Itzik Kadosh, who even before their engagement covered each of her twisted fingers with gold and diamonds.

He was seventeen years older than she was, and in

those days he was squeezing money and tears out of almost every nation in Africa. He began his business career by importing to Israel hollow gold jewellery, but by the time he met Sofia he had already become a major purveyor of tear-gas. Its choking, stinging clouds showered riches on him, while the trade in cheap gold was also flourishing. Itzik Kadosh's eyes twinkled brightly in their sockets, but they had brought down cataracts of tears by the time he acquired all the right business connections. By the time the real profits began to pour in, those eyes were surrounded by small wrinkles, and by the time he felt he had enough money to marry his temples were already turning silver.

Itzik Kadosh met Sofia when she was crowned queen. He saw her for the first time dressed in a ballgown with a nylon train and on her head a papier-mâché crown encrusted with glass gems. Six months later she would put on a wedding gown for him and drape her head in a veil.

'Ladies and gentlemen . . . men . . . men . . . !' echoed the loudspeakers when Sofia was being crowned the most beautiful girl of the technical-college system.

'Our beauty queen . . . een . . . een . . . is Sofia Azizyan . . . yan . . . yan . . .'

Itzik Kadosh saw her come up on to the stage and was struck by her languid beauty.

His young niece, on whose account he happened to be at the Givat Olga community centre that night, did not make it into the finals. When the ceremony ended he did not wait for her, but returned to his international gold and tears business. He didn't realise it, but the lure of Sofia's enervated loveliness had dissolved in his blood.

When he came back it was to persuade her to marry

him, because he'd discovered that since seeing her his breathing had become difficult and all his memories had evaporated. The look in her weary, seemingly indifferent, eyes killed his desire for other women, and he could not wait for the night when they would fall asleep together in a close embrace. Seeing her in her summer dresses that fluttered over her skin without daring to touch it, he did not so much fantasise about her luminous nudity as about the nightgown he would dress her in when she joined him in bed. Itzik Kadosh shed many tears because of her and there was a painful well of longing in his throat. He was thirty-five and in love with an eighteen-year-old beauty queen. He fell victim to a different kind of tear-gas – the scent of a desired woman. He did not miss his lost memories. His past was gone, and even his present seemed to dissipate without her.

Sofia toyed with him like an empress. She alternately encouraged and rejected him, set a time and place for a meeting and didn't show up. In those humid summer evenings of her glory he saw her flitting past him like a mocking songbird, her head crowned with a glittering papier-mâché crown and a retinue of admirers on motorbikes roaring after her.

'Itzik? What Itzik? I don't know any Itzik,' she would laugh calmly and disdainfully into the telephone when he called.

But only ten days after she'd given in to his pleading and agreed to go out with him they decided to get married. On their tenth date he gave her the last of the diamond rings with which he loaded her crooked fingers. Sofia felt the fingers bending under the weight and her wrists seemed ready to collapse.

Itzik had hardly finished popping the question, when she replied, 'All right, we'll get married.'

The reason she agreed was that she'd had a dream that he was crying bitterly on account of her. She heard herself speak, looked up from the diamonds and bit her lower lip, opening an old childhood scar. She tasted blood, and her heart grew fearful. She didn't know if she wanted him or not, because she never knew what she wanted or didn't want. So she agreed.

Deeply moved, Itzik Kadosh took off the metal chain on which she always wore the house keys around her neck. In its place he hung a golden link-chain with a pendant saying 'Itzik' in cursive. The pendant was caught on her lovely clavicle and sank into the hollow. Itzik thought that Sofia too felt the pangs of love in that well, and he filled it with kisses.

When he told her gently that he needed to go away again and would be back in two weeks, just a day before the wedding, she said again, 'All right.'

Never, in the wistful pre-wedding days, did she urge him to stop going away on his profitable trips; she never begged him to stay with her and did not complain that he was too busy selling hollow gold and tear-gas. She accepted his absence with the same tolerance with which she had let Maurice hog her mother's love and forgiven her father his absence during her childhood.

The night before his departure he stayed at her parents' place. Before everyone went to bed Sofia sat yawning while Itzik Kadosh told her father about the marvels of his journeys and the extent of his business affairs. Solly listened to him like a child, almost climbed into his future son-in-law's lap. Finally Iran laid a mattress for the guest in Maurice's room.

Sofia was in bed when Solly came in, took her hand in his and said, 'I talked to him. He's a good man. A really good man. But you, my little soul, you must do what your heart tells you, you see?' He petted and caressed her for a long time.

All night long Itzik Kadosh tried to listen to his betrothed, who was asleep in her room. He strained to hear her through the orchestra of the family's breathing, trying to discern some strain in her dreams of sadness or anger that would compel him to stay. His ears were filled with the crackling sounds of Iran and Solly's love-making, who had caught fire from his passion. In the morning he expected to see farewell tears in Sofia's eyes, but she didn't even wake up, and he left.

Meanwhile her mother and sisters planned her wedding for her.

'Wake up, Sofia, you got to get up now!' Iran tried to flush her out of bed, to take her measurements for the wedding gown.

'She's like somebody dead. I tell you a widow, God save us, feels more excitement than this one.'

'Enough, Mama, you and your nonsense,' Marcelle hushed her. 'Come, Lizzie, I'll hold her up on this side, you support her on the other side.'

They extracted her from the bedclothes, propped her up on their shoulders, and Iran's tape measure crept all over her. Sofia trembled in her dream.

'Tell me the truth, on the Bible,' Iran asked her daughters on the way to the dressmaker's house. 'Our

Sofia, is she taking him for his money? The truth, I want the real truth!'

'How can I tell?' the two replied in one voice. But Iran would have got the same answer if she'd put the question to Sofia herself.

Then they chose for her the fanciest and most expensive ballroom – the Venus Dome, which rose, proud and glittering, on top of a Tel Aviv hotel. With their lips daintily pursed they tasted samples of the many dinner courses, trying to guess which would appeal to Sofia, discussed the relative merits of Callas and Madonna lilies, and sent out numerous scalloped invitations, the words dictated by Marcelle and the decoration chosen by Lizzie. When the happy bridegroom returned, followed by a procession of breathless porters bringing new furniture and the latest electrical gadgets, humping chests full of kitchenware and knick-knacks, Marcelle and Lizzie almost fell on his neck with adoration.

Sofia was not very firmly present at her own wedding. The night before she dreamed that the wedding gown that had been made for her had a black train, but she didn't ask her mother what the dream meant. Her father trimmed his moustache down to a thin fringe, and her mother piled her hair into a tower. At noon on the day of the wedding Sofia took off the ten diamond rings and the gold link-chain and stood under the shower. The water drummed on her body like rain on a tin roof, and she stood still, gazing at the pale henna pattern on the palms of her hands, until the hot water ran out. She would remember nothing of the event itself, only the four bridesmaids in their bride-like dresses, because all evening she kept turning back to make sure that they were holding up the train to keep it from getting dirty, and meeting their black eyes. She did not appear in any of the wedding photographs, and Itzik Kadosh was so furious that he smashed the photographer's camera and drove him away without paying him.

'But I swear to you, the film with all her pictures got burnt out! I swear!' the man sobbed. He remembered that after the ceremony he went to look for the bride among the multitude of guests, but didn't find her, so he settled for the groom, who gave him a double smile, one for his bride. He also remembered the bride's little sister, who pushed herself into every picture, shouting, 'Me! Me! Take my picture again!'

But everyone said Sofia was a breathtaking bride, that her wedding celebration at the Venus Dome was extraordinary, and for many days afterwards people talked about the black dancers that her husband had brought from Africa to excite the guests with their bare buttocks and jiggling breasts, and the ivory necklaces around their necks.

That night, when Sofia lost her virginity, her heart felt deep and distant and her breasts hurt, as if they were choking Itzik's cries.

'What did you say?' Itzik Kadosh asked, falling still for a moment.

'No, nothing.'

They spent their honeymoon travelling around the capitals of Europe, flying from hotel to hotel, from bed to bed. When they returned, they went straight to their new home, a penthouse on top of a towerblock that scraped the sky of Bat-Yam. The tower was so high that its windows showed no views, only a thick crown of clouds that hung around them. Sofia would stand and gaze at them as at a mirror, but she saw nothing.

Whenever her husband flew off to Africa Sofia would return to her bed in her parents' house and sleep with her pathetic treasury of coins in the biscuit tin under the bed. In her dreams she heard only faint echoes that rose from her heart, and asked questions that had no answers. Pressed by her sisters, she would say that she was missing her husband, and in fact when she returned to their tower-top apartment she really did miss him. What she missed was the smell of a man who comes home after a day's work. Itzik Kadosh being far away and odourless, Sofia thought of him as a bridegroom seen in a dream, and often shed tears because of it.

During the summer holidays Matti was sent to sleep with Sofia in her double bed, to keep her from feeling afraid on her own. The Azizyan household she'd grown up in consisted of seven people in three rooms, and Sofia had only known the loneliness of being in a crowd. In her new home there was no one at whom to shout, 'Quiet now, everybody, I want to sleep!' or 'Who touched my money?' Nor was Iran there for her to cajole, 'Mama, tell me a story, but this time tell it just to me. You yourself mustn't listen, only I will hear it!' Not needing to force her way through the crush, or to fight for privacy, Sofia felt more lonely than ever. Whenever he returned from his travels Itzik Kadosh lavished caresses and hollow gold jewellery on her body. As she grew richer, her movements became more and more sluggish, and at long last she conceived.

'Mad about you, my queen!' Itzik Kadosh adored her belly, then flew off again, to redouble his gifts. Before she gave birth to his son she seemed to be in mourning for herself, and her bedsheets resembled rumpled shrouds.

Sometimes she peered into her wardrobe, rummaged in the bottom drawers and fished out the papier-mâché crown of her monarchy. Sofia would look at her fragmented reflection in the remaining glass gems but she did not dare to put it on her head, and would shove it back into the heap of rags that had once been her beauty queen's gown.

Yet her wedding shoes, which she had been so determined to keep, were lost and never found.

Walking past the hairdressing salon, half-hidden behind her big belly, she felt that her life before the wedding was as far away as the hair-washing basin in the recess of the shop. Sofia noted new clients inside, new hairstyles and new girl apprentices, whose eyes glittered when they stuffed one measly tip after another into the pockets of the glossy, skin-tight pants that hugged their rounded bottoms.

She felt her baby coughing when he was still in her womb. Iran told her it was nothing but wind, and that she should eat a lot of radishes to make it come out. Sofia knew that it was a cough which jerked the full sack inside her and jiggled her husband's name-pendant in the hollow of her neck, but she dutifully belched radishes and anxiety right until the baby's birth.

In the final days of her pregnancy she was utterly exhausted, as if emerging from a prolonged illness. Itzik Kadosh was ecstatic. His sisters and aunts, wishing to make up for his absences, climbed up to the summit of the Bat-Yam tower to perch on Sofia's bed, but became confused and returned to sea level.

'How Itzik can kiss that one I don't know,' they abused her in Moroccan on their way down. 'She keeps her mouth shut so tight, I bet it stinks like rotten meat.'

Only Itzik Kadosh's young niece, who had hung back behind the scenes when Sofia was being crowned beauty queen, knew that there was no unhappier girl than Sofia Azizyan in the whole network of technical-colleges.

'Mama! It hurts, Mama! It hurts, it's tearing me apart . . .' Sofia screamed in the delivery room.

'The pains of birth are just the beginning, little soul,' said Iran, stroking her daughter's face. 'Push, push.'

Sofia's baby was born eleven days before Grandma Touran died. He looked wrinkled and fragile like a washerwoman's hands. Everyone said he was absolutely the spitting image of Sofia, and he was named after his dead grandfather on his father's side. Grandma Touran died in a rage because of that baby. Her death intimidated the living, showing once again what a stubborn and determined woman she was.

'She decided to die, that granma of yours,' Iran fumed. 'She want to force us to do just what she wanted. Now I have to die to get even with her!'

Touran had not explained her demand but insisted that the boy be named Michael. Solly begged her to tell him the reason, but could not extract so much as a hint about the person she wished to commemorate. Nor did Iran explain why she refused it, and why she insisted on the name of Itzik Kadosh's father, whom she had never met.

Sofia said she didn't care what name they gave the boy.

So Solly had to disappoint his old mother, who had lately grown nostalgic for the clothes and necklaces she had brought from Persia many years before. The sweat of her last days soaked into heavy, mouldy fur coats. Her skin had a sheen like fluorescent light and gave off a smell of mothballs, and the moths which hovered above her head cast shadows on her pallid features. Solly wiped her tears with a lace handkerchief, leaving streaks of dust on her freckles, rubbed her feet and painted red varnish on her thick toenails, as he had done ever since he was a small boy. He tried to console her by asking her to be the child's godmother, but her pride was stronger than she was.

At the circumcision ceremony, when the baby was passed around by the guests who wished to bless him with their hands, Grandma Touran refused to touch him. In the kitchen Sofia refused to swallow her son's foreskin.

'Marcelle, you tell her,' Iran hissed, so no one could overhear. 'It's good for the depression after the baby's birth.'

'Leave her alone, Mama. She's been depressed ever since she herself was born,' Marcelle replied, and Iran hid the thin foreskin among the remaining pearls in the green jewellery box, until such time as Sofia could be persuaded.

Iran and Solly stopped quarrelling only when the baby fell ill at the age of one month. When the baby began to cough, Solly shaved off his mourner's beard, installed the tombstone on his mother's grave and returned home. A baby was dying in the house. Itzik Kadosh hurried back from abroad and was surprised to find his wife awake. He fell at her feet, sobbing. Sofia looked down at him over her violet silk nightgown and gave a faint smile. She was seeing his tears for the first time, and they looked exactly as they had done in her dreams – not only from his puffy reddened eyes, but from all the pores of his face. Itzik Kadosh wept for her the way other men sweat.

He began to say, 'I love y—' and stopped, because their son had again started coughing in that terrifying way.

He went up to his son's cot and looked at the baby, who coughed and coughed and wheezed, his poor exhausted lungs desperately gasping for air. His face turned red then blue, and all the blood vessels in his forehead and neck swelled and stood out on his skin. In terror, he opened his beautiful eyes that he'd inherited from his mother and stared at Itzik Kadosh's streaming tears. Sofia gathered him up in her arms, helplessly patted his back, and the coughs turned to barks.

'Sometimes he pukes in the end,' she shouted to his father over the din. 'Or he suddenly curls up tight, like a –'

Sofia spent a week in bed at her parents' house. She developed pneumonia, but did not take over her baby's affliction. When she recovered, she and her husband abandoned Bat-Yam and moved with their son into Grandma Touran's empty house, so that Iran and her daughters could help with the baby and enable her to get some sleep. Out of consideration for her, even the rooster and ducks that waddled under the orange trees kept quiet.

But Sofia was no longer able to sleep. Her reddened eyes watched Iran miserably burying her head between her sick grandson's little legs, crying and kissing and offering to sacrifice her life for his pretty willie.

Down on the ground floor of the secondary school, with its galleries and balconies that gave it the look of an amphitheatre, Marcelle Azizyan searched and found the seat on which she would sit in the coming school year. When the bell rang, she went out to the corridor, carrying a rustling bag of grapes, and found the love of her life on the upper balcony, leaning over the railing, looking brilliant in a patch of sunlight.

He had the face of a raven, dark skin and glossy hair, with delicate glasses riding on his nose in front of his small, too-close eyes, and his cheekbones gave a severe aspect to his smile. He struck her as looking intelligent, and she checked him out. His name was Yoel Hajjabi, a student in year eleven, a left-sided defender in the Givat Olga football team. He was unaware that she was following him, and never noticed the makeup mirrors she would hold up to powder her face and watch his reflection.

Since he never paid any attention to the tinkling of bangles that followed his passage up and down the staircases and the corridors, he was oblivious to its absence after she was expelled from the school. She was nineteen and suffering from periodic heartaches before he first looked at her and saw the stains of sadness on her face. The light from the living-room lamp shining on her poetry notebooks at night gleamed deep in her eyes, diluted with despair. She had already packed up the courtship manoeuvres she had learned from her sisters, and the art of seduction she had gleaned from books, wrapped them in old newspapers and stored them in the basement of her heart, when Yoel Hajjabi asked her, 'Are you Marcelle?' and a flock of blind old ravens flew out of her chest.

'Yes, I am Marcelle,' she replied, and six years after she'd first fallen in love with him she wanted only one thing – to fix a date for their wedding.

For six years she had conducted a passionate love affair with him, and he never knew. For six years she had been recording the chronicle of her love in her diaries, her carrier-ravens plucking out page after page and flying off to drop them into his heart's letter-box. For six years she sat on the terraces of the town football ground, longing to shout amid the supporters' roars the confessions that she whispered night after night at the dark window, to kiss him as every night she kissed the damp windowpane, and pierce his heart like the arrow that pierced the hearts she drew on the fogged patch she blew on the glass with the word 'Forever' scrawled below.

Her nights were so long that she had enough darkness to learn by heart the names of all the players in all the teams in the Second Division. Her gaze followed him from her first day in secondary until she got her last-term report which threw her out and into the technical college, where she learned hairdressing like her sister Sofia.

'A brain like God put in Marcelle's head is not for making streaks!' Iran yelled at the end of that year, but all the shouting didn't help. Marcelle was unable to concentrate on her studies. Her exam papers were devastated by angry red corrections, and her mother could no longer wave them like a fan to cool her face to impress her women neighbours. Solly was summoned from the sea to the classroom, and the smell of fish that hung about him cast a dank net of doubt on the teachers' eyes.

At the technical college Marcelle concentrated on her daydreams, wasted her potential, peroxided and hennaed her hair. In vain she rolled his name on her tongue, invented pet names for him and bit them into syllables. From time to time she visited the galleries of the mainstream secondary school, nodded to those of her former classmates who remembered her eyes gazing sadly at the rain, ignored the ones who forgot her, and pretended to be a stranger when they failed to recognise her under her colour-changing hairdos.

Then she mixed with the throng of students who filled the corridors during breaktimes, gazed up at the sunny balcony and felt the sweetness coursing through her veins. Yoel Hajjabi, the black raven, with the lithe and sinewy body, ran around among the horde of girls who waggled their backsides at him, kicked a ball with the boys, copied homework, but didn't see her.

'That one?' Sofia shrieked and grimaced as if she'd bitten on something bad when she accompanied Marcelle on one of her love missions.

'You mean that's what you've been killing yourself for? *Bah* . . .' She spread her crooked fingers and thrust them at Marcelle's sad eyes, as though to push them back into their sockets. Marcelle blinked impatiently, her proud lashes sweeping away the insult.

'Forget it. Just forget it! You don't understand.'

'And how I understand! I understand that you've been dying for his black arse for the last hundred years and he doesn't even know you exist. Shake your tail, girl, make eyes at him, do something . . .'

'How many eyes should I make, Sofia, eh?'

'And anyway, what are you doing falling for a skinny blind genius with glasses?' Sofia yawned, and Marcelle fell silent.

'The hell with that. Come, let's go, I'm freezing my arse sitting here.'

Her eyes were constantly searching for him, even in

places where there was no likelihood that he'd be found. She painted her lips such a brilliant red that all the men on the football pitch except Yoel stared at her mouth. She wore skimpy tanktops that exposed her tight vertical navel seductively in front, and the soft fleshy mound above the crack of her buttocks behind. She had more admirers than pairs of shoes, and when they stood near her they became dizzy from the perfumes that wafted from her curved neck.

But all Marcelle saw in any of them was a hint of his upper lip, his broad shoulders or his arrogant chin. Those who did not remind her of him she ignored. The sound of a motor-scooter zooming down the street would send her rushing to the window. Sometimes, on the boundary between night and day, when she handed her father a glass of black coffee, she would even see a resemblance between him and Yoel.

'Oh no! If even your gingery dad reminds you of that Yemenite football player,' Sofia sighed, 'then, sweetheart, your brain's really gone soft.'

Marcelle was the slave of her longings, with bangles on her arms and love's handcuffs on her heart.

Once, on one of her spying excursions, she came across him at the Book Week fair, pecking with his nose at the glossy pages of an astrology book. She went up and stood right behind him, her face almost touching his back, the top of her head at the level of his armpit. They were separated only by her nose. She saw that he was reading about Gemini.

'Do you have a book on astrology?' she asked the stall-keeper, all out of breath.

'What sign are you?'

Yoel Hajjabi's glance flashed at her from the summit of his body like the searchlight from a lighthouse sweeping over a desert island.

'Libra,' she gasped.

'That's in the second volume.' He indicated with his chin the volume from Leo to Capricorn.

Marcelle nodded nervously and leafed through the book. Her pink parrot nails clicked over the lines as if snipping their tails, and sank into the book's colourful cover to anchor her trembling body.

A confirmed believer, Yoel slammed shut the volume from Aquarius to Cancer. He didn't notice the dimples in her cheeks or in her elbows, nor the pale dimples in her hips under her skirt. He paid for the book and took it away, without considering that a Gemini man and a Libra woman make an excellent match, or that Marcelle had bought the second volume with illiterate haste, and was following close on his heels until she lost the scent of his cheap aftershave.

'What's the matter, my soul?' Iran asked one day when she saw her on the balcony, gazing wistfully at the distant horizon. 'You eating out your heart for some man?'

Marcelle didn't reply.

'No, *omri*, don't kill yourself like this. Doesn't it say in your books that for every finger on one hand there's a finger on the other hand, just right for it?' Iran demonstrated by pressing her fingertips together. 'Look, Marcelle, you see – they fit perfectly!'

Marcelle knew that she had the gift of appearing in the dreams of people who knew her. Her last, forlorn hope was that Yoel Hajjabi would dream about her, and that in his dream she would look beautiful and her hair would look great. In the end she gave up this hope too.

But when the years of yearning had almost run their course, when Marcelle thought about him mainly out of habit, the day came when Yoel asked her, 'Are you Marcelle?', and she replied, 'Yes, I'm Marcelle.' She could see that he was trying to recall where he knew her from.

On the advice of her sister Sofia, Marcelle put an ad in the personal column of the weekly crosswords magazine – 'A 19-year-old girl, good-looking and life-loving, would like to meet a suitable man for a serious relationship. Hobbies: reading, outdoor hikes' – and Sofia made her add 'horseback riding'.

For the next four months letters came pouring in. Marcelle was kept occupied designing the rejection postcards, meeting men at the café in the shopping centre, and turning down the obstinate ones who enclosed photographs. When Yoel Hajjabi's letter arrived her heart pounced on it like a creditor. The scent of his aftershave arrived ahead of him when he came to pick her up and take her to the sea, to look at the sunset.

On the way there, riding on the back of his motor-scooter, whose number plate was engraved on her heart, Marcelle thought that her father might as well have come along with them, since in a few hours he would be headed the same way on the first morning bus.

The sea sighed when Yoel touched her flesh. She watched his slender fingers in stupefaction, because she could see but not feel them, their touch was so delicate, as though feathers were stroking her skin. She kept looking at him with her eyes wide open, her gaze intense, because she couldn't believe that her body was feeling nothing.

'Your eyes are so sad, baby,' he said and fluttered his fingers over them, embarrassed by her gaze, like a virgin begging for the light to be turned off.

When his mouth touched hers Marcelle felt his body, though not her own. The waves were licking the sinking sun when his tongue thrust against her lips, pushed her teeth apart and entered her mouth, long as a foot, muscular and aggressive. The bell-clapper in her throat vibrated.

The seashore was empty. Marcelle could hear the crickets roaring in the thicket of beach lilies and saw fireflies lighting the route from her heart to his. He laid her back on the sand, penetrated her, and almost fainted when he came. His legs were long and tapered like the legs of a compass. Her bangles rubbed against him. He tried to slip them off her wrists, but could not.

'They're already part of you.' His cheekbones almost broke through the skin of his face.

'We're the complete set.'

They laughed, and he discovered the dimples in her cheeks. Then they climbed back on his Vespa and a swarm of late bees, drunk with nectar, whirled after them. Marcelle's hair blew in the wind, her skin glowed, and she clung hard to his waist, to keep from flying off.

'Not so tight, baby, you're hurting,' he scolded her fingers.

All the traffic lights turned green for them, and the scooter wheels crossed rivers of smells. They escaped the salty driftnet that the sea threw over the town, ploughed through sweet streams of ripening fruit and tingly-sour rivulets of cut grass. On every street they passed Marcelle saw people smiling at her, startled momentarily by the visible pleasure, and caught the fever of her love.

Marcelle, having drunk Yoel's kiss, likewise caught the wedding fever that had seized the household, and did not recover until they had found a ballroom and fixed a date. Yoel's family made the long journey from Miami to Givat Olga, and the henna ceremony took place in the bosom of Marcelle's family. Her mother prepared a grand feast for the occasion, set the table with the china that had been part of her dowry, and loaded the red roses of the porcelain with dishes she had cooked for the first time from recipes in the newspaper. She had shut herself away in the kitchen for three days and insisted on doing everything herself. When she emerged, she was followed by an aroma of novel spices that Maurice had brought from his shop. Afterwards Sofia laboured until nightfall to restore Iran's beauty which the work in the kitchen had worn away.

Yoel Hajjabi arrived bearing a bouquet of red tulips, and Iran was so moved that Marcelle had to swear three times that she had not told her fiancé that tulips were her mother's favourite flowers. The food was really delicious that evening, and Iran listened avidly to the compliments that Yoel paid her with a lover's generosity.

'Leave him alone, Solly,' she broke in between her husband and Yoel when they were discussing the young couple's economic prospects, talking with their hands marked with red henna streaks. 'Can't you see that our bridegroom wants to eat? Talk later.'

So they ate more and drank more, and Iran chatted till she collapsed. Later, when Marcelle and Yoel were divorced and Iran was too angry to speak to her, Marcelle tried to remember if that evening had really taken place or was a figment of her imagination. She was sure she'd seen Iran putting down her fork and the thread of her story and unbuttoning her son-in-law's waistband, to give him room for more of her new delicacies.

A few days before the wedding Marcelle asked Lizzie to bring her a sleeping pill from the hospital, and Lizzie brought two, round and pink and innocent-looking.

'But be careful, it's strong stuff. Maybe you should only take a half of one,' she warned her sister.

Years after she had lost and given up her battle with sleep, Marcelle rose broken and crushed from the bed of her exile in the living-room, and reignited the old conflict.

As her wedding day approached, Marcelle felt her pulse thudding in panic against the walls of her neck, the veins in her arms and the roof of her head between the temples. Her heart pounded wildly, swelling and shrinking in a shocking pattern, and her blood seemed to be throbbing audibly. She spoke gently to her body and tried to pacify it with delicacies, as she had learned to do from her mother. But her breathing grew shorter and shorter as though she were being pursued, and in her flight she saw herself growing farther from the charming young ladies of the paperback romances she used to read, who had garlands of orange blossoms woven into their hair and sweet cherubs hovering around their heads, and whose faces were radiant with the loveliness of happy brides.

On her last night as an unmarried girl, with her nerves jangling and her bangles ringing, she demanded that her sisters give back her lost share of the big bed in the children's room, and sent Matti to sleep on the living-room sofa. She tossed a pink pill into her gullet, and it slipped quietly down to her stomach. She sank into the unaccustomed softness of the cool bed, and evening fell. The entire household held its breath, people spoke in whispers and signs to avoid disturbing the bride, as if it were a house in mourning in which it is not done to raise one's voice. At last they all went to their beds to rest before the next day's festivities, and Marcelle heard the familiar nocturnal silence replacing the suppressed sounds of the day.

Once more the desperate nightly struggle of her childhood broke out, as in the days when her body trembled under the pictures of sainted rabbis and squashed the amulets and old blessings that were tucked under her mattress. The second pill also failed to soothe the jittery twitches in her belly, to calm her bucking heart and pacify the blood that rushed through it like a raging torrent of mud. All night long Marcelle heard police cars yowling in the streets, rushing to rescue good citizens who had been struck by some awful catastrophe.

When Solly left the house to go to the sea he found her sitting, looking pale and shivery, on the pavement outside, her sad eyes burning in the dawn light like forgotten street lamps.

'Don't be afraid, my little girl.' Her father tucked kisses in the palms of her tremulous hands. 'From tomorrow morning you'll be making coffee for your husband when he gets up. I'll make my own coffee, like I did today. Just make everything happen with good luck – all right, Papa's sweet girl?' He petted and caressed her. 'Now go upstairs, my soul, go on up. And what your heart tells you to do, that's what you do, all right?'

In the evening he trimmed his moustache down to a thin fringe, Mama piled up her hair into an architectural marvel, and Marcelle went to pieces.

'Ladeees and gentlemen . . . men . . . men! Please give a warm welcome to the bride and groom . . . oom . . . oom!' The loudspeakers in the Globe ballroom resounded in Marcelle's ears like the howls of a legion of demons. Trumpets and applause greeted her like the roar of an immense animal. The ceiling lights poured a hot dry glare on everything, and she saw herself reflected in a score of mirrors, dressed in a score of pale bridal gowns, shattered into umpteen broken reflections.

But then the two sleeping pills finally triumphed over her blood and Marcelle fell into the deepest sleep she had ever known. Her eyes were shut when she was led through the crowd of guests, her legs were melting under her on the way to the canopy, and she got married in a fog, her head resting on her husband's shoulder.

She could not be awakened. Nothing got through to her – not the brilliant lights and the photographer's flashes, not the music of the band and the blaring of trumpets, not Yoel's kisses and his soft slaps on her cheeks, not the coffee they poured into her or the iced water they sprinkled on her face. Matti was photographed instead of her – with the bouquet, the veil, the ring.

The guests, their faces coated with makeup and their lips pursed for kissing, crowded around her. Her mortified father and mother grabbed her by the shoulders and tried to shake her awake, and Lizzie and Sofia, both pregnant, used their big bellies to shove the advice-givers and the simply nosy out of the way. Then Yoel carried her outside into the fresh air, and the rumour circulated in the ballroom that the bride had fainted from so much excitement.

Maurice said she should be hidden in the cloakroom, to sleep among the shawls and coats till she woke up. But when the groom's family demanded her presence at the celebration her father carried her to the seat of honour, like a child who has fallen asleep on the sofa and must be carried to her bed, and made her sit beside her husband Yoel, though her head rested on the back of the chair. During the meal her sisters smoothed the skirt of her wedding gown to the sides, wiped her melting makeup and fixed her hairdo. But when the crowd got up to dance it was no longer possible to hide the disgrace. Marcelle slumped forwards and laid her forehead on the domed sweet *hallah*, while her solitary bridegroom shook hands with the well-wishers and danced like a widower with the single women.

The following day Marcelle woke up at noon and discovered that her love was dead. She uttered a little shriek, like the heroines of her favourite romances when the wind snatched away their hats. Her heart flopped over with shock. The hotel room in Eilat was empty, and her pale wedding gown was lying on the floor as though it had been moulted by a large animal. She was naked, and saw her bra lying among some curly gift-wrapping ribbons. Yoel was not in the room, but his spectacles were there, staring at her with astonishment. She didn't know what to do. Her eyes hurt, so she cried a little. Then she cried a lot, and her eyes grew dim, as though the tears were needles piercing them from within.

The thick fog of the longest sleep she had ever known weighed on her, but Marcelle knew that a disaster had taken place and tried to pull herself together. The harsh discovery that yesterday she had married a man whom she did not love today shook her so badly that she woke up completely. The magic was suddenly dissipated, leaving behind a bitter taste like unripe grapes.

She groped her way with sweaty hands to go to the bathroom and wash, but found nothing to hold on to and hit her shins on the furniture. After she'd bathed her face she suddenly understood what her mute body had been trying to tell her when her blood was storming and raging – her body had already known what her slow, stupid, hypnotised mind only now realised.

She dimly recalled that the previous night Yoel had carried her in his arms through the door of the hotel room. Like the heroes in the romances, though not quite. He had urged her to try walking from the bridal car, decorated with ribbons and balloons, to the hotel reception desk, but she'd collapsed. She also remembered seeing the carcasses of dogs that had been run over on the road. Finally Yoel slung her over his shoulder and her neck lay against his.

Years before our father's hair began to turn grey and recede, when Marcelle was a little girl who couldn't fall asleep, she liked to pretend to be sleeping in order to please him. Feeling the threat of the approaching moment when he and Mama would withdraw to their room and she would be left alone, she would shut her eyes and regulate her breathing.

'You see?' she'd hear him whisper. 'She's perfectly all right, my little girl. Sleeping like a baby.' He would gather her up in his arms with infinite gentleness, support her head so it wouldn't loll back, and hold his breath, to avoid meddling in her first dream and so trap her in the passage that connects the world of sleep with the world of waking.

In the dimness of the corridor that led from the living-room to the children's room, and unseen by Mama who was locking the front door, Marcelle would open her sad eyes and see her father's dearly loved, thick, sunburnt nape.

The night before, when her husband carried her, she'd seen his slim dark nape and her bridal veil trailing behind on the steps.

Suddenly it came to her that Yoel would soon return. His glasses indicated that he was nearby. She moved around the room like a blind person, bumping into the furniture, like a murderess looking for a place to hide the corpse of her love and thinking up lies to tell the police. Her blood ran cold with fear, then it grew hot with rage at herself. Through all those years Marcelle had confused Yoel with the imaginary heroes that her sad eyes cut out of the romances she read. She cut them out the way Iran cut out jackets and skirts using paper patterns from the Burda sewing books, and she pasted them into the wedding stories that her mother made up for the children at bedtime. She was so lonely and in love that she was unable to look into his raven's eyes and see that it was her dream standing in front of her – not a real man, with bulk and weight and colour, just a dream. If only she had known this the day before. If only she had realised that all through the past years she had merely travelled over the road-map of the land of love, never in the land itself.

Filled with self-pity, she looked back on the years of her love for Yoel and for a moment her yearning for him almost revived, but after so many years of imaginary love she couldn't bear to waste another day. She burst into tears just as he was coming in, because she knew what she was going to say to him.

'But, baby, it was you who wanted so much to get married,' he said after a long silence.

She saw that Yoel really loved her very much, that he was hurting from love, not from the affront or the disgrace.

He sat and she stood.

She stroked his face gently, because she knew that he was weak.

She looked out of the window and saw the carcasses of the dogs that had been run over. Then she turned and her gaze floated over the room like a lifebelt from a sunken ship. When her sad eyes ran aground on Yoel's face she wanted to cry again. But her tears had dried up, her heart was bitter, and only pity softened her voice when she said, 'But I don't love you any more.'

For a whole week she wandered through the streets of Eilat until she mustered the courage to get on the bus going north. She didn't know what she'd say to her parents, and was still overwhelmed by the new sensation in her chest, the feeling that her heart had become empty. Marcelle walked up to the third floor and stood before the closed door of the flat, at a loss as to how to do it, how to go in at all.

Iran was at home alone, slicing onions in the kitchen. The onion fumes stung Marcelle's face. She took great gulps of air and the tears broke from her eyes.

'Mama . . .'

Iran's face was also wet with tears when she turned round at the sound.

'Who's that? Ah! I didn't hear you come in, our new bride!' Iran exclaimed, sniffling. 'When did you get back, my soul? Where's Yoel?'

'Mama, I . . .' Marcelle approached her mother who opened her arms to embrace her, still holding the chopping knife covered with bits of juicy onion in her hand.

'Mama's own soul,' Iran laughed, the way mothers laugh when their children cry for childish reasons. 'The onion makes you cry, bride?'

'No, Mama, I . . .' Marcelle sobbed between her mother's kisses.

'Enough, my soul, stop! Have something to drink – here, drink!'

'No, Mama, that won't help me now.' Marcelle pushed away the glass of water, the oniony knife and the kisses. 'I'm . . . I'm getting a divorce.'

'Divorce?' The bitter word fell from Iran's lips, still coated with the sweet trace of her kisses.

'Yes. I don't love him any more.'

'What . . . ?'

'I'm not happy with Yoel, Mama,' Marcelle said, trembling all over.

For the first time in her life she addressed Iran as woman to woman, not as a child to her mother.

'That's no reason for divorcing, my soul.' The onion tears dried up completely in Iran's eyes.

Marcelle saw a dark void open in her mother's eyes, like a well of wrinkles, from which all the subsequent tears would flow.

'But I'm not happy with him, Mama. I can't find my happiness anywhere, I don't know . . .'

'Where did you leave it?' Iran interrupted in a voice that held both love and reproach. 'Where you lost it, there you must look for it.'

Iran didn't speak to her at all for a week, and then she fell silent altogether.

The story of Marcelle's marriage ended so soon, that the day of her divorce seemed more real than her wedding day. With her *ketubbah* folded up in her divorce papers, she returned to her lonely nights among the nocturnal geckos, and the moon taunted her with its distant beauty. She stopped working at the bridal salon, because it upset her, and instead looked after a paraplegic woman who lived nearby. The dimples did not reappear in her cheeks.

Now and then she tried to speak to her mother, took the Book of Psalms out of her hands and said, 'I don't know what's wrong with me, Mama. I don't feel good.'

'You got the curse?'

'No.'

'So maybe it's coming. Maybe that's why.'

'No, it's not that either.'

'Then you must be ovulating now. That must be the reason.'

'Yes . . .' She handed back the Psalms and gave up. 'Maybe that's it.'

In the pre-dawn mornings of her childhood her father's shaved wet face used to glow from within, like the radiance of a lampshade, as though his head were a lightbulb, but now when he came across her, a divorced woman lying on the living-room sofa, his light was extinguished. Sometimes Marcelle felt an urge to hide one of his sandals under the sofa, as she used to do when she was a child, so that he would hunt for it and be delighted when he found it, then she would wheedle him like the little girl she once was, saying, 'Pappy, Pappy, wait a little, I have such a pain here!'

'Where does it hurt, little girl?' He would kiss and kiss the child she used to be with his lips of a sea-creature. 'Here? And here also? Never mind. It'll be over by the time you get married.'

But Marcelle knew perfectly well that the reason for her misery was not that her period was due, or had just finished, or that she was ovulating. She knew that kisses wouldn't help, because her wedding day had come and gone. So she said nothing and Solly said nothing. Then Sofia returned home with her sick baby in her arms. Then Lizzie too came back, scented, bruised, with a phantom baby. Summer came and slowly burned up the whole house. It was so hot, it was impossible to close the windows and hide what had happened. Women's sobs and the baby's cough were heard all over the flat.

Sometimes when Marcelle looked up from her romance and saw her sisters coming home like wandering cows that had lost the bells hung round their necks, she wanted to say to them, 'Look, we never even solved the riddles of our dreams, and already we were married.'

We were in one sac, she thought, all of us in Mama's womb. When we were little girls the blood that flowed in our veins linked us together. When we grew up, the same sweat stuck to the shared skin from which we were all made. Flour, water and salt . . . And now, she thought, turning back to look at the Turkish film on television, its bluish light flickering on bluish bruises, now the thick glue of our tears is binding us once more into a single family.

When Mama noticed Lizzie's intense craving for figs in winter when she was a child, she realised that she'd inherited her father's passionate temperament. Long before Lizzie became a vampish young woman, Mama sewed strings of bells on to the hems of her skirts, to weigh them down and prevent the wind from raising them. When Lizzie was still growing Iran would unpick and re-sew the hems of her dresses by night, so that by morning they were longer and would ring gently.

'Wasn't it shorter yesterday?' Lizzie would exclaim in wonder at her miniskirt which suddenly came down to her knees.

'It's a skirt,' Iran responded, 'not a beard.'

But Lizzie had soon had enough of her mother's seamstressy tricks and intimidating bells, and wouldn't let her spoil her dresses with needles and safety pins. As her thighs grew longer, her skirts became shorter, and she tied a chain around her right ankle, because she had grown attached to the soft ringing that accompanied her footsteps. The tiny brass links tinkled with every move the adolescent girl made in her provocative, swaying walk.

Lizzie's eyes were always awash with pure transparent lymph, as though she was about to burst into tears. Strangers seeing the little girl in the street at once volunteered to look for her mother, because she seemed so lost. The lymph lost its purity when Lizzie was in a bad mood. It glazed over her eyes, giving them the appearance of cataracts, and her pupils shrank to pinhead size. Her mother could deduce her daughter's state of mind from her eyes, and wouldn't leave her alone until her pupils looked satisfactory.

But even more than the pupils, she watched over her hands, because Lizzie kept pushing her fingers and stroking herself between her legs. At night under the bedclothes, by day when we sprawled on the carpet in front of the television in the living-room, during lessons when her eyes were on the blackboard, and even when she was sent to stand in line at the grocer's till – she would part her legs, her back would arch, and her fingers would fumble under her skirt, exposing her thighs for all to see. Then her pupils enlarged as if she was drunk, while the odour of ripe bananas that rose from her flesh blocked all sights from her eyes and all sounds from her ears. This smell drove Mama crazy. She was afraid that one day she would find her daughter making love to herself in one of the neighbours' children's rooms.

Nothing helped – not Papa's fierce scolding nor Mama's reproachful shrieks. 'You're forgetting yourself again!' they'd yell in helpless rage, not realising that she remembered only herself. Furious slaps on her flushed, excited cheeks, smacks on her indecent fingers – nothing helped. Veiled by her mental cataracts, insensible in her dark corner, Lizzie played with herself. She taught Marcelle and Sofia that ice lollies could be pressed not only to the lips and tongue, but also to the nipples, and showed them how to make their budding breasts swell by fastening rubber bands around them.

When Lizzie was twelve the backs of her hands bore scars from the lighted matches her mother had punished her with, when in fits of despair she held them to the girl's hands till they burned out. But Lizzie's desire was not extinguished with them. She was struck with shame only when she saw her mother standing over her with fury in her eyes, with embarrassment when she saw her teachers staring at her with shock on their faces, and with confusion when she became aware of the vicious mockery of the neighbourhood children.

Gradually Lizzie learned to masturbate in solitude. Early in the morning she would climb up to the roof of the house, lean on the iron struts of the solar panels, and expose her body to the wind's kisses. Only the lizards could see her there. When at midday she saw the neighbours' children returning from school she would go down to the kitchen, sniffing at her fingers for the over-ripe banana odour of her shame, and describe to her mother what she had done at school that day.

'I love all my children like my soul, I'll be their sacrifice,' her mother unburdened herself wretchedly to her sisters. 'But my Lizzie, what can I do with her, she's . . . '

She never could find the term that would describe her, as though Lizzie's nature was beyond her limited Hebrew, and could not even be described in Isfahani Persian or Bengali.

'She's . . . she's . . . something else. God forgive me, she's from another world,' Mama sighed.

Lizzie's strange ways undermined Mama's delicate assurance. Confronted with them, she lost the competence of her motherhood. Her serenity, the calm with which she could take charge, her honest common sense –

all these fell away from her and left her once more a small, skinny girl, a helpless new immigrant.

She was unnerved by Lizzie's changing pupils and the soft humming she uttered when she was eating figs. The smell of over-ripe bananas made her nostrils swell, chafed her nerves and drove her away from the girl, whose bodily habits contradicted everything she had taught us.

Mama cried a great deal during those nights, but despite Mama's tears, Lizzie continued to delve into herself to find the hidden pleasure of her body, and the harsher Mama's punishments, the more her eyes glazed over and she withdrew into her pinhead pupils. She was beaten more than all of us, but also received the most kisses, because when Mama was utterly at a loss, she found her guilt in every part of Lizzie's body.

'Sorry, sorry, my little one, sorry,' Mama would beg, and would pet her compulsively with her hands which were burning hot, stinging and rough from the beating she'd given her. Their lips trembled, remorse kissed grievance, and they embraced each other till they became a mass of mutual consolation. Eventually Lizzie learned to make herself invisible and Mama stopped crying.

She kept herself secret. She withdrew into her loneliness, hid behind the shelter of her honey-coloured eyes with their cloudy film, and reduced herself till she evaporated. In moments of danger she willed her hands to be immobile, petrified her muscles and eliminated limb after limb from her consciousness, till eventually she vanished. That way the slaps did not hurt her, and only the bells of her skirts cried out.

She grew accustomed to people in the neighbourhood

elbowing each other or exchanging sidelong glances when she passed, and trained her ears not to hear their comments. She didn't hear her mother's voice when she was looking for her all over the flat, shouting, 'Lizzie! Come out from where you're hiding and go wash your hands!' Nor did she hear the neighbourhood children chanting, 'What a BAG of a SLAG!', any more than she heard the thunder that rolled against the blinds of the children's room on winter nights.

She stopped the sounds as they reached the threshold of her ears, pulled down the shutters, and the noise dropped, note by note, on to her eardrum and melted in its greasy yellow wax.

'Hello! Lizzie! Hello!' Mama would shout into the passages of her ears when she cleaned them with a towel after the bath. Delicate, almost unfelt tremors touched her eardrums then, like the quiver passing over an animal's skin. When she was sixteen or so, and wanted to hear the love-songs that the boys she lay with sang close to her ears, all that got through to her were some dim echoes, as if she were inhaling the narcissus scent of a woman who had passed hours earlier in the street.

In the early years of primary school the teachers complained that she was too absorbed in herself and did not listen when they spoke to her. Then they complained about her frequent absence from school, but eventually they stopped paying her any attention.

'And even when she is in class,' they said, sniffing, year after year till they gave up, 'I'm not sure she's really with us at all. You know what I'm getting at, Mrs Azizyan?'

Flushed with embarrassment, Mama's chin would nod furiously, the same chin that shook impotently when she beat Lizzie, and trembled helplessly when she cried at night.

Lizzie was always pretending to be somewhere – pretending that she was at school, that she was in the living-room, that she was asleep. She really was there, but her spirit was on the roof of the house, under the sun, among the dilapidated water-tanks and solar panels, between the third floor and the sky. There the bells on her skirts tinkled softly in the wind, as if they too were keeping the secret of her hiding place, and the burn scars from the matches glistened in the morning light like broken gems. Some days she didn't even touch herself, only sat there quietly with the birds, doing nothing, thinking nothing, not even looking at anything. Sometimes she remembered the sandwich her mother had made for her, lay down on her belly on the hot black tar and nibbled at it, humming between bites.

From this bird's-eye view she saw the top of her mother's head as she went out into the street with her old handbag tucked under her arm like a worn-out limb. Then she saw Mama returning home with the shopping bags, saw her brown hands emerging from the windows as she spread salted watermelon seeds to dry on the sills, or shook out clouds of grey house-dust like elderly thistledown, and saw the steam of cooking food curling out through the slats of the kitchen window. Sometimes she overheard Mama's out-of-tune singing of Hebrew songs she'd picked up from the radio; the mournful Persian songs of her childhood Mama only ever hummed softly to herself.

Lizzie was not afraid that she would fall off the roof; she was only afraid she'd be caught. From afar she watched Maurice returning from school, shuffling like an old man behind swarms of buzzing schoolchildren. She saw Sofia and Marcelle's schoolbags in the middle of a loving clutch of a dozen kids, in which they spun all the way home like the hands of a clock. Then she would nimbly climb over the parapet on to the fire escape, glide down rung after rung, and join the general hubbub, her pupils enlarged and her eyes glistening as if she was about to burst into tears.

Her body developed early. Her mound of Venus and the hollows of her armpits sprouted youthful fuzz long before the usual time. Her breasts also swelled in a hurry. They took the shape of the delicate wine glasses in the living-room sideboard, and looked pale as crystal in the light of the locked bathroom. Her pretty breasts and velvety mound felt like caresses lavished by her body on its inner walls, to console her for the burn scars on the backs of her hands, for her ears going deaf from insults and scolding, and for her hunger for love.

Though younger than her sisters, she had her first period a month before Sofia and six months before Marcelle. The house bled as if struck by a contagious disease from which only Maurice and Papa were immune. Eventually the menstrual cycles of all the women of the family coalesced into a single bloody week, as though set by the great pendulum of Iran's womb.

'Meat cooked with figs gets too soft too quick, you hear, Lizzie? Then it goes bad.' Mama would scold her and expel her reflection from the pots she wiped and from the surface of the soup before it was seasoned. But there was no one to forbid her to admire her beautiful breasts in the closed bathroom. Lizzie was repeatedly amazed by the sight of her breasts, which had grown all by themselves under the clothes that she tossed into the laundry basket.

She would stand in front of the mirror and turn half-way round, and see only her breasts. Her fingers trembled with excitement as they caressed the curves and followed their perfect wine-glass shape. The nipples stared at her from her reflection with a gaze that was rosy, sweet and proud. She would stretch her spine backwards to bring out the pale-blue map of veins that spread over the tender new flesh. Then she cupped them in her hands with her arms crossed, waited a little and abruptly exposed them, to surprise herself. Their loveliness struck the mirror like a blow and cast a hot breath on the glass surface.

Her eyes gradually fogged over as she contemplated her breasts and admired their profiles, and at last they appeared as if the air between her and the mirror was shimmering with heat. She longed to kiss them, and loved them more passionately than any other part of her body, more than she loved herself.

Marcelle and Sofia also loved them better than they loved the rest of her. When they took showers together their soft gaze would rest on her breasts. They stroked them to measure their circumference, to feel their weight that the air held up, and touch the glow they gave off. Lizzie would stand still like a tailor's dummy, looking down on the tops of her sisters' heads from the heights of her pride.

'There's no doubt about it, Lizzie's are the most beautiful,' Marcelle would declare with a radiant expression as Lizzie's breasts cast their light on her, and Lizzie felt a thrill.

'Oh yes, the finest I ever saw, so help me,' Sofia would shout. They always shouted when they wanted her to hear. Sofia sat on the edge of the bath, steaming hot water cascading behind her back, examining Lizzie's breasts from a distance with the appraising look of an artist examining his work. Marcelle racked her brains for suitable adjectives to describe their beauty.

'They're like . . . they're like . . .' she stammered helplessly, and the green tiled walls responded with an echo.

'On the Bible, Lizzie, honestly, they're the most beautiful. Better than the pictures of the naked women in Maurice's room,' Sofia assured her, leaning close to make sure Lizzie heard, then stood up because she feeling too hot.

'Like the Bible of tits! That's what they're like, the Bible of tits!' Marcelle declared triumphantly.

Lizzie, knowing what Marcelle was going to say next, shrank back anxiously.

'But like I said to you before, you got to take care of them.'

'Ouf, you and your nonsense!' Sofia waved her hands in the air to drive away the evil predictions so they wouldn't afflict her sister's breasts, but also to cool herself.

'Well, for your information, it's not at all nonsense!' Marcelle responded with dignity while searching for her bathroom slippers. 'It says so in all the women's magazines, every week. It says that when they grow early, they also sag early.'

Lizzie was seized with terror and stroked her breasts to calm them down. Marcelle reached and found her slippers wetted by the steaming vapour, and Sofia groped and found the door handle. Without the comfort of her sisters' admiring looks, Lizzie's proud nudity turned cold and bitter.

'Anyway, Mama says that a fig that's been rubbed with oil –'

'Yeah, yeah, I know – it ripens fast but doesn't have any taste. We've heard it a thousand times. But Mama also says that an unmarried woman has bugs between her legs, a crow in her brain and a poisonous snake in her heart. You believe that too?'

'No, but it's not just what she says, it's written, and anyway . . .'

They pushed open the bathroom door and went out. Their voices went on wrangling through the open crack they left behind, but no one peeped through it to admire her breasts. Lizzie again crossed her arms, shut her eyes in her ritual way, and uncovered herself all at once. But by now she got no pleasure out of it. The honey film on her eyes grew cloudy, and the mirror was hidden under thick, indifferent condensation.

Something was pulsing between her legs. Lizzie slipped into the bath, turned off the tap and the roaring current slowed down to a trickle. She knew no peace, only desire, desire to go out like this and walk about quietly, without any clothes or bells, all over the house. If she could, she would have climbed up to the roof like this and walked among the water-tanks in the soft evening breezes that would caress her naked body like the languid breaths of an immense fan. She rolled her eyes up to the ceiling, closed them, and touched.

She felt herself walking slowly, as if through a shallow swamp, her toes sinking into the soft layer of tar. The black stuff had melted in the torrid long summer break, and she revelled in its heat. Rosy evening clouds hovered over her head and flushed redder still. Happy little birds twittered greetings at her appearance, and big birds sang madly about her new breasts. They followed her everywhere and the sun couldn't go down. The neighbourhood children kicked balls up in the air and their eyes, following them, got stuck in the heights, their mouths gaping open, moist smiles of gratitude and respect on their lips. The flushed women in the kitchens whose windows hung wide open cut their fingers with paring knives, making their salad tomatoes bleed profusely, and sucked their thumbs with passion and anxious envy. Men dozing under newspapers switched off their radios in the middle of the news and rubbed their eyes to erase the post-prandial visions, their mouths suddenly filled with saliva, and they muttered like children who wake in the middle of the night having forgotten their native tongue.

'Come out of there, idiot!' her brother Maurice roared behind the door. 'There's other dirty people in this house who want to take a shower!' Lizzie felt the ticking inside her gathering speed. She opened and shut, opened and shut, and the scent of withered bananas rose from her like curls of incense smoke.

Lizzie's boys, tender and sweet as gift lambs presented by bridegrooms, clung close to her. They didn't know that her innocent eyes hid a blind self-love and were astounded when they found her silent lips open to kiss. They imagined that she didn't hear well because of the loud voices and music in the café, that she didn't say much because she was shy, and that they would only be able to dream about her splendid, wish-fulfilment body after seeing her to the front door of the Azizyan home and the automatic stairwell light had gone off.

Their restraint was honourable and crystalline as a wedding-gift vase. A picture of politeness, they would come in in the evening and wait for her between the mosaic lampshades, in the company of her delighted parents. Still the picture of politeness, they took her home through the empty streets at the required time, a little before midnight, their hands clutched behind them, anchored to the tailbone, their breathing as irregular from strain as the light from the street lamps. They walked cautiously, as if careful to avoid stepping on the invisible train of a bridal gown.

'They are such gentlemen, every one of them,' lamented Solly, aggravating Iran's sorrow. 'They're good boys, the ones Lizzie brings us. Boys from good homes, so nice and polite, really first-rate. But you see them just the one time and that's it, no more! I don't understand her. I really don't.'

Iran moaned in despair and Lizzie with lust. She unlocked the handcuffs of good upbringing that restrained the boys' hands, slipped her scarred hands into theirs, and led them, accompanied by the tinkling of her ankle chain, into the local park.

For a moment they were taken aback by her assertiveness and made dizzy for another moment by her boldness, then they surrendered in a daze to her imaginative love-making. Lizzie uttered loud moans, but in fact her desire was lacking. She enjoyed their expression when she took off her blouse, inhaled deeply the mortal fear that fell on them when she removed her bra, and watched everything from high above, from her roof. In the shadowy park, among the sleeping swings and empty roundabouts, her breasts gleamed palely and the wind silvered the leaves of the poplar trees.

She knew too well that they would soon droop and their radiance would dim like falling stars, that whether because of figs or bananas, bugs or crows or poisonous snakes, the pink nipple-eyes would soon lower their gaze with shame, then close. Her honeyed eyes filled with tears when she thought about it, but her boys didn't see that she was crying. As she fucked them, Lizzie submitted to her longings for herself and for the wind's fanning kisses. They begged her to allow them to come back and collapse on the park benches facing the beauty that silvered the poplar leaves, but Lizzie brushed them off with the same virtuous batting of her eyelashes with which she had allured them in the first place.

'Everyone gets just one bite of the cherry,' she said casually, drawing out the words like the chewing gum in her mouth. She chewed gum and blew pink bubbles through her lips.

Lizzie relished their alarm, their eyes staring with shock at the discovery, and nothing more. In the meantime she made her skirts shorter and shorter, powdered her breasts and shed her virginity time and time again. But she took care to hide her eyes from Maurice's inspection, so that he wouldn't see their whites growing clearer.

'The trouble with Lizzie's fellows is they don't have perseverance – that's her problem,' Solly speculated, rubbing salt into his wife's wound. 'There's nothing else wrong with her. You don't have to worry about her for no reason, Iran. Go to sleep.'

Eventually Lizzie abandoned the roof and the park benches in town, and went to train at a nursing college. Her over-ripe banana odour followed her to the hospital in Hadera and wafted down the long corridors, under the smells of illness and medications. There, within the hospital walls, she found her freedom, and her lust threw off all restraint, like ghosts in an abandoned castle. She was loved by doctors, male nurses, administrative staff, sometimes even patients. She would take off the white smock, the white dress, the white nylon stockings and shoes, and in the twilight between day and night and one body and another, she became pregnant.

Having poured her urine into a phial and pricked herself in the arm and squeezed some blood into a test-tube, she went to look for her baby's father in the maze of corridors and hallways.

She went up and down a lot of floors and stopped in front of a closed glass door on the fifth floor, and there she waited. Rough cloth curtains hung over her shoulders, the chill air pinched her nose, and her eyes patrolled the long corridor. The glaring light was reflected in the polished floor tiles, and among the vague forms of the patients and the patches of white smocks, she spotted the familiar gleaming smile of a medical student. She made him a sign to open the window.

'I'm pregnant!' she yelled through the glass.

'What?'

'I am PREGNANT!'

He touched his ear to indicate that he couldn't hear,

and before she could touch her belly by way of illustration, he pointed to his wristwatch to show he was in a hurry. So she fluttered her hand and gave up, and he walked away.

'Dr Lahav!' she shouted at a greying nape, but he didn't hear her either and walked towards the light.

Lizzie felt chilled. She wanted to leave the window and go to another ward, when the cafeteria manager, pushing a trolley with cakes and soft drinks, called down to her from the sixth floor.

'Hey, Lizzie, come on up!'

'What?'

'Come up here a moment.'

'You come down. I'm pregnant.'

'What?'

'I'm pregnant. I'm going to have a baby.'

'Don't move, I'm coming down! Don't move, Lizzie, I'm coming! You want to marry me?'

'What?'

There was neither time nor money for a ballroom, so they did without the henna ceremony and held the wedding in Ramlah, at the house of Hezi Moussafi's parents, where they also planned to live after the guests departed.

Iran said that Lizzie's pregnancy was a reason to die of shame, not to celebrate. Solly, who wavered between anger and embarrassment, kept his mouth shut. He did not trim his moustache down to a thin fringe, and she did not pile up her hair into fancy shapes.

Hezi's parents, a modest, elderly couple of bakers, their flesh as soft as unbaked dough, had waited years for his birth. He was born in Ramlah not long after they arrived from Iraq, and thereafter became the centre of their world. They saved up for him to go to medical school and opened another savings account for his marriage. They didn't ask why he was in such a hurry to marry, or why he had chosen such a strange and silent bride. They merely filled their little house with cakes made with margarine, pushed the living-room armchairs into the bedrooms, borrowed extra chairs from the neighbours, and brightened their veranda with colourful paper napkins like waterlilies.

It was the eve of Lag Baomer, bonfire night – that being the only one of the forty-nine days between Passover and Pentecost when weddings are permitted – and the whole country was ablaze with bonfires. Hezi had managed to find an available rabbi through the telephone directory, and he arrived half an hour early, a smiling man no taller than a child. Marcelle wanted to weave orchids into the hair of this sister who was so unexpectedly getting married, and Sofia wanted to curl her hair into corkscrews with her new electric curling machine. They also wanted to mascara her eyelashes and make up her face as much as she would allow them. But Lizzie washed her hair by herself and fastened it behind with a rubber band. She even refused to have a wedding gown made for her and offended her mother.

'For this I brought you up, Lizzie, for this?' Iran's anger contained so much sadness. 'For you to get married pregnant and in an old dress?'

'Enough, Iran. Let her alone,' said Solly. He took Lizzie aside, held her face between his hands and spoke into her ear. 'I don't know your fellow, Lizzie, but he looks like he's all right, and if you want to marry him, that's all right also.' As always, he stroked and caressed her with tireless patience. 'I only want you to be really happy, my soul, and for you to do what your heart tells you.'

Though her sisters made an effort to respect her odd wish to marry a man they'd only seen once, and to do so in a rush, with an unmade-up face, she saw that they recoiled from her, as though her indifference separated their glue into flour, salt and water. She chose a white woollen suit that she had in the wardrobe. Its skirt was so short that Hezi said, 'If a wind blows, they'll all be able to see your baby.'

Her eyes were gentle and vacant but she uttered a short chuckle, because his eyes were twinkling like someone who has just told a funny joke.

Except for a gold pin shaped like a raven that Grandma Touran had pinned on her before she went out, Lizzie did not put on any ornaments. She stood in the bathroom before the scratched mirror that held the memory of her nakedness, alone with the golden raven, looked straight at herself and said in a bitter voice, 'This is my wedding gown, and now I'm going to my wedding.'

When the few guests arrived they found her waiting for them at the door, smoking a cigarette. Hezi was nervous and looked for something to do. She followed him with her eyes and thought he was looking pale, as if he'd dusted himself with talcum powder. His ears flushed and his eyes darted this way and that. If one of the few hospital staff who had been invited were to put a hand on his forehead, it would have been found that the bridegroom was running a fever. She wanted to press her lips to his forehead, perhaps even press his face to her eyes and feel his temperature with her eyelids. She felt sorry for him – he scarcely knew her and now he was marrying her, believing in all innocence that her baby would resemble him and his aged parents.

The guests on the groom's side, taking Lizzie for a younger sister, asked her about the bride, and some even rebuked her for committing the sin of envy by wearing white.

'The way you look, doll,' one of Hezi's female relatives enthused, 'your turn will soon come. You just wait and see, it won't be long.'

Lizzie replied that she couldn't hear what was being said because the music was too loud, and went to join her uncles and aunts. Then the newly engaged Marcelle and Yoel Hajjabi arrived, followed by Sofia, who was pregnant and without her husband, and Maurice with Matti, who buzzed round the photographer, shouting, 'Take my picture! Take my picture!'

When her mother and father arrived with Grandma Touran Lizzie sat down with them. Her parents held each other's hands, she with her hair loose and he with his moustache untrimmed, raised their shoulders into a solid rampart, and shook the hands of well-wishers with their free hands.

Only as she passed through the masses of plastic flowers arranged all over the house, on her way to the white tablecloth stretched on four wooden poles to serve as a wedding canopy, did Lizzie feel any alarm.

More bonfires began to blaze not far from the open veranda doors. Smoke blew into the house and an acrid cloud hung over the canopy in the front room. The sky was as bright as at daybreak. She looked at Hezi and saw that he was unwell and his eyes were avoiding hers. The dwarfish rabbi he'd found looked at her hips, and she saw Maurice's eyes staring reproachfully at her breasts. Men she didn't know held the canopy poles. Her father stood waiting for her under the cloth. He smiled at her now, but the haze obscured his shy grin. Her sisters tossed sweets on her head out of straw baskets, and the sickly-sweet wedding music splashed at her feet.

Her mother took her right elbow and Hezi's mother her left and together they led her forward. Her legs felt heavy. She wanted to stop a moment, perhaps to feel the baby kicking or slapping her, or perhaps the baby would knock softly on the door and run away. But Hezi's mother, all worked up, pulled her along, Iran tugged at her in confusion, and Lizzie kept walking stiffly, like an old woman who has been sitting down too long. She walked so slowly that she felt she was moving backwards.

By the time she stood under the canopy her eyes were full of tears, but nobody saw them. Gradually they all began to weep as the smoke stung their eyes. A sooty veil hid Lizzie's filmy eyes and her blocked ears, and beneath the cover of tulle, lymph, soot and tears, nothing was real any more. Only black dust settled softly on the picture-frames on the wall, enveloped the curves of the china vases and dimmed the plastic colours of the floral arrangements. Someone closed the veranda doors, and Lizzie remembered her mother's stories about the ceremonial burning of corpses in India, how the hair caught fire first in a blaze of sparks, and how the burning coal of the heart burst open last of all, turned to ashes and was finally thrown into the river.

'Did you buy this ring yourself?' down below, the rabbi was asking Hezi.

'Yes,' Hezi replied quickly, breathlessly.

'For this woman?'

'Yes!' he said hastily.

'Wait, wait a minute,' the rabbi joked like a child. 'Look at her first. Is this the woman you had in mind?'

Everyone laughed aloud in relief, wiped their noses and eyes with the folded flowered paper napkins, and the music welled about them, treacly sweet. Applause rang out like empty embraces. The little rabbi spread his arms and bowed like a stage actor. Nobody noticed that Hezi Moussafi did not look at his bride, avoided touching her, and did not even kiss her at the end of the ceremony.

That night, lying on her back in his boyhood room which was now her home, Lizzie stared at the ceiling and knew that her husband had fallen asleep without loving her. For a moment she thought about her baby and for some reason remembered her Grandma Touran, who had stood all evening near the door, as though waiting to greet some late guests. Then Lizzie got up to pee, and found a bloodstain in her knickers.

After Lizzie's wedding came the summer which burned up everything, including her heart. Her pregnancy was imaginary, but her marriage was not. Hezi wouldn't look at her and didn't want to lie with her, so she lay with others. It made her sad, because she found his body sweet. She remembered how once, at the hospital, he had spilt his seed on the empty bed they'd found in a room somewhere, and when she'd returned there some hours later she'd seen a trail of ants leading up to the stain, as if it were a patch of vanilla ice-cream.

She lay beside him in his boyhood room in Ramlah, and longed for someone, for something, maybe even for him. Since she continued to work at the hospital, she also continued to fuck her lovers on all the floors and in all the wards. The rumours reached her husband down in the cafeteria, and he beat her up. Her tiny pupils did not deceive him. After a while she rarely went back to his parents' house or bothered to pretend that all was well. She followed her swaying shadow on the pavements, got drunk at the Mars Club, and when she came home she made no attempt to cover up the blue bruises left on her flesh by her husband. Only the humid air felt soft on her face, which looked pale, as if she were recovering from some old childhood ailment. All summer long the sweat streamed down the hollow of her back and trickled around her waist when she danced on the tables. Her ears could hardly hear any more, but anyone who caught a glimpse of her or heard the jangling of her brass anklet knew that Lizzie was on her way to destruction.

Maurice's heart did not murmur with love and not a particle of womanhood ever stuck to him. Small, bald and embittered, he was like a desolate planet in the cosmos. He smelled of shaving cream, and his skin tasted of talcum powder. The untrimmed nails on his two little fingers, hard and curved as talons, were yellow with earwax, because of his habit of pushing them into his ears and twirling them energetically, round and round, till he was satisfied.

He always looked older than he really was, with his eyes full of wariness like a man with a great deal of experience, only his body was small and flaccid. Because of his dicky heart he was exempt from military service, and instead burrowed into a little cavern-like shop near the market in south Tel Aviv, where he sold coriander seeds, peanuts and brown sugar. In that neighbourhood he also found women who didn't ask for much, women who wore their bodies as casually as an old shirt.

During the body-baring summer months Maurice would stand in the doorway of his shop, his eyes blank and his nostrils flaring, scratching his crotch and studying the phases of the breasts that passed through the street. Women sashayed past him, swinging their hips, their backs arched, their buttocks pushed out. His unblinking stare penetrated every fabric, undid every bra, ripped every bodice. Every day he saw whole life-cycles of breasts: little girls' nipples under school shirts, the swelling buds of adolescent girls and the conical breasts of young women in a hurry, the bulging udders of nursing mothers, as well as drooping breasts, pleated breasts, withered and collapsed breasts.

He would appraise the age of an approaching pair of breasts and wager a lunch with the neighbouring shopkeepers.

'Twenty-five, not a day less!' he'd declare exultantly. 'You'll see, a classical twenty-five. Here she comes . . . Hey honey, when's your next birthday? Hey, wait a minute, let me give you a present . . .'

Maurice inherited his father's fear of baldness. While his sisters laboured to pluck every hair on their bodies, Maurice shampooed his scalp with egg yolks, ate beetroots and plums, and fretted.

Consumed with envy, he watched the women growing up beside him, their splendid manes of hair which hung on their shoulders like waterfalls. He saw Marcelle and Sofia pounce on their clients' heads with knives and scissors, shearing hair, braiding it, curling it, straightening it, peroxiding and streaking it – as if those great bushes of hair were some kind of nuisance that needed to be tackled, while he counted another hundred or so more hairs that he lost to his comb every morning.

He followed his mother's advice and washed his hair with sage oil and myrtle extract, emptied on it whole tubes of strong-smelling pastes recommended by unscrupulous cosmeticians, and rubbed his thinning thatch with secret essences sold by miracle workers who published small ads in the back pages of the newspaper. Thanks to all these, as well as to his anxiety, Maurice's hair became thinner and scantier, and one by one ended up between the teeth of his comb.

Once he was quite bald he stopped locking Marcelle in the house till she tied a professional hair-straightening net on his head, and yanking Sofia from her sleep, yelling, 'Get up now, give me a shampoo and set!'

He tried to make up for the hair loss by growing a luxuriant moustache and sideburns which were as skimpy as the beard on an onion, and was surprised to discover that his neck and cheeks sprouted reddish hairs like his father's. Solly was pleased to see this proof of his seed in Maurice's body, and on Friday evenings offered him drops out of his bottle of coconut oil, to join him in anointing his reddish moustache and eyebrows.

'Take some, take some,' Solly would urge, blushing. 'That's why God grew a beard, don't you know? – because He was bald.'

But Maurice declined the offer. He shaved every day,

cultivated fashionable sideburns and yearned for the hair he'd lost.

One day he came home with the usual porno magazine stuck under his arm, carrying a hairpiece wrapped in brown paper. It looked dark and furry as a kitten.

'The stupid cows you go out with, they're sure to believe it's real!' his sisters laughed aloud, looking gorgeous. Marcelle's head was bristling with prickly rollers, and Sofia's head wore a hairdrying helmet. They teased him, mocked him, then took pity on him, tied an apron round his neck and invited him to come and sit on the purple fur seat in their room. The artificial mane spread over his skull, dusty and full of tangles. Their combs soon put life and bulk into it, but it was much too long. The alien hairs spread beyond his scalp and fell into his face.

'All right, you can trim it, but just a little at the sides,' Maurice commanded, breathless with excitement, imagining all the women he would conquer.

With Sofia giggling on his right and Marcelle joking on his left, their fingers pushed through the loops of their scissors, the metal blades whirled around Maurice's head. He watched Sofia's elegant fingernails, varnished a delicate pink, smoothing the hair over his right temple, while Marcelle's blood-red nails were trimming the hairpiece over his left.

'But can't you see? – it isn't straight here, it's not the same level!' he said to his reflection in the mirror. The song of the whirring blades of the two apprentice hairdressers began again. Perched on the purple fur stool, Maurice shut his eyes and his lashes fluttered in the intense storm of his inner feelings.

He visualised tall women with tiny breasts falling at his

feet, and short women lifting their yearning eyes and their dreamy nipples to him. He imagined red-haired women with saffron tufts between their legs, pale women whose pubis sprouted ginger curls, women with long hair that swept the floor, and girls whose hair was cropped short-short on top as well as down below, young girls whose hair and bed habits were equally wild, and severe-looking women with sleekly gathered hair and boundless lust.

'Hey, you blind or what? Can't you see that it isn't the same here as on that side? You think it's going to grow back? It won't grow back, you idiot!' he shrieked, his eyebrows quivering on his forehead. His sisters went on splitting their sides with laughter.

'Your weddings – please God, I hope your weddings turn into funerals, you goddamn stupid cows! Give me the scissors!'

Stressed and sweating, Maurice held the hand-mirror between his knees and slipped his trembling fingers into the scissors. His balls bulged in his too-tight trousers, his body was small and skinny but he had big hands. He tried to correct the cut of the false hair, snipped ends with meticulous care, looked at himself this way and that, but when had finished the wig was too short, and the remains of his real hair showed under its edge.

Iran thought that the passages of Maurice's heart were closed to love. She was afraid that if an opening was made and a woman entered through it, the heart murmur would become audible, break out of his chest like a desperate cow's moo, and kill him. Perhaps that was the reason she looked askance at his women, whom he conquered easily and discarded just as lightly.

'I think,' Iran confided in a wretched voice to his sisters, 'that Maurice doesn't like the dirt that a woman's body makes. He doesn't understand how good it tastes.'

But it was not only women's smell and flavour that Maurice had difficulties with. Their touch, too, was hard for him to bear. As a lover he was hasty and selfish, because his loneliness did not leave him for a moment.

He could only really let himself go between the breasts of his whore, because he recognised the loneliness in her eyes and knew that she saw the same thing in his. She regarded him as a good and generous customer, not on account of his long pinkie nails or his smooth compliments, but because of the many little gifts he brought her.

Maurice's little shop stocked not only heaps of intoxicating spices, but also various delicacies. Bridegrooms would come to him for elegantly wrapped boxes of chocolate truffles, sparkling wines and little baskets filled with nuts. 'For the mother-in-law, right?' he'd trot out his usual joke. For determined suitors he packaged chunks of stoned dates, bags of dried figs and little bottles of rosewater. He gave no such presents to the women who let him screw them for nothing, but the silent whore from Salameh Street, between whose thighs he had lost his virginity, received not only the usual payment, but also lovers' gifts: cakes of halwa and of marzipan, small packets of cloves and mustard seeds.

Her ageing glassy body was white like arrack when a chunk of ice is added to it. Her nipples were wreathed with grey whiskers, as long as the feathered ruff of an old eagle. He was twenty-two when, after prolonged hesitation, he put down the billiard cue at Tony Montana's

Meeting-Place, and mustered the courage to climb up the spiral staircase that led to her flat over the club.

'You ever fucked someone?' she asked, seeing his shaking hands.

'Yes, yes, sure . . .' Maurice steadied his hands and the tremor moved into his throat. In the silence that fell when she sucked him, he could hear the clashing of billiard balls down below and imagined them rolling about on the green baize. He looked at the top of her head bobbing up and down, her grey hair dyed a smoky blonde. When she moved up his body he saw that she didn't shave her underarms and that her thighs were still firm. Her voice hardly got through to him.

'I don't have enough money,' he whispered to her false pearl earrings, but she went on. Since then he'd been back time and again to that whore whose skin was white as cloudy arrack, climbing up and down the spiral stairs in the billiard club, and her anise odour clung to his hairpiece. That Sunday, too, when Matti came home from boarding-school in honour of her birthday, Maurice went to his glassy whore after closing his shop. Before leaving her he pulled on his cowboy boots, which added a couple of inches to his height, wriggled into his suede jacket and walked to the main bus station in Tel Aviv. His flared trousers slapped against his shins. The platforms were empty, and he stopped to sit down and rest in every one of them. Once on the coastal road his thoughts flitted from one idea to another, but by the time he arrived in Givat Olga his mind had come to a halt on the subject of his mother.

When he was an only child and she was a young girl, she used to bring him to this place in the evening. During the day the station was full of people and a haze of exhaust fumes, but in the evening it looked like a ghostly abandoned plaza. Maurice would pick a dark, empty bus that appealed to him and his mother would poke around under the front door till it hiccuped, opened and let them climb in.

'Now you sit here, mister driver,' she would say, placing his little hands on the big steering wheel, 'and I –'

'Hey, lady, lady, you don't have to push!' Maurice would shout, enraptured and scared in equal measure.

She would give him a coin with her bleach-smelling hands, receive an imaginary ticket and sit down. He remembered the sense of power that made his little legs swing back and forth, and the dangerous darkness that lay in ambush for them beyond the wide windscreen. How he loved her then.

Excited and slightly dazed, Mama would pull the cord to ring the bell, get off the bus and on again, pay the driver and travel to her destination. The stars fell from the sky on her head and twinkled out of her hair. All his wishes came true. Finally, flushed and breathless, Iran would pick him up and clasp his body that had gone numb from sheer joy, support his head when it drooped in sleep on her shoulder, and walk home.

But it was a long time since they had sat together and watched the porthole of the washing machine, or searched for flying diamond chips in the dust particles that hung in shafts of light. In those days she used to laugh like wine glasses clinking together when she talked about the daughter-in-law he would bring her.

'Oh, yes, my Maurice, when you have your wedding

I'll grow a peacock tail – what do you say? – instead of a bridegroom's mother's dress.'

Later she would urge him irritably to hurry up and get married, lecture him on how to court the girls, and feed him puffed fenugreek seeds that gave his skin the bitter-sweet smell of love.

'Come on, then, Maurice, get on with it! . . . The body of a man without a woman, it pinches him like a new shoe from the shop.'

But after the epidemic of weddings ravaged the family, his mother went on searching for a bride for him only in bitter coffee dregs, and her potted herb-garden also withered and died. Since his mother had reached the age when women lose their monthly period, their confidence and sanity, she'd done nothing but cry.

Now and then he also cried, because the tears that washed through the house stimulated his eyes, the way running water from a tap makes reluctant urine start to flow.

The bouquets he had sent the girls he courted had long ago withered and died, and when he saw that they too faded after they married he was meanly pleased that they had turned him down. He saw his sisters, too, being swept into marriage, the way beach sandals abandoned on the shore are carried off by the waves. The three big girls were all married in one year, one after the other, catching the wedding fever as if it were a contagious childhood disease to which he alone was immune. Then he saw Sofia and Lizzie thrown back on the shore of their parents' home like seaweed, like sea-shells, like unwanted guests, stunned with grief and stinking up the house with the scorched smell of their memories.

When Maurice went to bed he would take off his hairpiece, crawl under the blanket with the leopardesses, and start fantasising about his beautiful bride. Beautiful, but not too beautiful. And smiling – that too was important. With eyes like black glass and a swan-like body.

And she should have a big heavy arse, he thought, and breasts the same size. So he would have four equal globes to play with. All his own.

And a long neck and luminous skin. What a wedding he would have for her! A fabulous wedding. And what a bridal gown he would buy her – she'd look like a queen. And there would be singers and a band and fireworks. Whatever she fancied, he wouldn't begrudge her anything. She would stand between his mother, with her hair piled artistically, and his father, with his moustache trimmed down to a pencil-line. They'd be proud as peacocks, those two. And when she smiled at him under the canopy he would hold her hand and squeeze it hard.

He might also drink champagne from one of her bridal slippers.

It would be like the scenes he saw in Turkish films. She would smile shyly behind her hand when he spoke words of love into her ear. Shy women are the most attractive, they're real treasures. And she would never get suntanned. He didn't like it. And in the winter she would let the rain fall on her, and her hair would smell like the bay leaves that are cooked in hot soup. And she would be intelligent, too.

Intelligent, yes, but no fancy stuff. They would dance the first slow dance of the wedding feast, and forget the guests around them. They'd dance cheek to cheek and then belly to belly. Her nipples would stiffen and her breasts fill with blood, swell against him and blush. Yes. And the blush would spread to her face – how lovely – and to her thighs.

Her name would be short and simple, Osnat, perhaps, or Anat.

Or maybe Sivan Azizyan.

And they would have a nice house to come home to, and on cold evenings he would light a paraffin stove in their living-room, and on it he would place a pot with water, and add to it orange and tangerine peel. And she would ask in her soft voice, 'What are you doing, my Maurice?'

'You'll see, you'll see in a minute,' he would answer, and snuggle against her breasts and her hair. And as the smell of paraffin mingled with the smell of citrus peel and spread through the house like a fresh, warm whisper, she would sniff and purr with delight and say, 'Aah, that's good, my Maurice, that's nice . . .'

Part Five

Matti Azizyan's Birthday, from Noon till Evening

IT IS POSSIBLE THAT in other days, when life was much simpler, Matti's stamina would have won her an honourable place among her people. Clad in leopard skins, she would have led the hunt for zebra and deer. But in Givat Olga's suburbs, in the Azizyan household, Matti's presence was intolerable. When she was exiled to the boarding-school, where she got a Ritalin tablet stuffed into her mouth every four hours, she calmed down. The other disturbed children who had been placed there, behind the high wall with barbed wire along the top, also swallowed Ritalin with water and calmed down. Matti wanted to run away, but she had nowhere to go, so she declined slowly behind the wall, beyond which were tall cactuses and normal children who shouted at her on their way to school, 'Loony! Dummy!'

At first Matti refused to swallow the pills. She spat, scratched and bit. Then she gave in, and thereafter everything proceeded slowly and dully. Nothing remained of the two wills that had ruled her, and she allowed the pills to dominate her, to empty her black eyes of their wildness and fill her up with a great oblivion. Her medlar pip, which had once been small and luminous white, cracked and split wide open. Sometimes she hugged a tree, a bed, a counsellor, and longed for her mother and father, but then she would remember how they'd all recoiled from her after what happened, and her eyes darkened like shutters closing on a small room.

'Don't worry, Moni, I won't leave you,' she would whisper to the shadow that walked with her along the wall, but was growing paler and dimmer from day to day. The pair of white horses that lived at the school accompanied Matti and her fading shadow till lights-out at nine in the evening, and gazed over her shoulders at the world beyond the high wall, their lovely eyes full of boredom.

After she had been at the school for two months Iran came to see her, carrying two baskets. She sat on the edge of her bed and shouted, 'Matti! Matti! Matti!'

Matti did not respond. She stared at the silent thorny field outside the window, explored the caverns of her nose and split the frizzy ends of her hair. Iran unloaded her baskets, stuck one into the other, and all the way back to Givat Olga on the number 641 bus wept bitterly with sorrow and remorse.

'Maybe you were simply boring her?' Solly suggested to his wife and wiped her tears with his hands.

'You don't understand,' Iran sobbed. 'We let them make the girl into a plant. You won't know her. It's a different girl. A crazy girl.'

A month later Solly took Iran's baskets and took bus number 641 to the boarding-school. He sat with Matti in front of the cactus thicket and talked to her politely, as to a stranger, with tender words and a spongy tongue.

Matti gazed at him with her beautiful eyes filled with boredom, and was too shy to touch him.

'I don't know what it is . . . She's not in this reality.' Solly's voice shook when he handed the empty baskets to his wife. He had shed his own tears of sorrow and remorse by himself, all the way back to Givat Olga.

But Matti was in this reality, only she had become dozy, and her dreams were filled with weird visions. Sometimes she fell asleep in the middle of the day, slid under the desk and slept on the floor. At first she suffered occasionally from nausea and dizziness, but these passed. Only the nervous tics in her facial muscles did not go away, and made her stare at her distorted reflection in the formica surface of the dining-hall tables, the soapy puddle in the shower cubicle and the glass of tea given at supper. There were no shop windows at the school, nor any mirrors, like the ones that hung at home between the mosaic lampshades, in the bathroom, in the girls' room and in Mama and Papa's bedroom. In the morning, before swallowing the first tablet, Matti needed to recall what she looked like, to remember that she was two people and to be like Moni. Like the white horses who wanted to leap over the high wall, she too tried and failed, and a moment later she was given a pill to swallow, and four hours later another pill, then one more, and already they were turning off the lights.

When Matti had been at the boarding-school for three months her parents took the number 641 bus and travelled without any baskets to bring her back home.

'She's become like a robot, they're drugging her silly, that's a treatment, that is?' Solly punished himself and his wife.

'Better she should make hell at home,' Iran decided. 'We can't live like this, with Matti stuck in that place with all the retards!'

When they arrived at the school Matti was in the shower. Her father stood by the door and her mother sat on her bed, to surprise her when she came out. Wisps of vapour curled out through the slatted shower door, and with it the words of the song Matti was singing to herself under the current of warm water.

On the way back Iran wept with deep emotion and relief. The staff had assured them that Matti was showing great improvement, that the facial tics would stop after a while, and that there was no reason to take her home just yet.

'And her eyes have some light in them again, don't they?' Solly asked repeatedly. 'Did you see it?'

'And she's eating all right,' Iran agreed, and asked, 'And she has some colour in her face again, did you see?'

After six months at the school Matti was so calm that she was sent home on her birthday, to spend a day and a night with her family. She patted the white horses in farewell and waved her hand to the blank-eyed children who lived surrounded by barbed wire. The staff gave her six tablets of Ritalin, which Matti put in her pocket and did not intend to swallow, but felt them now and then to draw strength from them and to calm down. Now, too, when she stood with her completely shorn head in front of her mother in the brightly lit bedroom, she fumbled at the Ritalin tablets which mingled in her pocket with the pearls she'd stolen from the green jewellery box, while the market vegetables that had rolled on the floor were being put back in the basket.

Evidently Lizzie was not dead, because Matti saw her waking up on the sofa. Lizzie whimpered with pain as her body recalled the beating Maurice had given her earlier that morning.

Matti stuck her hand into her other pocket, felt the sharp scissors and the paper coins of her face that she'd cut out of the album photos.

'What kind of girl are you, eh, Matti? My God, how you look now. I could die,' Iran muttered, stunned. And added to herself in despair, 'Crazy, acts like crazy.'

She captured Matti's cheeks in her hand and squeezed them hard with her fingers. With her other hand she tried to smooth the remaining hair, but gave up and recoiled with cold aversion. Her lips were dry and it was plain to see that she badly wanted to cry, but her tears held back, undecided whether to spill over or be re-absorbed into her eyes. Matti saw this and thought that if she could come up with something bad to say, not something really awful, just something bad, her mother would grasp at it as it left her lips, and allow the tears to flow.

'I'm going to shower,' Lizzie groaned and crept away in a glimmering of sequins down the corridor of the Indian gods from the living-room to the bathroom. Iran noted her blue bruises until she disappeared behind the closed door and the sound of running water followed. She took a deep breath of the air in the corridor, which was still echoing with Lizzie's moans of pain, and turned to look at Matti.

Matti tried to feel what her mother was feeling, to know how to help her, but Iran seemed to her to be a different mother, somebody else's mother. She remembered how once, when she was a pre-schooler, she'd suddenly screamed, 'You're a bad mother, I'm sick of you, I want a different mother, somebody else's mother!'

'A different mother? I'm killing myself and you . . . All right, fine, a different mother . . .' Iran had simmered all the way to the market. 'Here, choose one for yourself!'

The fingers which had squeezed Matti's arm with a double strength of anger and affront, and dragged her all the way from the house to the market stalls, suddenly let go. Her mother disappeared among the mounds of watermelons, and after a long time reappeared, red-eyed, from behind a stack of cauliflowers.

Matti looked at her mother's wet eyes as she stood in the Indian gods' corridor and saw that she was just like Matti on that day – a small frightened child wandering among other children's mothers' baskets. Now her mother was lost in the big market that had once been her life. She saw that her mother couldn't understand what she had done that made her into a bad mother, causing her children to turn out as they did. And just like Matti when she was crying after being beaten, her mother too didn't understand why everybody kept yelling at her, 'Bad girl! Bad girl!'

Iran sighed as if she heard Matti's thoughts and nodded sadly, as if in agreement. Matti went up to her, to help her with the heavy basket, to remove the strange kerchief from her head, to stroke her sweating neck and say in a voice sweetened with a smile, 'Mama love, darling Mama . . .'

But Iran thought of something else, because she suddenly clapped her hands together and fluttered her eyelids, and said in a decisive voice and dry lips, 'All right, OK, go to Grandma Touran's house, tell Sofia that I'm making lunch, she must bring the baby here and eat. I have to talk to all of you.'

'What about?' Matti asked.

'First go and call her. I'll make mashed potatoes, all right?'

'You will?' Matti asked in disbelief.

'What's the matter, you don't like mashed potatoes no more?' Iran's voice shook with uncertainty. 'Mashed potatoes and meatballs, the way you like them, no?'

'Yes. Mashed potatoes and meatballs.' The familiar words soothed Matti's heart like a cool compress on a feverish brow.

She obeyed and went down the stairs very slowly. She did not rush from floor to floor as she used to do, did not spread her legs or fling her arms out, nor did she slide like the wind down the iron banister. Her eyes did not widen with the delicious fear, and her voice did not pierce the shadowy stairwell with a cry like a raven. She held on to the cold metal and walked down the steps like an old woman. The banister was painted black, but patches of rust showed through the smooth enamel the way the bald patches showed through her cropped hair. She walked down the sixty steps that divided the Azizyan house from the ground slowly, like a person gathering memories by way of provisions for a long journey ahead, stringing them on a single long white thread.

She stopped beside each of the neighbours' doors and stood cautiously on the rough doormats in front of them. She let the sounds trickle subtly under the doors and into her ears, and the faint smells of cooking that curled out of the pots reach her nose, and the murmurs of conversation resound softly through the walls and break on the shore of her thoughts. She was feeling cold, so she wrapped herself in all these sensations as if they were an old shirt and worn trousers, soft and pleasant after repeated washing. She felt she was trying on the clothes of all the inhabitants of the building, as though she was everybody's youngest sister, who did not resemble any of them but nevertheless took on whatever had become too tight and ragged and uncomfortable, so that they could continue to live in all those rooms and buy themselves new things.

When she reached the ground she stopped in the shade of the guava trees, whose sweet musty aroma filled every breath she took. Sunlight and shadows played on her face. She picked one fine-looking guava and bit it, but at once spat it out and threw the fruit away. It tasted like a rotten pear, as if the touch of Matti's teeth had poisoned it. The medlars too shrugged loose from the tree branches when Matti approached them and committed suicide. All that was left on the upper branches were some bird-pecked fruits. Across the street, under the orange trees in Grandma Touran's yard, the rooster was courting the ducks, and the ducks yowled like cats. Beyond the yard a new building rose unexpectedly, and a plane flying very low rattled like an old sewing-machine. Dogs smelled her from afar and barked only at her.

Matti wiped her mouth on the back of her hand and stood still, perplexed, her pockets full of the calming pills and the paper coins of her face. She shut her eyes and took a deep breath.

'Take it easy, Moni, take it easy,' she said to herself and crossed the narrow alley towards the orange trees.

When she knocked on the door of her grandmother's

house she remembered the day she stole a cigarette from Grandma Touran's packet and tried to escape into the oleander thicket behind the house. Grandma Touran grabbed her by the ear and a smile spread over her old face. Matti shrank into the pain and awaited the slap.

'Why steal?' she heard her say when she let her have her ear back. 'Ask me nicely and I'll give you.'

Her grandmother taught her to inhale the smoke, hold it in her lungs and exhale. Matti remembered her saying in her rasping, choking voice, 'Enjoy it, let your insides enjoy it.'

Sofia opened the door and the memory slammed shut. Her long hair with its blonde streaks blew in the current of the opening door, and the bald patches in Matti's scalp shivered. Sofia was so beautiful and so surprised to see her looking like this that Matti felt ashamed.

'Yes, I got a haircut,' she mumbled, looking down at Sofia's furry house-slippers.

'So I see,' Sofia laughed tiredly. 'So I see.' Her gold earrings made her head sway from side to side, as though they were a pair of scales in which she weighed her mind.

'Mama said you're to come and eat,' Matti said very quickly and emphatically. Sofia noticed the tics in her face and thought that her little sister was shorter than she'd remembered.

'Wait, sweetie, wait a bit, come in a minute.'

Matti stepped back in confusion, because Sofia, in inviting her in, moved aside and revealed the interior behind her, the big bed in the middle, and the baby lying on it. Matti's eyes fell again to the floor.

'It's all right, sweetie, it happened a long time ago,' Sofia's voice dropped to an eleven-year-old's level. 'Babies don't even remember such things. It's nonsense.' She drew her sister gently into the house, and Matti felt her hand trembling.

'It's nonsense, isn't it? Isn't it?' Sofia said to her baby in a babyish voice as she went back to him, her pelvis swinging in semi-circular motion, as if she were wading through deep water. Matti followed behind, staring at the satin hem foaming around her sister's slim ankles.

Matti was thinking about Sofia, her very big sister, and how when she returned from her honeymoon and her husband went off to Africa, she'd asked Matti to come and sleep with her in the tall tower in Bat-Yam, because she felt lonely and afraid to sleep alone, and Matti would listen in the dark to Sofia talking in her sleep.

'Let's be friends again, please, my auntie Matti, all right?' Sofia spoke for her baby.

She sat down on the bed and Matti joined her, repressing all movement in her muscles. Sofia gathered up the baby and very carefully laid him on Matti's lap, which slowly opened to receive him.

'He's heavier,' Matti said without a voice or a smile. Tears choked Sofia's throat and she rubbed her neck to drive them away. Matti felt the baby's heart beating inside her own, but she didn't look at him. She was looking at her sister and saw the gold chain tightening around her neck and the pendant with the name Itzik rising and falling in the hollow of her throat. Matti remembered Lizzie's baby, which they were keeping away from her, saying it was a phantom.

'Cuddle him, Matti, don't be scared,' Sofia said to her, but Matti didn't dare. But she did manage to tear her eyes away from her sister, where they had sunk so deep that they saw nothing, and turn to look at the baby.

She saw that his eyes were big and beautiful, and were exactly like Sofia's – the spitting image, absolutely spitting.

'See, Moni, it's so nice to look the same,' she said in her heart, and her muscles softened.

The baby babbled something, in the same voice Sofia used when speaking for him, and Matti thought that he looked sweet and innocent when he wasn't coughing. An ordinary baby, a bit like a boy, a bit like a girl. He put out his hand to touch her face, like a blind person who needs his fingers to get to know a face, but his arm was too short and the little fingers wriggled. She leaned forward to him tenderly, but her mind's eye conjured up imaginary scissors snicking the sweet air between them, went snip-snip and cut his face out in a perfect circle. The baby wrinkled his forehead, as if he recognised her.

Suddenly she jumped up. 'Mama said you must come to eat lunch!' She averted her gaze from the baby and chucked him at his mother.

'She's cooking!' she shouted in agitation and swallowed all the saliva in her mouth. The delicate fleshy hollows behind her knees were suddenly filled with sweat.

Sofia clutched the baby with one hand and with the other wiped the tears that had suddenly washed over her face. 'Mama's making lunch?' she murmured sadly, as if she'd just woken up. 'That's a good sign. Wait, I'll just put something on and I'll go up with you.'

It was already twelve-thirty. Sofia thrust her pelvis sideways and propped her baby on it. Outdoors the summer was over. Matti went up the stairs with her sister and nephew, and as she entered her home she again smelled the scorched smell. By now Lizzie had come out of the shower, her hair wet, and Marcelle had come back tired from the paralysed woman's house.

Matti stood at the window and looked down at the yard on which the new building cast a shadow. Cats ambled among the guava and medlar trees as if they owned the place, flirting their tails to provoke the dogs, who smelled Matti from afar and barked only at her.

There weren't any pebbles on the windowsill, and Matti stroked her arm which had braced to throw one.

She saw that the charred patches on the ground left by the Lag Baomer bonfires had not yet faded, saw the two stones marking the goalposts for the football games in which she hadn't taken part for the last six months, and the oleander thicket which had always been her perfect hideaway. Then she saw the procession of neighbourhood kids streaming home from school and crouched down to watch them without being spotted.

The guava and medlar gangs, schoolbags on their backs and lunch bags dangling from their necks, followed by their younger brothers and sisters, were shouting, joshing and laughing, confident in themselves and their togetherness. Matti observed each face carefully, like a hitman looking through a gunsight. The closer they came to the house the further back she withdrew, dissolving into herself, into the pocket which held the six Ritalin pills.

Matti had been sick and hadn't been to school for a long time, but nobody came to give her lessons. Today was her birthday, but nobody was giving her a party. It hurt her to look at them, and she went on hiding long after the sound of trainers and sandals stomping up the stairs fell silent, and after the last flat door that opened to them had been slammed shut.

'It's just you and me, my Moni. That's all,' she said under her breath, and then the sound of meatballs sizzling in the pan struck her rigid back. Matti turned round, because it seemed to her that the hissing sound coming from the kitchen was her mother's laughter, and that she would shortly see her flesh quivering with amusement as if it was being fried in hot oil.

But Iran was standing at the filthy cooker, frying pan in hand, smoke in her eyes, her shoulders slumped. Sofia was peeling potatoes, Lizzie was slicing cucumbers and Marcelle was washing the dishes.

Matti waited for one of them to look up and search for her, for one of them to raise her plucked eyebrows and crease her forehead and call for her, for all of them to suddenly think of her, turn round, or even just turn their heads, and be seized with momentary alarm as they remembered that the baby was in its cot and she was loose and crazy in the house. But they went on frying and peeling and washing dishes in silence: even their bangles and anklets and gold necklaces did not tinkle. The only sounds to reach her ears were the sounds of sighs and running water, of sizzling oil and chopping knives.

She looked at the floor of the flat, from the living-room to the kitchen, over the carpets and to the balcony. Her lashes swept the dust and dirt to the windowsill, and there stopped. A column of big, round-bottomed ants, coloured black and bronze, marched up to their nest in the corner of the window lintel. Matti crouched down again, as if to hide from view, and observed their burnished bodies which glistened in the autumn sunlight. They reminded her of the fat boy who had provoked her months before, and whom she'd tied down on a nest of red ants. That was at a time when Matti was forbidden to eat sweet things, both because she'd inherited her father's weak teeth, but also because her mother had been told at the clinic that perhaps sugar was making her such a bundle of nerves. But the fat boy couldn't care less. He'd stuck out his red tongue and taunted her with chocolate wafers, chewing them one by one and speaking very slowly, sucking the words as if they were sweets:

'Na-na, na-na-na! Matti's an idiot, goes to special class!'

'You watch it!' Matti gave him fair warning a moment before she erupted.

'Matti's an idiot, will be a street sweeper! Matti's cra –'

She remembered how he'd clutched at her arms when she tied him with wire to the lamp-post, how he'd shaken her hard to make a good little girl or boy fall out of the wicked girl, one who would be her own spitting image and would say to her, 'Enough, Matti, stop, he's a poor little thing.' But she'd flung him down to the ground with a thwack. She remembered the agitated ants crawling over his thighs and stinging him, remembered how he'd shrunk away from the strange tickle and started crying in a strange, silent, inward way, making pink ripples pass over his flesh, and how the ants had discovered his sweet fat and fallen on the treasures of his sticky skin, and how she'd looked at him without pity and seen him as a big lollipop which had been sucked and thrown away, moist with childish saliva.

Matti glanced at the baby. Sofia's eyes smiled out of his face. More and more ants marched into the hole in the wall, like a procession of children going home after school. They advanced steadily, as if the house had been abandoned and they were taking it over.

Matti waited and waited, still as the statue of an Indian god. The procession came to an end; only a few stragglers still walked along the window frame. She caught the last ant in the procession between her finger and thumb as in a vice, and threw it out of the window. She looked out to see it falling down, storey after storey, but by the time she leaned over the sill the tiny glittering ant had been carried away by the breeze. Its family had disappeared into the wall. Matti thought that it would take the ant a very long time to find its way back home, and that its family would have forgotten it by then, and she regretted throwing it out of the window.

An anonymous arm appeared from a window in the opposite building, holding a striped cloth and shaking it. Bits of bread fell out and whirled on their way down.

She heard behind her the glassy clatter of plates and the metallic ringing of knives and forks. The kitchen drawers moved woodenly in and out, dishes touched the table like toes dipping into cold water. Matti's face grew very serious. She became taut as a spring and a knot of anticipation swelled in her belly.

'Matti! Come and eat!' She heard her mother's voice, abruptly puncturing with the needle of routine the airy balloon that was compressing her lungs up to her throat. She wanted to run over to her with empty lungs, to fling herself at her with all her weight, to hug her and kiss her, to eat more and more just to please her. But she couldn't move, because she needed to hear it one more time, one last time.

'Matti, where are you? Food is ready!'

She wanted to rush over and tell her mother and sisters something terribly funny, something that you can't help laughing at, that you wet yourself laughing about, to make Sofia stop sighing, and Marcelle break her silence, and Lizzie hear something at long last, and Mama laugh the way she used to, the kind of laugh that brought a mist of happy tears to her eyes and made her chew over the joke till she gasped and said, 'Aye-aye-aye, some character, eh, this Matti of ours!'

But then she thought that Mama's muscles had become so tired that she wouldn't even be able to smile, no matter how funny the joke that Matti made up for her.

'I went to Moni's grave today.'

'What?'

'Yes, it's exactly eleven years today. Also I met a rabbi there and he said that you must all change your names. He said the names I gave you when you were born are all unlucky, so he said I must give you all new names.'

'What?'

'Yes, he says I should call Maurice Shalom, Sofia I must call Geula, Lizzie must be Tikvah, Marcelle Brakhah, and Matti Mazal [luck].'

'What?'

'He also says that the baby must now be called Nes [miracle], and that when all the names are on your identity cards and you have been blessed in the synagogue, you'll soon get used to them.'

Iran Azizyan spoke, and her words were so acid that

they corroded her daughters. Matti didn't understand why they needed to change their names, but she saw that her mother's breath was scorching Sofia, Marcelle and Lizzie, and again smelled the burnt odour. They were sitting round the table, eating the meal she had prepared: mashed potatoes, meatballs and a fresh salad. Her husband was at sea and Maurice was in his little spice shop. The silence flowed in the kitchen between her and her daughters, like frying oil that had turned black from repeated use.

Their silence grew longer and thicker, and Iran felt it assaulting her on all sides. Sofia closed her eyes in despair, as if she would never open them again, Marcelle's eyes looked sadder than ever, and Lizzie withdrew into a blank stare that saw nothing.

'Why?' Matti asked finally, her eyes moving over her mother's face, like the eyes of a grown-up wondering about a child's expression.

'Mmm . . .?' Iran placed her tremulous hands on her hips and her elbows stuck out like blunted arrows.

'Why must we change the names you gave us when we were born? What's wrong with the names we've got?' Matti really didn't understand.

Suddenly the flab on Iran's arms began to shake. Tears burst out of her eyes and flowed like a heavy shower.

'Cause . . . cause . . . I don't know wha-wha-what to do . . . I don't know, don't know what to do for you chi-chi-children, what I can do . . . I don't know any more . . . I want to ki-ki-kill myself cause I don't know what more I can do for you . . .'

Iran had inherited her emotional nature from her mother, whose heart became ill from excessive use. When she realised what Iran was like, she said to her, 'All the women are like that, my *omri*. Really really. Your father says all Persian women cry a lot, even when it isn't necessary. Poor things, what can we do, that's how we are.'

Iran's daughters knew that she was suffering greatly. Since the summer had burnt everything down she'd stopped eating sweet things, only sat beside the sick baby and prayed to God. For months the house had been darkened, and she read to the baby out of the Book of Psalms a dreadful sad story that he couldn't understand, and had still not reached its end. Iran expended so much pity on her children, and agonised so much in her empathy with their pain, that she became a different woman, somebody's else's mum.

Their mother, who had always been just their own mama, had suddenly changed. Their mama, who could be in all the rooms at the same time, whose only friends were her sisters, who never went on a trip without her children, who spent an evening away from home only to go to a relative's wedding, bar-mitzvah or circumcision, who had never sat in a café, who had no occupation or hobby except her motherhood – she had suddenly become a different person.

Years after giving birth to Maurice, Iran was once again a little girl without breasts, an adolescent girl coveting the world's despair, a strange woman made up of wrinkles. She had resigned her post of mother, packed up all the family's troubles and withdrawn on her own into sorrow's small, private and shut-off chamber. Pain was like a new hobby she had discovered, and she even neglected their father in order to indulge in it.

Her children saw her distancing herself from him, carrying between her teeth all the loves that had died, that were never born, or were stillborn, and refusing to share her prey with him. Solly Azizyan was as fine-textured as his vest, bashful as a guest, and he had loved her for so many years, longer than he'd loved himself. He saw that her eyes had lost their brightness, that they no longer met his, and that she hid them behind her defiant hands when she bent over the candles she lit every Monday and Thursday morning, the days when the Torah scroll is taken out of its ark in the synagogue. He saw the Book of Psalms shaking in her hands and her fingers moistening its cover with their sweat. At night she either came to bed late, or pretended to be asleep, and he breathed in the sweet odour behind her ears until he fell asleep. Every night she soaked their bed with her tears, and slipped out of it to go to the synagogue before he woke up. He knew that it was from him that she hid her lovely hair under kerchiefs, and that it was to repulse his red lips that it began to smell of the lavender of old age.

One night, on his way to the shower, he found that he'd forgotten to take clean underwear, and returned absent-mindedly to the bedroom. His wife was sitting on the bed with her back to the door. Her black hair tumbled out of the pious kerchief, with which she stifled all her desires. Her hair was long and tired-looking, with a faint bluish tinge of greying, and it looked dank and greasy after many days of neglect.

The sight of her exposed hair broke open the apple of longing that was choking Solly's throat. He was filled with such intense lust, and was so astonished by it, that he fled from the room without the socks. Before undoing the first button of her blouse, Iran turned round, listened for the sound of rushing water coming through the wall, and only then began to undress. She did not know that her husband had glimpsed her uncovered hair, and that at that moment he was agonising in the bathroom like a virgin lad who had peeped through the window at a woman undressing.

Twenty-eight years had passed since he'd first seen her, cast his love-line, hooked her and pulled her in. Lately she had become a different woman, somebody else's wife. Sometimes, when their glances happened to meet, Iran saw her husband looking at her as he had done that winter evening, a long time ago, before the roof had been tarred for the third time and the rain played a metallic tune in the tin buckets which caught the drops falling from the ceiling. That evening when he'd come home from the fish-market stall she'd opened the door to him with her hair done in a new style that Marcelle and Sofia had devised for her, not long after they'd begun to learn hairdressing at the technical college.

All that afternoon she had sat among the singing buckets brimming with rainwater, while her daughters trimmed and shaped her long hair.

'It'll look terrific on you,' they said, and dyed it the colour of aubergine.

'Out of this world,' they said, and fed the hair with creams to make it curl.

'Fabulous!' they breathed, and puffed it out with the hot breath of an electric hairdryer.

In the evening there was a power cut and the house was lit with candles. She heard her husband's footsteps on the stairs and got up. She opened the door and stood there, beautiful, loving and smiling. But Solly, exhausted and confused, stopped on the threshold. His eyebrows, those cornices under his forehead, had not withstood the downpour through which he'd come and his eyes were full of water.

'Oh, sorry, I made a mistake,' he mumbled damply, blushed and pulled the door shut. He did not recognise her and went to look for his wife.

But his wife didn't know anything except how to be his children's mother. Ever since they were tiny, when they would hide in the laundry basket, play peekaboo behind the armchairs in the living-room and pop out of the kitchen cupboards, she'd promised them that if ever they were hungry she would take bread out of her mouth and give it to them, that on each hand she had a special finger for each one of them. Her children grew taller, became adult, but her heart did not rise with them; it remained near the ground as it had always been. She still looked for them behind the heaps of dirty clothes, the remains of the three-part sofa and the depleted kitchen cupboards. They had grown but her heart remained where it had always been, at the level that children can easily reach. At this level what was there for her to do except weep? She knew how sorely her daughters needed love and how badly Maurice needed a woman. So she tore her love for Solly out of her heart, as if it were the bread she needed to feed them. But she could find no use for her fingers.

Pity they grew up, she sometimes thought, then caught herself and rephrased it: pity they grew up so soon.

All she knew was how to be their mother. For them she emptied the chambers of her heart that were as high as ballrooms, turned its wide basement into storage space and filled it with all their sorrows. And when a woman's heart becomes so stuffy and dark, she cries all the time and turns to God to find answers.

Wearing her wooden mules and lavender kerchief, she boarded the bus that departed early in the morning from the Sephardi synagogue, together with the old men and women who like her made the rounds of the sainted rabbis' tombs. Under carob, fig and olive trees, in remote niches, caverns carved out of the bedrock or grand marble pavilions, Iran clung to tombstones and entreated God to help her children.

'Please make my Marcelle go back to her husband . . .' she whispered at the iron gate of the women's section at the tomb of Rabbi Meir Baal Haness in Tiberias. She tied a scrap torn from a cotton shirt of Marcelle's to a low-hanging olive branch, to ensure that the patron saint of marital harmony would rise from his resting place, carry her plea to heaven and persuade God to heed her. She believed that before long Marcelle and Yoel Hajjabi would get together again, and like all loving couples visit the Sea of Galilee, gaze upon the Golan mountains and undo that knotted scrap of cloth. But when she returned there on her own, she found Marcelle's coloured flags till fluttering in the breeze and fading under the blazing sun.

'Please give health to Sofia's baby, please . . .' she wept silently at the tomb of the Baba Sali in Netivot, which had become mouldy from the untold tears that had been shed on its stones. She saw the lame and the crippled and the sick come to beg for recovery, and her heart filled with hope. Like any desperate person, she comforted herself with tales of the miracles wrought by the worship of the sainted rabbi, about tumours that shrank and vanished and paraplegics who got out of their wheelchairs and walked.

'Please make my Lizzie stop all that stuff . . .' she murmured with a pious expression at the tomb of Rabbi Shimon Bar-Yohai in Meron, laid a little stone on the dome and stuffed a written note into a crack. Cataracts of wax from memorial candles brimmed over from the niches.

'Sofia needs to be strong. Strength for living is needed for Sofia . . .' She butted her forehead at Rachel's Tomb in Bethlehem, breathing in the scent of myrtles.

'Give my Maurice a good bride, Maurice needs a wife . . .' she whispered in the crush that thronged the tomb of Yonatan ben Uziel.

'Put some quietness into Matti's heart, so it won't burn her up . . .' she sobbed beside a band of yeshiva students who were praying devoutly at the crowded tomb of Dan ben Yaacov at Eshtaol. When she set a candle-flame to flicker its light on the low, sooty ceiling, her tears glistened and vast-bottomed women comforted her lavender-kerchiefed head with caresses.

This day, after Maurice had beaten Lizzie black and blue and Iran's lifted arms all but cracked the ceiling in her despair, she'd been to the grave of Matti's dead twin and then also called on the grave of Grandma Touran. It was there she'd met the rabbi who instructed her to change the names she'd given her children. At home the Persian copper vessels were turning green, the delicate crocheted mats turned grey and the scales of the goldfish faded to silver. On the kitchen table the mashed potatoes cooled, the meatballs shrank and the chopped fresh vegetables wallowed dully in the salad. The girls' faces went blank and they didn't say anything. Their mother wept.

Marcelle gazed at her sadly, looking at her the way you look at a new acquaintance when you are introduced. First at the eyes, then at the face, and lastly, furtively, at the form of the whole person. She saw Iran's sobs shaking her whole body.

My mother, she thought with a twinge, and felt the fine hairs on her arms standing on end.

Marcelle would have liked to say what she had wanted to say to her mother a couple of months before, when she was still working at the bridal salon, Classic 2000, and Iran, who happened to be in the area, came in to say hello. Marcelle was filing the nails of an excited bride and the radio was playing the last hits of the summer, when she glanced up, saw an old woman come in, and went on working. A second later she realised it was her mother, her face webbed with wrinkles and her back stooped.

'My soul . . .' Iran began, embarrassed.

Marcelle couldn't utter a sound, because the words that leaped into her mouth – 'Oh no! Mama, look how we ruined your face!' – were not to be spoken.

She kept silent then and was still silent now, her fingers fumbling with some invisible crumbs on the kitchen table.

Because at such moments you don't say what you really want to say. The powerful words lurk in your throat, growling, their hackles rising, making the eyes flash a warning look, but they remain unspoken.

If those big words had not finally tucked in their tails

and slunk away, Marcelle would have stood up and said, 'Why, Mama?'

She would have extended her hand with its umpteen tinkling bangles, soothed her mother's tremor, and whispered, 'Why do you take all our troubles into your heart? Why don't you look after yourself, instead of crying all day and all night? Why don't you take better care of your heart, our Mama?'

The words she didn't say were boiling inside her. She would have asked, 'Why do you love us so much? I mean, love us too much, just like that, without limit, without ever drawing a line and saying, That's it, no more! How much can I stand on their account? How much can I take to heart? Finish, otherwise it's going to kill me. You should be thinking, like, This is me. That's my body. And this is where my flesh ends and there's some skin on it. Then there's a bit of space, all right? OK, so in this space I'm going to put all my children's troubles, right here! Between you, Mama, and myself, between you and Sofia, you and Maurice, Lizzie, even Matti, and God knows who else! I mean, you don't need to cry and cry the whole time. Each one has his own mess and his own shit, so let each one cry for himself. By himself. Cause those are our pains, Mama, not yours, so stop now! Just stop! Cut it out!'

Then Marcelle would have taken a deep breath, swallowed the saliva that foamed with her agitation, and said, 'Honestly, Mama, look at it – nothing has happened to you. Everything's all right, thank God. You're not divorced, you're married, aren't you? You still have your husband, thank God. You are healthy, your children are healthy, your husband sleeps beside you in your bed at night. It wasn't you who got pregnant with a phantom, you didn't go deaf, you didn't marry somebody for no reason at all, and you didn't lose a child, and your husband doesn't beat you, does he? You're not rotting alone in your room like a stinky old dog, without a wife, without children, without love. No, that's us! Us! You understand what I'm saying? That's us, Mama, for heaven's sake! So, right, I know, things have got tough here and every one of us is crying tears of blood because of the shit we're in, and it's a mess, OK, so we cry our eyes out, because it's a shame – but it's a shame about us, Mama, not you! We are not you, Mama love, can't you understand?'

But Marcelle said nothing. She didn't even have the strength to get up and touch her mother. Her head rested between her hands, her elbows on the table and her fingers digging into her cheeks, as if she had to hold her head so it wouldn't roll away before she could set it on the empty plate. Her sad eyes travelled over the dirty floor, caressing it with their velvety touch. Iran didn't see the golden fuzz stiffening on Marcelle's arms, and couldn't read the blurry script of the weary thoughts that passed behind her glasses: 'Enough tears, Mama, it'll be all right.'

If an unseen hand had not snatched the big words from Marcelle's mouth before they were ready to be uttered; if the only thing left in her mouth had not been a dry, hollow, scratchy twig with a few cotton threads dangling from it, loose ends such as, 'Did you get some sleep?' and 'Come and eat', 'We're out of sugar' and 'Yes, I must tell Maurice to bring some'; if Marcelle had not been so very silent, Sofia might have stood up now and hugged Iran.

Even if without saying a word. It had been many days since Iran had been properly hugged.

If Sofia had done that, Iran would have stood before her, would have rested her forehead against her daughter's neck, would have sunk her nose between the prominent collar-bones and let her tears wet the diamond necklaces. Sofia would have bent over her and patted the shaking back, felt the gap between their bodies in her mother's breasts and gazed at the living-room through the kitchen door. From that angle Sofia would have seen the wedding photograph of Iran and Solly on its shelf in the dresser, soft and curling from the humid years. There Iran was smiling in black and white, under a silvery glass globe that hung from the ceiling of the ballroom in Jaffa. Her breasts were high and upthrusting, visibly lovely under the pearly gown.

Those breasts of her mother's, both in the photograph and against her bosom, would have given Sofia the strength to say to her in a soft voice, 'Look at that, Mama love, you had four children by the time you were twenty-five, and then Matti also.'

The words would have given Sofia extra strength, and she would have tightened her embrace. Then she would have stroked with her fingertips her mother's floury arms, warmed the flabby breasts with her palms and caressed the watery belly.

'You were just a child. What did you know about life anyway? You gave us your soul. But look now, your belly is empty and we're big, thank God. Not children any more. That you gave birth to us means that . . . it means that you gave us life, but you gave it to us to live, didn't you? So enough, you breastfed us enough, changed our nappies enough, you don't have any more babies. And you're not a girl any more either. So enough with all those sainted tombs that you go to like going to a clinic. And you can't change our names, we already have names. And we don't need any more magic tricks and rabbis either. Please. It'll all work out in the end without them, you'll see.'

But Sofia didn't stand up, did not hug and did not speak. She only stared at the open window, her eyes as black as the eyes of the Indian gods in the corridor. Tears filled her but did not brim over. She hugged her own shoulders, as if she were two people, her own sad shoulders and somebody else's arms. Now and then she touched her jewels, to be sure that they were still there, that she could lean on them in case she stumbled.

If Sofia had stood up and spoken, perhaps Lizzie would have said something too. Maybe not much. Maybe without getting up from her chair. Maybe without even looking at her mother's milky moon-shell eyes. But she too would have said something like, 'Enough, Mama!'

Her raven eyelashes would have fluttered at her sisters, to seek their support.

'Right, Marcelle? We need you to be stronger, you're our Mama, isn't that so, Sofia? What a shame. Where are your eyes in the middle of all these wrinkles you collected? Where are your tits inside all those rags you got on? And what about your hair, eh? The only thing that hasn't changed is your Persian accent.'

Iran would have cracked a shy grin, Sofia and Marcelle would have chuckled softly, and Lizzie would have drawn strength with every word and cried out in agitation.

'Eh, Mama love? What happened? Did the world die? The sea get burnt up? Yes, yes, laugh a little, it'll be all right, we'll get through this. What did you say I must be called now, Tikvah, right – hope? OK, so believe me, Tikvah Azizyan's word is like a rock. I swear by Tikvah everything will work out all right.'

But Lizzie also failed to utter those words that, if left unsaid, sink into the tongue, dissolve in the mouth, combine with the bodily fluids and turn into tears, sweat and urine.

Lizzie got up and went to the bathroom, leaving her mother and sisters in the kitchen with the silence. The silence had come into the house before the summer, like a fat, important guest who climbed, perspiring, up the stairs, and had a chair quickly brought forward for her to sit on, leg over leg. The guest had stayed on, day after day, her gaping suitcases filling the rooms, and already she was opening the fridge, propping her feet on the table and feeling very much at home, like one of the family. And now the silence was in the rush of water Lizzie flushed in the toilet, in her moans of pain as she walked down the Indian gods' corridor, in the squeal of springs when she lay down on Mama and Papa's bed, and then in her sudden shriek:

'What's this? Who did this to the photo album?'

'What? What did she say?' Iran asked Marcelle, who was clasping her head in despair, and Sofia, who was hugging herself as if she were cold and resting a cheek on her shoulder.

'What happened, Lizzie?' They rose and went out of the kitchen, leaving Matti on her own, reflected in the salad spoon, the oil in the frying pan and the empty plates.

Matti stuck the earpieces of the stethoscope she'd hidden under her shirt in her ears, pressed its end to her frightened heart, and suddenly heard the little voice of a child.

'Matti? Hey, Matti!'

She turned her head to the sound.

She tried to say, 'Moni . . .' He was standing in the kitchen doorway and holding his hand out to her. Now Matti couldn't tell whose reflection she saw in the salad spoon, the oily frying pan and the empty plates.

'Come, Matti, let's get out of here.'

'My Moni . . .' She was unable to say it.

'Come on then, leave them alone.' He opened the door. 'It's our birthday today.' And out they went.

He looks so much like her.

'No, Matti. Not downstairs. This way, this way.'

So much like her. She is unable to move.

'Come on then, what's wrong with you? Watch out for the plant.'

Moni grabs her hand and pulls her along the third-floor landing, to the flat of the couple without children, who went to work and left it empty. He waits for her to come in and shuts the door after them.

Matti looks at his black eyes, the black snakes of his eyebrows, the thin upper lip and swelling lower one, and the slightly prominent ears.

So much like her. The spitting image.

He's at the same level as she. He smiles at her and it's just like her smile.

'My Matti,' he purrs, presses his cheek to hers, crushes

her nose against his shoulder and hugs her hard. Matti's hands are shaking, but Moni's hands are as strong as the hands of a grown man, and his skin smells like a newborn baby. Only his hair and eyelashes move slowly, as if he's under water.

'Matti!' Iran's voice echoes through the whole building. 'Matti, where are you?'

'You know,' Moni slips out of her arms, 'I'm dying, dying of hunger.'

He pulls her along to the kitchen and opens the fridge.

'Hey look!' he laughs into the fridge. 'Come here, you won't believe this . . .'

He takes out a round cake, coated with chocolate and decorated with tiny, multi-coloured sweets.

On it is written 'Happy birthday, Matti!' in white whipped icing.

Matti counts the candles. Eleven.

'This cake must've just now dropped from the sky!' Moni beams. He sticks five fingers into the cake, claws out a big chunk and puts it in his mouth.

Now the icing says, 'Birthday, Matti!'

'You know what?' he says with his mouth full. 'I think it really suits you, your hair like this.'

Moni passes his open palm over her head and sucks the chocolate off the fingers of the other hand. Then he pushes his eyebrows into his forehead, pulls in his cheeks and touches his fishface grimace, as if his teeth are hurting.

'So how about it?' He grins and gives her chin a little pinch. 'Shall we go? We have all the time in the world. Come, let's move.' He takes the cake in one hand and her hand in the other, turns the door handle with his elbow and sticks out his head to make sure there's nobody on the landing.

'All right,' he nods to her to come out. 'What a stink . . . Again this burnt smell. How did you get to sleep last night?'

Matti can also smell the charred stink. She doesn't take her eyes off him, follows him closely like a person being rescued from a burnt house, groping her way through the blackened ruins, her hair singed and her skin scorched. Moni goes down quickly; already he's looking up to her from the second floor.

'Kill me if I can figure out how you managed to dream that dream last night,' he says.

Matti stops.

'You stopping again?' He comes up to her. 'What's the matter with you? Give me your hand.'

'What dream?'

'You know, the one with the white cat and the flying parade.'

Now she remembers. She was riding the white cat that used to live in their house, and her mother and father called her from high above. She looked up and saw her mother riding on a pigeon and her father on a big fish. They waved to her and flew on. Then she saw that everyone was flying after them – Maurice on an owl with yellow eyes, Grandma Touran on a duck, Marcelle on a crow, Sofia on the back of her blue baby, who was flapping his arms as he did when he had a fit of coughing, then Lizzie, holding on to the ears of her phantom baby. They all flew away, but the white cat didn't know how to fly.

'How did you know what I dreamed?' she asks him when they get to the bottom.

'Matti, Matti, Matti . . .' he sighs. 'What sort of question is that? It's me, Moni, you forgot?'

'So you . . .?'

'What?' he yells, bending his ear with his hand. 'Speak louder. Now I'm here I can't hear everything!'

'So all the time,' Matti raises her voice which quavers in the wind, 'all the time you could hear what I was saying to you? All the thoughts that I thought real hard so that you'd hear?'

'Sure I heard. Did you think I was deaf?'

They cross the street, and Moni leads her to the oleander thicket behind Grandma Touran's house, the best hideaway in the neighbourhood. He creeps under the branches to where they enclose a private, round room, and holds out his hand to her. Matti looks back and sees the white blossoms fluttering in the wind, sweeping away the traces of her bare feet on the ground and falling on her path. Inside the oleander room she feels her toes and knees stinging, and discovers that in the time since she was last here the ground has been covered with a carpet of nettles which has lifted up into the air the packet of cigarettes and box of matches that she'd hidden there after Grandma Touran's funeral.

Nobody knows about my hiding place, thinks Matti, and suddenly feels cold. Looking over Moni's shoulder, through the curtain of leaves, she sees their house looking like a big concrete bitch crouching to pee among the guava trees.

'First of all, show me the pictures you cut out.'

Matti takes all the picture circles out of her pocket and lets them fall on the carpet of nettles. The scissors also drop from her hand. Moni is holding a lighted match.

He lights the candles that stand on the remains of the cake.

'Happy birthday to us, Matti,' he says and kisses her on the forehead. 'Don't forget to make a wish!'

But before Matti can make her wish, Moni blows out the candles. She feels the wind passing under her skin and wants to cry.

'What did you wish?'

'That you never . . . that you never leave me again.'

'Great! Just what I wanted to hear! And now, give a big welcome to the magician! Look at this magic, Matti. Snap!' He's holding another burning match. The fire tickles his fingertips, and then burns away all of Matti's smiles.

'Look, look, Matti, see how pretty, they're burning!'

Matti watches and sees herself being consumed. She burns well, because it was a good match that flared noisily, stank of sulphur and irritated her nostrils. Her tears fall on the nettles. She sees her neck burning, then her face, the naughty eyes and the crazy eyes and the prominent ears, and the hair that had once been long. The bluish flame melts the colour off the paper, and when her last smile disappears all that is left are some little black scraps.

'Maaattiii . . . Maaattiii . . .' Sofia is shouting from the window. 'Where are you? Come home!'

Matti peers through her tears and the curtain of leaves and sees Sofia disappearing from the balcony with the baby slung over her shoulder. She looks back at Moni. He puts out a finger and touches a tear. The tear dries up. He touches another and another, till all her tears dry up.

'Matti, my little girl,' he says and comes closer. His

finger moves down the wet trails, slips over her chin and makes shivers run down her neck.

'My little twin,' he whispers and kisses her eyes. Fresh tears appear on his lips. His kisses drive the shivers away from her neck and they plunge down to her stomach.

'You won't leave me again, will you? Not ever?'

'Sure,' he whispers to her. 'You missed me an awful lot, didn't you?'

Matti nods, and Moni kisses the flattened bridge of her nose.

'You look so much like me . . .'

'And you are pretty, aren't you, Matti?'

Matti nods again, and Moni laces five fingers into her trembling hand.

'And I love you, because you're my soul, my eyes, because you're my life, Matti.'

His other hand gathers her remaining fingers.

'And now we're stuck together for ever and ever.'

Matti nods.

'Now you'll come with me, Matti. You'll do just what I tell you, promise?'

Matti nods.

All at once the twenty fingers tighten together.

'One inside the other, like two seeds in one fruit, remember?'

Matti nods again.

'Now take these scissors.' He peels away one hand and slips the cold metal loops over her bare fingers.

'You'll do exactly what Moni tells you?'

Matti opens the five fingers of Moni's hand that she's still holding and they unfold like flower petals. She looks at the lines in his palm to see if they resemble hers, brings his hand up to her nose and sniffs the new-baby scent of his.

'You hear me, Matti? Even if it makes a little blood come out and hurts you a little bit, you'll do it.'

'Matti! Matti!' Marcelle is yelling from the third-floor window. 'Come home!'

Moni raises his head and looks anxiously at the balcony.

'Look, Moni.' She slips one loop of the scissors over her thumb and the other over his. 'It's like rings.'

'Right, right.' He is swallowing nervously and not really listening to her.

'You'll see,' he says, 'after you do it, we'll be together always.'

'Let's play bride and bridegroom!' Flares blaze in her eyes, stirred by the wind. 'Please, Moni! Please let's!'

'Later, sweetheart, later.'

'No, now! I want to now!' she begs. 'I want it to be me too!'

'All right then, tell me what I must do.' The wind grabs the open casement windows of Grandma Touran's house and slams them in alarm.

'Nothing. We've got rings, we've got a cake and flowers.' Matti looks up with a big smile at the low oleander canopy. 'All I need now is a veil.'

The wind draws back the curtain of branches and Matti can see a little white cloud sailing in the cold air. She steps out of the hiding place and sees the cloud hovering over Grandma Touran's house, swirling in the wind, then floating down to her, very slowly. A dusty old veil, laced with wilting lilies, comes down and rests on her head. It is starting to rain.

'Matti, come inside now! Come in this minute, I'm telling you!'

She does what Moni tells her to do, and kneels between his arms.

A dirty grey rain makes silvery threads drop down through the white oleander blossoms, dangling and fraying as they fall. Hard little raindrops drum on the bald patches of Matti's scalp, dissolve the black ashes left from her photographs, and mash the remains of the cake, from which tracks of white icing and tiny coloured sweets spread in all directions. Amid the new-baby smell of Moni, through the veil that the rain has pasted to her face and the wet oleander branches, Matti sees the guava and medlar gangs trooping down gaily, noisily, to the courtyard and dancing in the downpour. She sees the first-floor housewives rush to the washing lines, the second-floor housewives hurriedly taking down their washing which the rain has polka-dotted, and on the third floor a woman closes her balcony windows and peers out anxiously at the street. The rain's thin fingers draw fine lines in the film of dust that has built up all summer on the windowpanes, and thin rivulets run down the wrinkles that the summer has etched in the woman's face. Matti sees her mumbling mutely through the window, 'Matti . . . Matti . . . Matti . . .'

'Look, my soul,' Moni whispers in a tender, wet voice, 'look, you're wet all over, my beautiful bride. And you're barefoot, on top of everything else . . .' He wipes the mud off the soles of her feet.

'We can't get married with you barefoot, my twin.' He pulls off his right shoe and presses his foot into the bed of nettles.

'You'll do what I tell you, all right?'

Moni bends over and puts the shoe on her right foot.

'Exactly the same size,' Matti whispers in wonder, looking at their four feet, one pair bare and the other clad in Moni's silver shoes.

'Listen to your heart, my Matti, listen to what it tells you and do that.' He moves the stethoscope amplifier over her heart.

Then he kisses her on the lips, a long-long kiss, hands her the scissors, slips the loops over her fingers and opens the blades wide. The rain comes down harder, and Matti's heart is roaring.

She looks into Moni's blazing eyes.

'Pppprrr . . .' he growls into the stethoscope, almost deafening her. 'Ppprrrr . . .'

The growling rasps the inside of her head while the scissors scratch her neck. Matti shuts her eyes tight, frees one hand from the scissors and rummages in her trouser pocket. She fishes out her six Ritalin tablets, puts four of them on her tongue, opens her mouth to the rain and lets it flush them down into her throat.

'Moni!' Matti's eyes remain shut tight.

'Moni!' she screams through the stethoscope amplifier into her ears. 'Go away from me, go away now! Don't come back! Enough, my soul, please, enough!'

She doesn't see her words drowning like the small stones in the puddles that are forming among the nettles, doesn't see the cats fleeing from the rubbish bins, or the guava and medlar gangs abruptly stopping their dance, staring in terror at Grandma Touran's empty house, then rushing off up the stairs. Behind her eyelids which remain squeezed shut she can only hear herself, screaming into her own head.

'Go away! Go away! Go to your place and don't ever come back here!'

She hears the voice of a baby being washed under rushing water. It sounds dull and faraway.

'Matti, my soul . . . Mattiii myyyy souuulll . . .' She hears the baby crying, but the yellow water with its myriad tiny bubbles turns red, runs into his throat, foams with his breath, fills up his lungs, and he glows and dims, chokes and turns blue, kicks and drowns, till he falls quite silent.

When Matti woke up evening had almost fallen. It was still raining a little, but the wind had grown tired. There was no one with her under the oleander canopy. She felt her neck, and found a little cut on the front of her throat. She dug a hole in the ground under the nettles and put into it the scissors, the veil and the pearls that remained from her mother's wedding gown. She also took the stethoscope off her neck and buried it in the ground with the rest.

Then Matti covered everything thoroughly and went home, hopping on one foot all the way.

The front door was wide open and Matti stood wet and amazed in the doorway. The house was so clean. She saw the eyes of the dancers holding up the lampshades twinkling at her, the terrazzo floor tiles were gleaming and the Indian gods glittered at her from the corridor. There was clear water in the fishbowl where the two goldfish were swimming. The copper vessels in the side-board were shiny; even the imitation cut-glass wine glasses looked real. On the wall the woman was again sleeping among the roses, the huge peacock spread his tail and the king of Persia was once again embalmed in his uniform.

Lizzie was standing beside the balcony door, dressed in one of their mother's old pallid dresses, her hair tied back and her face shiny with sweat, wringing a floor-cloth into a bucket.

'You're back,' she said when she noticed Matti, and looked up and down at her wet clothes. Matti thought Lizzie was going to sneeze, but instead she smiled and stretched out her arm.

'Look! Look! They've grown!'

'What's grown?' Matti asked, puzzled.

Sofia came out of the girls' bedroom, her baby under one arm and a bowl of wet washing clasped in the other. Marcelle emerged from the bathroom with a bottle of bleach in one hand and a floor mop in the other. Iran came out of the kitchen with an egg in each hand. They stopped where they were, hair gathered behind, faded old dresses on their bodies, and stared at Matti as if she'd flown in through the window. Even Sofia's baby gurgled at her and smiled. First they looked into her eyes, then at her shoulders and finally at her chest. Then they all smiled and exchanged melting glances.

'Congratulations, my soul. They're starting to grow on you. Good luck!' Lizzie said to her.

Matti looked down at her wet shirt and was so amazed that her heart beat through all her pores. When she raised her head she saw Lizzie kneeling in front of her.

'I'm a sacrifice for your pretty tits,' Lizzie said, her eyes shining, and placed a kiss on each of her swelling nipples.

Then Marcelle and Sofia and Mama approached, bringing with them the odours of washing-powder, bleach and fried onion, and knelt in front of Matti, their faces wreathed in smiles.

'I'm a sacrifice for your lovely breasts, my soul,' they all said and kissed each nipple. Lizzie looked at Matti, her little sister, whom she had not seen for the past six months, during which those small buds had made their appearance. Lizzie cupped her own breasts in her hands – under her mother's pale old dress, under the sweat, they felt softer than ever. She thought that she, Lizzie, and certainly also Marcelle and Sofia, had surely grown new breasts in the past summer, new pairs in place of those which had budded there ten years before, and that with these breasts, with this new flesh, which they alone could see rising, would also grow whatever was needed to work things out.

A NOTE ON THE AUTHOR

Dorit Rabinyau was born in 1972 and lives in Israel. Her first novel, *Persian Brides*, was published in eight languages and was awarded The Jewish Quarterly-Wingate Literary Award in 1999.

A NOTE ON THE TYPE

The text of this book is set in Linotype Sabon, named after the type founder, Jacques Sabon. It was designed by Jan Tschichold and jointly developed by Linotype, Monotype and Stempel, in response to a need for a typeface to be available in identical form for mechanical hot metal composition and hand composition using foundry type.

Tschichold based his design for Sabon roman on a fount engraved by Garamond, and Sabon italic on a fount by Granjon. It was first used in 1966 and has proved an enduring modern classic.